I0831742

Moments in the Sun

Moments in the Sun

Akili'Ka Mbonisi

Published By: Poetic Blasphemy
An Imprint of Mbonisi Graphics™
Virginia Beach, VA.

A Publication of Poetic Blasphemy
An Imprint of Mbonisi Graphics™
poeticblasphemy.com/books

Cover Art Designed by Mbonisi Graphics™

Library of Congress Control Number: 2010902645

Paperback
ISBN-13: 978-0-9788420-2-4
ISBN-10: 0-9788420-2-4

Hardback
ISBN-13: 978-0-9788420-5-5
ISBN-10: 0-9788420-5-7

Printed in the United States of America by Lulu.com

To Joanne,

My ever giving mother.

"Cease trying to be the sun and become a speck.

....

Don't pretend to be a candle; be a moth,

so you may taste the savor of Life..."

-Rumi

Contents

Moments in the Sun

Prologue

The Unwanted

A siren howled down London's rain drenched streets into the night. Curtains of rain swept the ground, pummeling the hull of a speeding wagon. Hurried, the ambulance skidded around turns as its driver made no attempt to negotiate the oncoming craters in the black asphalt. Rain pounded the front glass, immediately sheeting it between windshield wipes. Its passengers, more bruised than worried, securely anchored themselves in the tousling box and steadied the stretcher on which a screaming, sweat and blood soaked woman lay attached to an intravenous drip swaying precariously. The wagon was inadequately lit and stuffy from the night's recycled air. It was filled with all sorts of technological equipment, bottles of solutions, and carefully boxed bandages that became dislodged from their shelving now and again by the rough ride. There was barely enough room in the back for the three of them. This did not hinder the two paramedics, however, who sat on either sides of the patient working tirelessly to stabilize her.

PROLOGUE

"Please, Miss, you have to breathe," the woman paramedic implored with a concerned expression on her face. "I know this is difficult for you right now, but if you hang in there a few minutes more, you have my word that we will soon be at the hospital where you can safely deliver your child."

Her voice was distinctively Celtic, tender and melodic. She had a kind freckled face and wore her ginger hair back into a knot that splintered into escaping curls from the bumpy ride. She was suited in a uniform that was obviously made for a man, yet it did not detract from her feminine demeanor.

The patient bristled again in pain. She grabbed the other paramedic by his arm and barked through her clinched teeth.

"Tell that driver to turn this meat wagon around. I believe he missed a few potholes back there."

The two paramedics responded with uncomfortable yet understanding smiles. Immediately the ambulance came to a screeching halt, jarring its occupants inside.

"Oh, how lovely," she complained, throwing her hands in the air of the cramped space. "Now you are going to try and shake my baby out of me. That's right, pay no attention to the screaming pregnant wo —— . Damn, can you be a bit more rougher."

And with that, they rolled her stretcher out of the medical transport onto the cobblestone paving and jostled through the hospital emergency doors. The clatter of the wheels dissipated into the bustling cacophony of voices, cries, noises, and scents that thickened the air.

"Like I promised Miss, safe and sound," the paramedic reassured.

The silent paramedic, who sat on the other side of her during transport, was conveying something about her condition to the doctor in a low whisper. It seemed grave, but she did not care. Her worries melted away when she caught sight of a familiar face standing amongst the chaos. His face, of which his black rope like locks draped partially over, was smooth, deep brown, and calming. She could no longer hear the clamor around her, only the mouthed words that never left his lips.

"I am here. Everything is going to be okay."

A smile came over her face, and the lights dimmed until there was nothing more than darkness.

A middle aged Scandinavian gentleman pushed through the emergency doors as if he owned the building. Judging by the expensive clothes he wore, he could at that. He paused, holding his head high as if to proclaim his presence, and although worried, his arrogance hid it well. Making his way through the busy room, he found the front desk and announced himself to the receptionist.

"Frey, Arthur Frey. I was told that my wife was admitted here. She is full term in her pregnancy, and I would like very much to see her. Now," he resolutely added with an air of aristocracy.

The receptionist, a heavy build pale woman with hair pinned up by the use of several number two pencils, was slightly taken aback by his audacity; however, in dealing with countless others who believe that money positioned them above the rest or entitled them to special treatment of some sort, she examined the roster, tapped her pen on the counter with a drummer's flurry and pointed to the crowded waiting room answering.

"Frey. Yes, the doctor will be right with you. Please take a seat."

The waiting area, a thick translucent glass and partially breeze block constructed room, was set to the left of the information desk. Its entrance was twice the width that of conventional doorways, minus the door. Although near full capacity, its occupants were silent. Frey, with his coat draped over the left arm of his well tailored designer suit, stepped inside and surveyed the room. There was an empty seat to the right of him, and after a quick glance at a distorted reflection, attempting to examine his hair, he reluctantly planted himself in the seat directly across from a dark gentleman with long black dreadlocks and wearing a blood stained shirt. The gentleman stared unblinkingly, as if appraising Frey. Then after what seemed a very long and uncomfortable moment, the gentleman opened his mouth to speak, but was interrupted.

"Mr. Frey?" said a man standing in the threshold of the waiting room dressed in green scrubs.

He was a gray headed and bespectacled gentleman, a bit taller than Frey, whose bags beneath his eyes seemed to magnify themselves in his thick wire framed glasses perched low upon his nose.

Frey sprung to attention at the sound of his name.

"My wife, I need to see her. Now," he said testily, indicating that he was a man unaccustomed to waiting.

"I am Dr. Druid, one of several surgeons who had to operate on your wife tonight. Could you please come with me, sir," he instructed.

They both walked in the direction of the operating room, Frey falling in step with the doctor.

"Operate?" he this time more nervously inquired. "My wife and child, are they okay?"

"They are stable; however, three things I must inform you of, Mr. Frey," he said with a sound of foreboding sentiment in his voice. "First: Your son is doing well in the NICU. That's the Neonatal Intensive —"

"Yes, yes doctor I know. Get on with it."

"Well..." said Druid.

He paused for a moment, carefully weighing his own words, then nonetheless continued.

"...that's where I will personally escort you after you have seen your wife, sir," he added, giving particular emphasis to *sir*.

They stopped outside the operating room in which Mrs. Frey was being fussed over by several doctors.

"Second: We are very concerned about your wife's condition. She has lost a lot of blood on the way here, and the paramedics did an excellent job at keeping her stabilized for now. According to her records," he went on, "she has had a history of high blood pressure, and she is —"

PROLOGUE

"Code blue operating room 1b STAT," an urgent call over the intercom interrupted.

"Coming through! Coming through!" yelled a few nurses impatiently, wheeling more equipment into the room that was now bustling with urgency.

Frey wheeled aside in order to avoid the oncoming trotters.

"Doctor," one of the nurses called as she poked her head out of the door.

And without a thought, Dr. Druid dashed through the swinging doors of the operating room in which Mrs. Frey was being attended.

After some considerable waiting in the corridor to hear the progress of his wife, Frey snapped to his feet once again as Dr. Druid stepped out of the room, somber.

"She lost too much blood. We did all that was humanly possible. I'm sorry Mr. Frey. Your wife is... She didn't pull through. We have —"

"I want to see her," he demanded in a harsh whisper, with one hand raised, signaling that he had heard enough.

"Very well."

Frey entered the room alone. It was quiet now. The doctors, who had all been working to save her life, were rapidly peeling off one at a time till there were none. The lights were a bit more turned down than what they were before. The body of Mrs. Frey lay there peacefully. She had always been a stunning looking woman, and now she appeared to be a bit angelic. Long dark brown hair and facial features that hinted of her Hispanic heritage, accented her beauty. He had not realized just how beautiful she was until now or had somehow forgotten.

"Catherine, I know I've ignored you for many years, mea culpa," he said, confessing yet finding no tears. "I hope it's not too late for you to forgive me. You've always been kind and giving. I know you would have made a wonderful mother."

Just then a thought occurred to Frey, and he darted out of the door, where stood Dr. Druid waiting.

"Now take me to my son."

"Mr. Frey, about that third thing that I need yet to speak with you about," he cautiously mentioned in a very clinical tone as the pair of them proceeded to the elevator.

There were several people standing silently, awaiting the arrival of the lift. Dr. Druid walked over and pushed repeatedly at the already lit button. He held off in silence out of respect for Frey's privacy. A distant expression stole upon his face, illustrating a man whose brain was coping with more than enough issues at one time and searching for the right words to transition this unique situation. Behind the doors, the elevator locked into place with a deep clanking sound. A bell chimed, the doors to the lift opened, and the both filed in with a few others, dipping the elevator slightly with their weight while taking care as to respect the personal space of the other passengers. Dr. Druid prodded the well worn number three amber colored button and stood there silently, bouncing slightly on the balls of his feet, head tilted upward counting the numbers as they lit with each corresponding floor. Frey stirred inside impatiently, and the chime inside the elevator signaled the arrival of their destination. The pair of them filed out into the corridor, Frey again falling in step with Druid. They arrived at the NICU where Druid used his badge to gain entry through the electronically locked door. Druid continued explaining while they walked.

"As unique as your case may seem, your situation is not unlike many others. With a little understanding —"

"Come off it," snapped Frey impatiently. "Is he deformed or has he some developmental delays I will have to deal with for the rest of his life? What is it? Give it to me straight doctor."

They stopped in front of an enormous window in the corridor, where babies in their warmers lay swaddled behind the thick pane. The doctor motioned ever so slightly to the nurse to bring the baby. She walked over to the warmer labeled FREY, reached down and effortlessly lifted the swaddled bundle and brought the baby closer to the glass. There he could see it, the unexpected horror.

"I see what you mean doctor. It's worst than what I thought. The baby is —," said Frey, searching for a handle on the moment, the right words to cut through his utter shock.

He then became enraged, roaring.

"He's... he's!" sputtered Frey, "bloody Black dammit all —"

"African British," amended Druid. "And Mr. Frey, here at St. Agnes, we have counselors for cases such as this," he assured, attempting to stem the flow of Frey's anger.

"I don't care what the bloody hell you call that... that thing, and I don't need a counselor!" said Frey, throwing a towering temper, his voice now at full volume. “I already know what I am going to do!”

“What will you do then, sir?”

“Bloody hell —— are you cracked? Not a damn thing!” he spat. “It’s not my baby, not my problem!”

With that, he turned on his heel and proceeded down the corridor, leaving a slightly taken aback Dr. Druid still planted in his spot.

“And what of your wife’s body Mr. Frey?” he called out to him after quickly gathering his stunned senses. “We need to discuss some arrangements ——”

“I don’t give a damn what you do. You can BURN it for all I care!”

35 Years Later in The U.S.

Like I said, there are far too many victims in the world: Too many people are not taking full responsibility for what happens to them, thus bringing misfortune upon themselves and those closest to them. The world is in chaos, and the only things that you can control to some degree are the things that happen to you," voiced James to his girlfriend Veronica in a most ardent tone. "What? Why are you looking at me like that?"

"I just love it when you get all fired up and philosophical like. You are so passionate about your views, and I just enjoy hearing you make a big fuss. Don't hold back now. You just go ahead and let it all out," Veronica joked, then reached over to the driver's side of the car and caressed his face.

"You're mocking me now," he muttered, tightening his grip on the steering wheel. "Okay, I will keep my views to myself."

"Oh come now, baby," said Veronica. "I really do enjoy you when you are expressing yourself so. It's one of the things I love about you."

"What else do you love about me?"

"I love your..." she said pausing in mid thread, distracted by the flashing lights up ahead. "I wonder what's all the fuss? You know, what's going on up there?"

"What's going on is you're saying what you love about me."

"Seriously James, I wonder what is it that has stopped traffic?"

They could see at the intersection, that traffic was frozen in all directions. A cherry sports car with tinted windows was pulled over in the left turn lane of a busy highway by a squad car with brilliant red and blue lights that flickered and rotated. The officer stepped half way out of his vehicle, one foot planted on the ground and the other inside. His voice boomed, commanding the occupant of the car to turn off the ignition and stick both hands out of the window. A few minutes went by as a shadowy figure behind the dark tinted glass, silhouetted by the lights of the arrested traffic, fumbled in the glove compartment for something. This did not imbue the already suspicious officer with trust. Another squad car joined, and the second officer, fully stepping out of his car, drawing his weapon low at his side —— with index finger pointed along the barrel —— bellowed the command again. Finally, the driver side window rolled down and a young man stuck his hands out.

"Slowly open the door from the outside. Keep your hands up where I can see them. Exit the car and walk slowly towards me!" shouted the lead officer vociferously.

CHAPTER ONE

The young man made to do as he was instructed. His appearance was curiously disheveled and simultaneously very fashionable. He was suited in an overly large jacket and trousers that hung low on his hips, giving the bizarre appearance of a disproportionate human, elongated at the top. The bottom of his trousers bunched at his immaculately white Nikes. Forgetting himself, he motioned to readjust his pants that were adorned with a hidden belt that gave them no support.

"Put your hands up!" they roared.

"Man I just wanna —"

"I said keep your damn hands up!" barked the other officer now drawing his weapon and pointing it at the young man.

The young man — appearing accustomed to the sight of a gun — surveyed the officers appraisingly, then locked eyes with the lead unemotionally, and after a few moments, slowly acquiesced to the officer's demand.

"Sir, listen to me carefully. The next thing you are going to do is turn slowly and place your hands on the roof of the car!" shouted the officer clearly in a rehearsed and monotone fashion.

The night was cool, and a slight breeze carried the fresh smell of donuts from a nearby coffee and pastry shop that was opened all night. His palms and fingers were sticky, sweaty, and an acute uneasiness passed over him. He had never drawn his weapon on a person and believed somehow the young man knew this. He would rather be parked in a lot outside some twenty-four hour grocery store talking with a fellow officer at present, than to be pointing his gun at someone. The officer had a dreadful feeling welling in the pit of his stomach and wanted this to end without bloodshed. Just a few hours and he will be home safe and having a chuckle with the wife about how nervous he had been, standing with his forty-five shaking the bullets and screws from it. If only he knew what the young man was thinking at that moment. Then suddenly the young man reached again, his hand entering inside the front of his opened jacket beneath his shirt. He tugged on a large shiny object that glinted in the head lights of the squad cars.

"Gun!" cried the second officer.

There were two loud pops, then silence.

A Misunderstanding

Just minutes before the gun shots rang, a balled and well built dark gentleman dressed in black and driving a stolen car had joined the cue of drivers awaiting the traffic signal. He was in an irascible mood over a business deal and grew tired of his contact, who was on the other end of the cell phone, evading his request. His irritation grew by the moment, and when he had enough, his tone became threatening.

"How long do we have to keep snatching these damn cars before I can speak to Sergei. This penny ante nonsense is a waste of my time. I tell you what, get me Sergei and do it as if your life depended on it. I don't care how you do it or how dangerous you think he is. I promise you, I'm ten times the horror. Trust me, you don't want to be on the wrong side of my good nature."

He flipped his phone close with a sudden snap, and before he could stow it in his leather jacket, it rang.

"W'sup. Oh, Rose. Why are you calling me on this number? Is everything okay? Good —— So what do I owe this pleasure —— No, that's not such a good idea. Can this wait until I get back? I know you feel you can do whatever the hell you want to do, but I need you and our daughter to stay the hell away from here. I promise you after this is over, I will give it all up, and we can be a regular family. So please, stay in Alexandria —— You what? That's just like something you would do. Dammit woman! No, it's too late to turn around and head back. You're nearly here. My aunt Bess' place is on the way. Stop by and stay until I get there. She will remember you. Stay away from the city. What I am doing is far too dangerous to worry about the both of you being anywhere near it. So for once, do what I ask you to. Okay? Thank you. Night. Got to go, baby."

He closed his mobile, dawning a curious look on his face. His eye had fallen upon the young man who was accosted by police officers, and he had a feeling the situation was soon to get out of control. He opened his mobile again, then dialed.

"Put him on the phone. What do you mean who? You know who I'm talking about. Put Sam on the phone. Now," he added sharply.

He stared. It was all he could do to remain seated. He could intervene if he so desired; however, he knew the situation would exacerbate from his interference. Being in possession of a stolen vehicle would cause more problems than he cared to deal with. He could only sit there like the rest of the commuters, quiet, helpless. Yet, he was not amazed.

CHAPTER TWO

Presently, the sound of two gun shots startled James and Veronica in their seats. Although they were safely nestled in the BMW fifteen cars back from the intersection, where their eyes fell upon this horrible account, it was nonetheless unexpected and very disconcerting. The silence in the car swelled suddenly. Lights filtering through the windows from the street lamps and cars lights silhouetted their frozen forms. An ornate necklace hung from the rearview mirror, casting its reflection on their features which faded in and out of the darkness by the illuminating lights. They were in utter bewilderment of what had just transpired.

"Oh my," gasped Veronica in a whisper. "Did you see how they — how they —? I mean it was totally unlawful, wasn't it? I don't understand it. How could something like this happen? How can they do that? It's just wrong. James Benjamin O'Neil, are you listening to me?"

Any other time the sound of his full name would cause him some mild irritation, but he remained non responsive. James could no longer hear her voice. It was being pushed somewhere in a surreal like distance by what his eyes took in. Like everyone else who witnessed the scene, his mind was transfixed on the atrocity, eager to get a closer look. He alternated between acceleration and breaking, inching forward, anticipating his turn to survey. Incrementally the cross traffic proceeded with drivers and passengers alike, craning their necks to see the evidence of what had just transpired. The green light again gave James' queue permission to proceed forward. James and Veronica could see out of the driver's side of the car one officer seated, crouched down on the median with his face in his hands and the other officer, who bore a look of astonishment. The young man, whose identity was obscured by the looming officer, lay lifeless in the street, contorted and soaking in a pool of his own blood. His belt buckle beneath his shirt was exposed to the night, glinting like a beacon, calling onlookers to a tragic misunderstanding.

The sound of Veronica's voice and the cocktail of street noises inundated James' muted hearing, swelling themselves to the forefront of his consciousness.

"Oh, damn... damn. Did you see that?" he exploded out of nowhere, as if snapping out of a trance.

"Yes Jamie, I saw it. Did you not hear me talking to you? Honestly. I sometimes wonder where you go when you zone out like that. I was saying," she spoke rapidly in order to reiterate. "That poor man —— the officers —— it all escalated so quickly. It's such a shame. And to witness it, I don't think I will ever be the same again."

"No justice, no continuity, no love, it's just chaos. That's what I was talking about," he said, finding more volume in his voice. "The world is in crisis. There's no order in it all. That man did not have to die like that. I think this all could have been avoided somehow. The officer could have been a bit more acute and slow to shoot. And that guy should have known better to reach the way that he did. What was he thinking? It was a volatile situation waiting to explode."

CHAPTER TWO

"I wish you wouldn't work yourself up so, your pressure, my good sir."

"Will you stop sounding like a..." he paused, searching for the words, "pristine white girl, I'm trying to —"

"Jamie baby, but I am," she said smiling, gently stroking his cheek with the back of her hand. "I am — pristine — white, and you are not all black yourself," she added, affectionately tapping her forefinger to his chin while smiling.

He felt her words were kind but a reprobation nonetheless. Indeed he was not entirely African American. Although his features and hair style made that fact unapparent, James himself was the product of two people from different cultures. He resigned himself to accept what he had always known to be true; that being, he appeared at first glance and chiefly African American.

"Yeah, I know. You're right. Let's get away from here. It's depressing."

On that note, James gave the car more gas, accelerating from the tragic incident. As they proceeded, the pair could hear the sound of the approaching sirens in the distance. And the blaring howls dissipated in the deep and unperturbed night that swallowed them in its calm.

A half an hour past, and they presently drove around steadying one another with exchanged glances and overtures of affection. Nothing could be a better remedy for their nerves being on edge than to be in the company of one other.

Veronica was a breathtakingly stunning woman with long dark hair, of which she wore down when meeting with James. It fell upon her shoulders and draped below the center of her back. She spoke more with her eyes, raising and furrowing her brow slightly in a flirtatious manner, constantly indicating to James how sexy she thought he was.

James, always confident in his good looks, blushed unnoticeably beneath his brown skin. His hair hung in ropes of black locks down his back and was loosely tied, giving a disheveled appearance that only someone with his handsome looks could pull off. And although self assured and well adjusted to compliments, only she could invoke the elation of fluttering butterflies within him. It felt good to be important to someone and to be desired as much as he desired her.

Veronica reached over, took his free hand, and covering it with her own, she placed it in her lap. She had a strong need to touch and be touched by him. James felt that all too often feeling welling up inside of him, urging him again to profess his love for her, but he stifled the words and smiled. He felt that he had far too often bore his feelings when he should have been silent. He could not help how he felt. Veronica was both beautiful inside and out. His breathing became irregular and his heart pounded in his chest. His insides writhed and erupted hot lava. He gripped the steering wheel tightly with his left hand while trying to focus and drew long deep breaths in order to master himself. She had always affected him this way and appeared to somehow had more control over the impression he made upon her. Veronica knew that his passion was rising to the point of no containment and saw him struggling with it. She stroked his beard stubbled face again with the back of her hand, smiling knowingly at the words that he had not voiced.

“I know baby,” she whispered. “I know... Now take me home.”

“Promise me something, love,”

“What is it?” she said, taking in his somber expression.

“Promise me you won't let me embarrass myself,” he said trying to steady his voice and not sound too grave. “I am not sure sometimes if I am... well, a bit too intense.”

He managed a feeble smile. She leaned in and kissed him. His nerves steadied.

“Don't worry, baby, you're doing fine.”

After a fashion, James pulled up in front of her condo and a sense of panic washed over him. There was so much that they did not say and do. Veronica sat there immobilized by some invisible force. She did not want to leave him this way and knew she was making it difficult for the both of them to say goodnight. She wanted so much to throw her arms around him and say, let’s just leave... now and run away from here.

“Go, please,” he whispered. "Go before —”

He silenced himself, reached up at the cabin light and disabled it. She stepped out of the car as he lowered his hand to feel her body against it, gliding away as he curled his fingers. Veronica always enjoyed the feel of his hands touching her; it sent shocks all through her. She turned around, shut the door, leaned into the window and looked into James' eyes. It was there, just at the opening of her lips forming.

"I know. I love you too, Veronica."

She leaned in and touched his hand one last time, then forced herself to turn and leave.

James watched Veronica until she disappeared safely into her home, then drove off feeling thoroughly satisfied that he was able to meet with her today. He spent the trip home reflecting on the night's events: the quiet and secluded birthday dinner with Veronica in his honor, the shooting, and the drive home with her, all of which he recounted in vivid detail. How beautiful she always looked, particularly with her hair down.

It was not long before James arrived home. Tossing his keys onto a poorly managed table littered with letters, bills, and advertisements. He picked up a hand full and thumbed through a stack of letters, which were mostly from the same sender, then threw the lot into a basket on the table with other unopened letters. He caught sight of his medicine sitting on the counter of the kitchen's pass-through to the left, where he placed as a visual queue and daily reminder to help regulate his blood pressure. James opened the bottle, tapped the recommended dosage and returned the bottle back onto its resting spot. He absentmindedly repositioned his Louisville Slugger bat that leaned against the side of the tiny table and swallowed the tiny pill without water, then pushed the play button of his machine to check his messages.

"You have three new messages," the machine droned mechanically. "Message one, beep."

CHAPTER TWO

Hi Jamie, it's your mother. Happy birthday sweetie. I know you don't like to make a big to do out of them, now that you are much older. Remember we have dinner here at the house this Sunday and bring that sweet young woman of yours with you. Also, I heard from Red. She is in town. Oh, and Jamie, have you spoken to your father yet? Are you still stock piling his letters in a bin without reading them? I am only asking because he asked about you again today. Remember to take your medicine. Love you Jamie... Night sweetie.

"Beep, message two."

Yo. Happy birthday, dog. It's me. I'm just calling to see how the night went with you and your woman. We got to chop it up soon... you know. Testing out the new whip right now. I'm loving it and got to get new personalized plates. Since you on vacation, I'll be by your spot tomorrow to —— Damn, being pulled over... call you back.

"Beep, message three."

Hey sexy man, I'm missing you already. No one is here; I want to tell you that I do love you, and thank you for a most pleasant evening, and I hope to have many more such ——

"Beep."

James hit the erase button, interrupting the message. He could hear no more of it. He enjoyed listening to Veronica's voice, but presently he was sadden by the thought that tonight she would not be with him. And although she does profess to the contrary, he felt she would be home, comfortable, and nestled in bed with her husband.

3

Resilient

Far on the other side of town, in an operating room of a very poorly funded hospital, doctors worked earnestly to save the young man suffering from two enormous gun shot wounds to the chest. It is nothing less than a miracle that he has made it thus far. Because of this young man's resilience, the doctors are determined to give him the best care that their years of medical knowledge could offer.

"He's in v-fib. Two hundred joule. All clear!" shouted the doctor.

Lying there, the young man felt as though he was hurtling through a deep black void. Moments of his life flashed beneath his eyelids: A police officer was yelling and pointing a gun at him, his mother complaining about his attire, his first kiss, people screaming in pandemonium, the sound of a shot gun being cocked, and many other images flashbulbing themselves. And as though reaching in and pulling a moment from a hay stack of jumbled thoughts, his mind rested upon a single coherent event.

"Twitch!" a voice bellowed.

It was hot, and a hazy light illuminated his thoughts. His eyes began to adjust. He was standing in a grocery store, and a furious man outside was approaching with three other companions, all with guns in tow. One of the gunmen called out again.

"Twitch — Twitch bring your punk ass out here right now, bitch!"

The man's deep voice roared with sheer loathing, penetrating the thick brick and glass of the store. Many of the cashiers who witnessed the arrival of the ruffians left their stations in fear. Customers abandoned their places in lines, withdrawing to the rear of the store for safety, while other stood there in utter shock at what was happening.

"Kyle, customer service up front please," a tentative voice to the young man's right called over the intercom system, doing his best to conceal the shock of it all.

Overhead, the bounding of heavy footsteps ran across the ceiling and trampled down the stairs to the left, bringing with it a wild eye Kyle carrying a camouflage duffle bag. He stomped fearlessly over to the left of where the young man stood, unzipped his bag and pulled out a shotgun with countless rubber bands around its brown sawed off handle. He cocked it with alarming intent and propped it onto his shoulder as if to say, *come in and get me.*

CHAPTER THREE

"This has gotten way out of hand, William," muttered the voice to the young man's right. "I'm going home."

"You go, man. I got to see this," said the young man, completely transfixed on what was happening.

The sound of the clock punching a time card exploded into the sound of a defibrillator sending electrical current through his body, pulling him back to the operating table. Again, everything went black.

"Three hundred joules," the doctor said. "Clear!"

For a brief moment, every groping hand on the gunshot victim withdrew, and the paddles sent a shock through the young man's body causing him again to rise in one great pulse.

"Epinephrine one milligram IV-push. NOW! Who's with me?" said the doctor, her voice growing even more urgent.

And a nurse bustled over to the intravenous drip and injected something into the transparent tubing.

"Clear!"

Again, another massive pulse surged through the young man, and a silence fell over the room. All eyes were fixed on the heart monitor. Five seconds later a heart beat registered.

"That's it, come on back," encouraged the doctor. "Come on back."

Reminiscing

Saturday morning was greeted with the songs of birds perched in their tree hung nests and with those who had found the comfortable resting places of heavy electrical wires tied taught between massive wood splintering poles. The sun chased off the remainder of the night's mist, which had left well manicured lawns besprinkled with dewdrops, accenting cobwebs made by diligent spiders during the night. The Local Pilot dated August 28th lay strewn near front doors, welcome mats and flower beds with all the accuracy of a poorly compensated and hastened newspaper courier. Its headline blared:

High Speed Chase Ended In Shootout.

Last night, officers of the 23rd precinct, pursued an unknown man at high speeds and cornered him at the intersection of Virginia Beach

> *Blvd. and Witchduck road, where the assailant immediately exited his car brandishing a firearm and was shot by one of the two officers on the —*

The rest of the article was skewed by the manner in which the paper was unceremoniously rolled and banded. Large black slippers appeared next to this particular wrapping, and the owner of 427 Redgate Avenue reached down to collect his day's post. His eyes fell upon the headline, and to James' surprise, there lay the previous night recounted in deplorable detail. He unconsciously backed himself into the house while scanning the article, then turned and leaned against the door, automatically locking it. James stood there resting on the door for a while trying to take in the story as told by the press. It was blatantly inaccurate of what he had witnessed.

"What gun?" he croaked out loud in his morning voice to the post. *"Cornered? This is all wrong. Something is not adding up,"* he thought this time, refraining from speaking out loud to an inanimate object or so to himself.

James tutted reprovingly and shook his head, then resigned himself to resume thumbing through the newspaper.

> *Capt. Samuel Mahony, the newly appointed head and instrumental figure in the major shake-up of the*

corruption in the 23rd precinct, was asked about the weapon many witnesses said they did not see. He simply stated that "there is an investigation underway," and he could not comment. See ***CHASE A4***

"Well," said James this time aloud, "someone's paying attention to the details."

❦

The sun fingered its rays between the kitchen blinds, and its warm glow was trapped by thin layers of yellow curtains diffusing its light onto the textured white walls. A black marble top island stood in the center of the room, compartmentalized with a number of shelving, cabinets below, sink, oven range, and four high chairs made of black wrought-iron and leather covered cushions, two on either side of its wide girth. It was crowned by stainless steel cookware hanging overhead, glinting in the light that stole through the veil curtains. Wood cabinets dressed the walls with an interior design that blended its doors with that of the pantry and refrigerator. And the counters ran wall to wall, punctuated by a large pass through to the left of the entrance that flowed into to the grand room, completing this ostentatious look.

CHAPTER FOUR

James' house shoes quietly shuffled across the carpet, then like sand paper crossed the threshold of the kitchen's hardwood floor, and he noisily slid a chair from beneath the island, plopping down in his favorite. He placed his hot tea, of which he had brewed before collecting the news, onto the counter and continued to scan the paper. This was always James' favorite time of day, where he basked quietly in the morning light, enjoying a little music, news and taking in the morning post. This day was quite different from any other serene day of the year. It was the first day of his sabbatical, possibly the first day of a new profession interest, and his best mate William would be calling on him soon, so the pair of them could fill most of the day with typical male bonding rituals, such as watching a DVD of an old boxing match of Muhammad Ali, discussing the voluptuous delineation of female co-workers, and taking William's new car for a spin. This new car idea appealed to him more, for it would surely keep his mind, at least for a few hours, off Veronica.

William had been his best friend since childhood, and the pair were students working their way through college in a retail grocery store about fifteen years ago, long before James became a copy editor at Quill And Parchment Books. He broke off from his reading, reminiscing. A slight grin formed on James' face as he took a long pull of Earl Grey, reflecting on a time when he and William were back in Oakland, working for a store that lost more money than it could procure from its clientele.

Back then, it was what seemed the hottest day of summer. Clouds were for miles no where to be found. The heat and fumes from the baked asphalt distorted cars in the distance. Shade from trees and building over-hangs offered no relief from the scorching sun, and sweat soaked shirts appeared to be the order of the day. The air was oven hot, roasting head tops and wilting hairdos, some had fallen flat in greasy curtains of both curly and straight, while others were tied back away from sweat stung eyes. Shoppers busied themselves in the strip mall of Acorn Shopping Center. Its proprietors, feeling the taxing heat that the summer offered their escaping comfortable air conditionings, had thrown their doors ajar, attempting to persuade an occasional breeze.

Acorn Super Market was the largest store in the tiny mall and by far the most tolerable of the heat. Because its doors were in a constant flux of opening and closing by bustling customers, its cool interior struggled in combating the mounting heat. James recalled that day the heat brought more with it than uncomfortable perspiration.

Kyle Coster, who was known by most as Twitch, the store's security guard, had physically accosted a man and a pregnant woman on the front end and accused them of theft before surprised and incredulous looking customers. Twitch was a very tall and lanky man whose arms were bowed at his side as if he was waiting to grow muscle in the place where there were none. His movements were jerky and mechanical like, giving the appearance of a skeleton impersonating a robotic cop, and he spoke in a mono tone fashion worthy of a character from an old black and white police movie.

CHAPTER FOUR

"Sir, come with me to the back," Twitch had instructed in an intimidating manner."

What had happened after that was classic and to this day very hard to believe. The wide eyed man motioned, pointing behind and over Twitch's shoulder.

"What the hell is that."

Twitch turned in apparent alarm to see what was it that had excited the man so. And in that split second of opportunity, the man wrenched his arm from Twitch's grip and darted out of the door, leaving his pregnant companion behind. And Twitch, feeling ego bruised and scandalized before a host of witnesses, seized the woman by her arm and frog-marched her to the warehouse in the back where he cuffed her to a metal ladder that was bolted to a wall.

William had witnessed the entire matter and lost no time in informing James —— who had always been at logger heads with Twitch over his practice of arresting people —— that Twitch had once again overstepped his boundaries as a security guard. After William's retelling of the incident, James had found the pregnant woman in the back, just as William said and was incensed by what he had seen. The scene in the front of the store became chaotic shortly thereafter, with guns and with people running about screaming.

That was so long ago, and it remained nevertheless very fresh in his memory. The newspaper headline had triggered those thoughts. And now, being completely happy and free from that stressful existence, he placed the post aside for his later perusal, rocked his chair back on its hind legs and took a long draft from his cup, thoroughly enjoying his solitude.

5

The Letters

Twenty minutes or so flew by before James abdicated himself to tackling his mail. He strolled over to his paper littered table, that stood tucked in a tiny alcove of the foyer, and resolutely gathered the lot of mail addressed to him from his father. Placing them in order according to the dates, he extricate an envelope that stood curiously from the rest. It was sullied and worn with wrinkles from much use of handling and turned face down with something scribbled on the back of it. And to his good fortune, there written on the back of the unopened letter in purple ink, a poem that he believed to have been lost. James was not as organized as his father when inscribing his thoughts. Whether it was along the margins of the daily post, on a paper bag, a napkin or on his arm, it matter not. When inspiration washed over him, he would utilize what ever tools were available.

"Ah... there you are. I thought you were lost with the rest," he whispered, casting his eyes upon his jumbled cipher then reading.

fold the sun

strange thing about sunshine
sunshowers
sunrays
and sunflowers

sunrays
and sunnydays
can be folded into your pocket
like veronica says

i keep her close
no matter the distance between us
sun rise
sun sets
sun baths
sun reflects
yet i could never forget
her smile

it burns a hole in the pocket of my trousers.

He paused for several moments, taking in his words. At the time he had written them, they brilliantly expressed his feelings. Now, however, they felt shopworn and somehow less impressive. Then suddenly a self convicting feeling stole over him, and he realized there was no putting it off anymore. He had run out of excuses of being far too busy to reply, not to mention the little time it would had taken to read his father's letters. After all, he had time to scribble on the back of this one, and that was condemning in itself.

CHAPTER FIVE

"Enough of this," he thought, and returned the letter back into the collection.

The truth of the matter, it was James who was not putting forth the effort to mend the rift between him and his father, and he realized this. One thing was for certain: James' father had always been there his entire childhood without fail and showed no signs of abandoning their father son relationship, no matter how strained it was. James, remembering the message his mother left on his answering machine the previous night, felt for a moment ashamed of himself. It had accomplished the desired effect, and he was absolutely convinced she was in cahoots with his father.

After sequentially organizing his father's letters, James stood there for a few moments breathing deeply, contemplating the weight of it all, as if preparing to dive into a pool of ice cold water. Again he deliberated, noting his father's address. *Alexander Frederick O'Neil, Swissotel The Howard, 12 Temple Place, London.* He then took particular notice of how is father always used his full name when addressing letters. Any other time, he would devote long hours at signing autographs and books for his avid readers, using his well known pen name, Alexander Frederick.

Then abruptly, and with great determination, James tore open the first letter in an attempt to chase away apprehension. He recognized the script. It was not typed but in one of his father's hand writings. James' father had in the past displayed an incredible ability to write distinctively different in more than one hand writing, which was one of the things James admired about his father. This time it appeared much more cramped and slender looking as opposed to the free flowing and open loops which he managed in the past in demonstrating.

The letter was written on a cream colored parchment that smelled oddly of his father's study at O'Neil Lane. James hesitated; fond memories rushed to the forefront of his mind, and he jerked his head slightly to clear the images. Slowly he began to read.

My Dear Son;

I hope this letter finds you thriving in the best of health. Although we have for some time now remained distant, you dwell constantly on my mind, and I long for the days when we may again sit hours conversing or simply enjoying a stimulating game of chess. Moments such as those live close to my heart. I cannot change what has happened, but I accept responsibility in the cause of such. Perhaps you will see your way in allowing me to disclose the circumstances leading up to our estrangement. Hopefully, this letter will act as a precursor. In knowing and understanding details of these events, perhaps you will find in your heart a little forgiveness. Your mother tells me that you have moved out of the guest house and that you visit frequently, and she enjoys your company hours on end. I have asked her to plead my case with you, so that you will find it in your heart to forgive me for the things that have happened and for what I will divulge to you. Your mother feels that I should leave well enough alone; however, you remain and always my son. I cannot tell you it all in one letter. I will do my best to tell you as much as memory serves. Please wait until I have told you the full account of what you understand as the truth before judging me or even your mother. After all these years and so many regrets, one in particular I hold in my heart still. We never told you that we adopted you at birth. I know this comes as a blow, but we love you and no amount of paperwork can make our love for you any less. There exist more that you need to know, son. Bear with me. I will tell you all in the fullness of time.

Live and love with all your heart. Moments in the sun belong(s) to you, my son.
Love,
Dad.

6

Pandora's Box

James collapsed the letter quickly in his hands as if he had read something atrociously obscene. His eyes widened, shifting from left to right wildly searching. His heart hammered out of his chest into his throat; hot needles pricked his body all over, and he began to feel slightly light headed. Everything around him became a gaussian blur: His sight unfocused. The television that played quietly in the living room, the morning twittering of birds, the sound of intermittent sprinklers watering lawns, and the sound of traffic that ambled by, all of which became muted. He was frozen on the spot, his senses were dulled, and he did not know what to make of it all. His mind spun circles trying to grasp a handle on the moment. And when comprehension informed his groggy thoughts, he was stricken with complete outrage.

"What in the —— !" James roared, his voice tailing away at the end and echoing through the house.

CHAPTER SIX

James shook his head reprovingly while he mastered the urge to curse out loud. His lips pressed together, tempering himself. After a few moments of gathering his composure, his temper abated. He unrumpled the letter and reexamined it. Perhaps he had read it wrong or somehow misinterpreted. He read the letter again, this time with deliberate intent. And sure enough, he had in fact understood it perfectly clear.

"Huh, there is no *s* on the end of that word. It's *Moments in the sun belong...* The subject is plural," he muttered, with an air of indignation and admixed disappointment.

Had he been lied to all these years? His life, all that he believed he was, was a lie? All those people who claim how much he favored his father, how very much alike the pair were. Had they been lying all this time? Naturally, even his mother had offered, on numerous occasions over the years, how much like his father he was. Why would she say such a thing? Who and where were his real parents? James felt it was just like his father to drop a bomb like this, such a flare for the dramatics. What was he thinking, putting something like this in a letter? Didn't he deserve a little consideration, at the very least to be told in person? After all, his father did have a home here in the states and could have waited until he was once again in town. James posed one question after another to himself, and to his dismal expectations, no answers were availed. He knew very well that a person to person conversation was out of the question. He would rather have not known he was adopted. And now it would seem, Pandora's Box has been opened; there is no putting back the monster within.

His mind grounded back into action, posing more unanswered questions. Was it his mother who talked his father into the adoption? It would make sense. What in the world has this new information to do with what his father had done? It was unforgivable, and his mother seems to have no problem with it. He felt tired, worn out from the emotional roller coaster. He started to feel guilty. Hadn't his parents given him a comfortable life? It was more than what most other children he knew had. Hadn't they loved him just as much as any parents would love their own? Coming to grips with the reality of it all, James realized that he owed this small request of his father; however, realizing and doing were altogether two entirely different things. It took this long for him to read this one letter, many of which he should have already. He accepted it will take some adjustment on his part. James also realized that he will have to read all of the letters in order to have all the facts, at least all as told to him by his father.

And as these thoughts raced, the music emanating from the television heralded the local morning news, and its all too familiar melody seeped its way through the heavily jumbled contemplation of James' mind.

This is Channel 3 Morning News with Laura Sanchez. In international news: Today marks the 35th anniversary of the disappearance of self made multi-billion dollar business tycoon Arthur Frey, of Frey Enterprises. Arthur Frey disappeared shortly after the death of his wife Lady Catherine Barinard, one of two estranged daughters of Lord William Barinard III and the Duchess Darlene De'Monet. A shroud of mystery surrounded Lady Catherine's death and Arthur Frey's disappearance. Inspector Garrison of Scotland Yard is to this day unable to ascertain what exactly happened to the billionaire tycoon, who also had been their primary suspect. It was believed by many, and still is, that Frey ——

"If I had your money, I probably would disappear too, leave all of this madness behind," he said sardonically, speaking over the news caster while preparing to open another one of his father's letters.

Twiddling it with both his thumbs and forefingers, as if fanning himself, he quickly unfurled the envelope with renewed interest.

The news caster continued her report.

Up next on News 3: A string of violent robberies last night. One victim shaken, relives her horrifying experience. Plus, the most frequently stolen cars of the year. And if you think crooks are only looking for luxury, think again. Find out more on how local law makers are cracking down on the recent outbreak of car theft. But first, police chase ended in another shooting. We have an amateur video clip taken with a bystander's cell phone. We must warn you; this is alarmingly graphic.

James glance over his shoulder at the television to discover last night's events again unfold before his eyes and gaped. He stared for a while, and to his enormous surprise, a grainy, color depraved video showed spectators in one of the passing cars; they were undeniable. It was he and Veronica peering out of the driver's window, attempting to get a closer look.

"Oh no, this is not good, not good at all."

7

The Book Store

James sailed quickly across the room to the television and squinted his eyes to make out the figure lying on the ground. This was, however, to no avail. He then looked back at himself and Veronica, and taking under consideration the grade of the video, he realized that they were barely distinguishable in the grainy and pixelated broadcast and thought perhaps the situation was not as serious as it may have seemed. And just as the tension in his chest abated, the phone rang. James absentmindedly reached over to the glass-top coffee table without taking his eyes off the screen, still squinting as he studied; he fumbled clumsily before gripping the receiver. Immediately from the receiver, came an upset woman's voice speaking rapidly, her words falling over themselves in a panicked whisper.

"It's on the news — I mean, we're on the news."

"Good morning pretty," James said warmly. "I know. I see. And you look great."

"Now you pick this moment to be facetious?" she said, still whispering.

"Don't worry, I can barely tell who we are."

"My goodness Jamie, if he finds —— if someone recognizes us ——"

"Not to worry," he calmly said. "Everything will be fine, just fine. Okay?"

"You think so?"

"I'm more than sure."

But he was not sure. He did not entirely believe things were going to be fine. Although he could not bear to see Veronica in such a worried state, it did not matter to him as much as it did to her that someone may have seen them together. He secretly welcomed the idea of exposure and felt he had more urgent matters pressing him, now that he had put aside his resentment and read his father's letter. This was, however, not the time to fan the flame of insecurity. He consoled her for a while longer, and when her apprehension subsided, James felt he should tell her about the letter, but in person, if at all possible. He longed to see her, and what better reason could he have to spend stolen moments with her.

"Veronica, I have to tell you something —— something important. Can we meet in the library or some other place you would feel comfortable? I have something I need to show you as well. And no it is not a ring, nothing that grave," he solemnly amended, guessing her thoughts, dispelling any trepidation that this was a preamble to proposal of marriage. "It's about my father, his letters. And I prefer not to do this over the phone, if that's okay with you."

"Jamie ——"

"Please, Veronica?"

"The book store. I'll meet you there in forty-five minutes," she said in a hurried whisper.

"Okay, see you there."

And with endearing intimations, they ended the call. James dashed immediately to his bedroom closet excited and pulled out his favorite white shirt with the mandarin collar Veronica loved so much. He was quite a smart dresser and took particular care in wearing cloths Veronica found him irresistible in. His wardrobe consist of formal and professional attire with a flare somewhat of a high fashion male model. He knew it was but a small part of the attraction she had for him, and it was a plus he always smelt —— as she often reminded him —— good enough to eat.

On the way, James took a route through a deprived and forsaken neighborhood he remembered from his childhood long ago. Colonial Park was not the straightest route between the two points of his home and the book store; however, this mattered not, for he was feeling quite in the mood for a bit of nostalgia.

Upon entering the neighborhood, passing beautifully constructed churches and equally shabby corner stores, James became sick with astonishment at its bedraggled appearance. He cast around, taking in more of the surroundings and was greatly disturbed at what he had seen. He wondered how could people live in such conditions? How could they go about their daily lives with the site of it all constantly reminding them of their arrested development?

There were contents of open garbage bags and toppled containers that lay strewn curb side hither and dither, exposing their contents of fast food wrappings from some local restaurant. In addition, it was evident by the emanating smell, that several days of festering in the open sun, heaped a particularly rotting odor. Now and again, discarded fish and maggot infested meats mingled with the air of the stifling summer heat. James' stomach objected, and he rolled the windows up hastily and turned the air-conditioner on to stay the stench. The now silent scene was a movie, viewed in passing through the windows of the quiet interior of his car. He gaped at old yellow stained bed mattresses, furniture, and very large appliances, such as refrigerators that lay doorless on their backs, and broken air conditioners, unceremoniously tossed out in front of unkempt yards, that were sparse and browned by the sweltering heat.

Apartment buildings were bricked and tall. Some displayed fire escapes in their backs, and others revealed webbed clotheslines spun in circles by an occasional breeze, flapping dingy and color faded clothes in carousels. An astonishing amount of beautiful cars, moreover, lined the streets, sometimes bumper to bumper, in a stark contrast to this societal atrocity. James did not remember the neighborhood looking like this when he visited it as a child. He thought, perhaps children eyes are more forgiving. Its dilapidated buildings with broken windows brought to mind his fathers words: "*It could all be taken away from you in the blink of an eye, son. It's important to appreciate the things you have.*" His father's deep voice had instructed —— years ago when teaching James how to swing his new Louisville Slugger ——long before James was able to comprehend its meaning.

As true as this may be, James could not help wondering why did the tenants of this community allow their environment to come to such conditions unbefitting for human habitation. This appeared to James as a self destructive act.

"Goodness. What happened here?"

He blew a sign of astonished relief, muttering the word *wow*, and felt instantly appreciative for the life his parents gave him.

The streets were becoming far too narrow, and its many years of pothole worn surfaces were taxing James' car suspensions. He therefore turned on to Church Street to avoid more of the same and found the road was kinder, smoothly paved, and the homes quickly became aesthetically pleasing. How odd this was, he thought as his eyes fell upon a group of men approaching rapidly and who seemed a bit out of place, waiting for something or someone. James could have sworn he knew one of the men, but craning his neck at this point was out of the question. He was driving far too fast to get a good look. He therefore ignored the moment of familiarity, and his mind returned to the morning's earlier events and now found himself dwelling on his father's letters, particularly the one he so reluctantly had the displeasure of reading. And he tittered irritatedly at this.

Barnes & Noble Book Store was located on the corner of the very busy Constitution Drive and Virginia Beach Blvd. It stood first in Columbus Village, a small shopping plaza consisting of quality stores such as: F.Y.E. Music, Bed Baths & Beyond, a Schlotzky's Deli, David Nygaard Fine Jewelry, Bagels 'N More, Lens Crafters and a Regal Stadium that set apart in the distance from the rest of the buildings, due to the amount of traffic it generated weekends from enthusiastic movie goers. The parking lot of the tiny mall was often used as a shortcut to avoid long traffic lights, and today was no different from any other.

James found a vacant spot amongst the congestion, and after activating his car alarm with a high chirping hiccup, he headed towards the entrance and proceeded inside the green doubled French doors. Directly leading into a tiny foyer was a knee high wooden rack holding a variety of advertisements against a four foot long wall. Another set of glass French doors stood as a gateway, buffering outside disturbances. Inside, its cliental were a united nation of many who loved the taste of coffee brewed at least five hundred ways to tantalize the pallet. Its many high windows allowed the sunlight to intermix with the incandescent lighting, creating an absolutely perfect setting for reading. Those who were not at their ease sitting at small tables, quietly chatting and sampling the various flavors of coffee, were quite at their leisure perusing books and magazines.

The residual sound of outside traffic seeping into the interior's serene mood, was muffled into silence by the closing doors' vacuum. James paused inside before a magnificently large multi pyramid display, constructed with colorful hardbacks of best sellers. One of the titles stood out from the rest and made him smile: *Love Needs No Excuse: It is its own license.* He scanned for Veronica and caught sight of her standing in the fiction section, reading an encyclopedic size of a book. Although he had seen her last night, his heart leapt at the sight of her, turning flips that made his stomach felt as though the bottom of the floor had fallen from beneath his feet.

"Veronica," his lips silently framed her name.

She was dressed in a white short sleeve shirt that was cut slightly above the waist line of her jeans, complementing her shape. She brushed her dark hair away from her face, slowly tucking it behind her ear with her fingers as the light through a tall window shown upon her grace. James drew a long breath and could have sworn for a brief moment he smelt her hair.

He walked over to her excitedly, and she raised her eyes slowly from the book; her head tilted slightly with one eyebrow flirtatiously raised, smiling. Their eyes locked, and the pair mastered the impulse to throw themselves into each other's arms.

"So, what is it you want to show me?" she asked, now taking in James' appearance and redolence. "God, you smell so good. I could sop you up with a biscuit," she whispered, breathing him in even more, moving closer, and purposefully brushing up against him while she stowed the book back onto the shelf.

"I —— um —— you look beautiful," he sputtered, losing his thread of thought from Veronica's close proximity.

And when she did not back away, his eyes betrayed him, and he made to kiss her. A nearby grizzle-haired woman was eyeing them curiously.

"Careful, we are ——"

"Yeah, I know," said James, his heart now hammering in his chest and breath labored.

He took a step back and a moment to collect himself, and at the same time, he pulled from his attaché case a stack of letters and handed her the one he had read earlier.

"This is what I have to show you."

"Who are they from?"

"These are from my father. I've read that one so far. Well, I was going to read another, but you called," he finished weakly, sounding as though making an excuse for why he had not read more.

Veronica smiled.

"Good, you are reading them. Now let's see. How choice," she said, unfurling the envelope, appreciating the parchment on which the letter was written and taking note of the state of it and James' earlier attempt to smooth the wrinkles from it. She took a moment to read the letter, all the while shaking her head. The farther her eyes traveled down the parchment, the more stricken her expression became until...

"No way!" ejaculated Veronica, clapping her hand over her mouth as an after thought.

At this sudden outburst, James turned his head to the right and smiled uncomfortably at the grizzle-haired woman. Then the pair of them began quietly laughing at themselves.

"Oh baby, I'm so sorry you had to find out something like this in a letter. Are you okay?" she asked after gaining her composure.

"I'm better now. You should of heard me wake the neighborhood when I read it. Took me twice to make sure I understood it right."

He bore a forced smile underneath his disappointment.

"And you had no idea all those years that you may have been adopted?"

"None whatsoever. Looking back, you would think I would have felt more of an outsider as a child. You know, how some people who find out they were adopted, tend to have grown up knowing they were different than the rest of their family? I never would have thought it."

She reached over and gently caressed his cheek with the palm of her hand, then remembering her surroundings, she quickly retracted it, and with a massive effort, she averted her eyes from his to concentrate on the letter in hand.

"You know Jamie, this *s* on the end of *belong(s)* —"

"Yeah I know, the perfect Mr. Frederick made a mistake."

"What do you mean by —— Wait a second. I've seen this phrase before, written purposefully as it is in this letter."

She turned the envelope over and read the name *Alexander Frederick O'Neil.*

"Jamie, is this who I think it is?"

"Yeah, it's my father," he said in a nonchalant tone.

"No sweetie, that's not what I meant. Is your father *the* very introverted and highly illustrious poet philosopher Alexander Frederick, who was responsible for the internet conspiracy theory *FEMA Martial Law,* which is now a movie?"

"Boy, talk about your long titles," he said under his breath. "Yeah, so what?"

"So what —— ? Are you kidding me? Why didn't you tell me?"

"I never got around to it. What? I would have done," he said sounding a bit too defensive.

"It's okay," Veronica assured him in a soothing voice, while taking notice of the return address. "Does he live in this hotel, in London?"

"No, he lives in the countryside, but from time to time stays in London when he is conducting business, often as long as a year or more. Needless to say, my parents have an odd relationship that I have yet to fully understand. I guess living in two places keeps people from popping in on his privacy. Perhaps that's what keeps their relationship —— What?"

He adopted a quizzical look on his face.

CHAPTER SEVEN

"I only ask because... Well he is one of my favorite writers. And the internet drama he caused was incredible, a stroke of genius."

"I suppose you'll be needing an autograph or something?"

"Well, now that you mentioned it," Veronica said smiling broadly. "Could you? —— Gotcha," she added, taking in James' look of shock. "No, my love... nothing like that. But what he has written here makes a lot of sense," she continued, deliberately steering the conversation back on track.

"How's that?"

She guided him over to the section marked Philosophy/ Poetry and ran her fingers along the books till she got to Frederick. There were seven books of his there, one catching her attention, remembering she had that one as well as many others in her collection: *Poetic Blasphemy, The Awakening; The TOLM, 360 Degrees; The Lost Book; Kisses;* and the latest, *Love Needs No Excuse: It is its own license,* all sat there upon the shelf in hard back. She extricated one from the shelf, opened it and read from the top of one of the pages a quote.

"The annotation here says it's taken from *Moments In The Sun.* I'm sure it's a book or journal of some sort. That would make sense if it is a particular thing, which would account for the *s* on the end of the word. Listen to this one. You don't mind me reading this, do you?"

"By all means, have at it."

She began to read.

I find moments in the sun
you
heavy in my hand
fingers curling rays
spilling over me.

I want to grow inside of you.

She sighed with a smile accompanied by a distantly satisfying expression on her face.

"Would you like a cigarette now?"

"Cute, Jamie, real cute."

"And you read this piece because...?"

"Because your father is constantly quoting from this book no one has ever read or seen. He does this in all of his books, as if there is some unknown finished volume. Oh, how I would love to sink my fingers into that. Well my point is," she went on, "I think this book has been written for you. He's telling you this in a cryptic way."

"That's a bit of a stretch. You think?"

"Yes, I do. And I'm sure you've read your father's work."

"Sure I have. He's my father, right? Well, at least he was, up until these letters. I don't know what to think now."

"I think you should read the rest of the letters, and if you need to talk about them, I am here. I can read them for — I mean to you, if you like.

"Thanks, pretty. I'll keep that in mind," he said mildly, assuring her that he was not wholly dismissing her offer.

"Now, is there something else you would like to talk about? There is more. Isn't it?

"Why do you ask?"

"Because over the phone you said you had something to tell me, my love. And in the letter, Jamie, your father made reference to something that had happen and is now seeking to make amends for. I suppose it's in the rest of the letters. These two somethings are the same. Yes?"

"Yeah, ask me again later," he said with a reassuring smile, indicating it was perfectly permissible to pursue the matter at another time.

Indeed, there was something more, but James was not prepared to tell her now, here in a book store amongst the prying ears of strangers. He had, however, kept it to himself for many years and now remembered it fresh as the day it happened.

"You are not taking Jamie away from me, Alex," his mother Elizabeth had said many years ago on a cloudy autumn morning, tension constricting her voice in a whisper and straining to contain her anger.

"The boy has the right to know, Bess."

"You shagged some bloody posh bitch," she said, her voice rising in anger, "and had a child, knowing how much I wanted one. Now that you are a big time author and all that tosh, you want to *temporarily,"* she stressed the word, "move back to England and take the only thing I have left. You think I don't know what you're up to. Don't you? You and that scared face womanizer of a friend Cornelius Robertson whoring around. No Alex, Jamie stays with me. You can go back to London and shag your —"

"Keep your damn voice down, woman," James' father snapped maliciously.

However, it was too late. James had walked into the room long before they realized he was there. His face was in utter shock and incredulity, slowly turning to anger. His father seeing this, yanked off a necklace from around his own neck, walked over to James, shoved it into his hand and left. James was seventeen years at the time of his father's unceremonious departure, and it was the last time he saw his father on a regular basis. It was a lot to take in, and presently, James wished he had asked his father about the sister or brother he had not known.

"Jamie?" said Veronica, presently jarring him out of deep thought. "Are you okay?"

"Yeah, you're probably right about the journal, though. I'll read the rest of the letters soon and tell you all about them. And I'll question my mother about — Oh, by the way, my mother has invited me to dinner. Do you think you can see your way in coming with me? Please, it means a lot to me."

He bore an imploring look that Veronica found hard to deny.

"I don't know Jamie," she said weakly.

"Before you say no, I should tell you, she asked if I would bring you."

This statement from James came as quite a surprise to Veronica. She was flattered that James had mentioned her to his mother and was equally touched and simultaneously discomposed by his desire to introduce her, knowing her situation.

"Yes," she said in an effort to please him. "I really need to get back now," she added, returning the book to its original place on the shelf.

"Wonderful. Will is suppose to come over today," he said, averting his eyes from her gaze and turning.

"Jamie, wait," she whispered, her voice cracking with suppressed emotion.

"Yeah?"

She cast around for words to articulate her pent up emotions and found but a few.

"You have created sensations of which my heart has never known. You are light's fullest dimension. You are love's truest intentions."

He was spellbound, at a lost for words, struggling with leaving. And out of nowhere, throwing caution to the winds, she kissed him.

Appearance and Perception

James was feeling so elated by the time he returned to his car; he nearly missed a business card that was wedged between the windshield and wiper blade. He snatched the card from its resting place and was about to toss it as rubbish before recognizing the word, SORRY, written in large letters. He pulled the card closer and read the note.

> SORRY to have left without exchanging my insurance information with you. I accidentally bumped your car door. Here is my card. Please call me for any repairs that may be needed.
>
> Frank

Worried, James' eyes ran up and down the car doors, searching. And to his very happy surprise, he found only a small scratch.

CHAPTER EIGHT

"Got to get this car alarm looked at," he murmured, breathing a sigh of relief.

He flipped the card over to read, FRANK NEFER, The Law Office Of McNeal & Nefer.

"How about that, an honest lawyer," he quietly chortled to himself.

He got into his car while taking note of his father's silver ornate necklace that swung from the rear view mirror and push the memory in his mind aside as easily as he did the necklace, reaching past it and throwing the business card into an unkempt glove compartment. He turned the ignition and took off into the direction in which he came, hoping he had not missed William's call.

Feeling quite pleased with himself, he turned on the radio to listen to some music for a change. James was never much into radio; it annoyed him far too much to keep it tuned to one station, commercials playing one after another ad nauseam, accompanied with a few songs every now and again. He had always felt when technology becomes an irritant, put it away or get rid of it all together. However, he was in a mellifluous mood now after seeing Veronica and felt even the radio could not dampen his spirits. He pushed the seek button on the console repeatedly, hoping to stumble upon a familiar song.

"... to say congratulations to Marcus Bell, winner of last night's LOTTO Jackpot in the amount of—"

He pushed the seek button again. And after sometime of prodding, he happened upon an old favorite.

"I won't go... I won't sleep... And I can't breathe... Until you resting here with me," he bellowed in a cracking voice, forcing notes out of tune at the top of his lungs. "Ah yes, Dido."

He laughed at himself, thinking what William would say if he heard him singing this type of song and in a moon howling manner.

"Bruh, we're gonna put that in the little black box and throw it into the bottom of the ocean."

James did not care; he was alone in his car with tinted windows raised, and could sing loud as he cared to.

"I won't leave... And I can't hide... I cannot be... Until you resting —"

He paused, turning the radio off in order to concentrate on what he had seen. No, surely he must be mistaken. He needed a closer look. James pulled slowly up to the group of men hovering about a parked car, cursing fluidly with one another. They were all dressed in overly large t-shirts and black trousers that sagged low in the back, adorned by non-supportive belts that miraculously managed to keep their pants from falling well below the buttocks area. Some exposed their under garments while forming a scrum at the base of their pants with the hemline dragging, effecting the all too popular peculiarity of a disproportionate individual, elongated at the top half. The third gentleman stood over the two, as if giving directions on how to change a tire, while the forth busied himself with the door on the other side of the car. James was now absolutely certain of his familiarity with the third guy and suspected there was something quite erroneous about their conduct. He rolled down his window.

"Yo, Stephen!" he bellowed.

"Handle your business, B," issued a strong baritone voice from one of the men crouched down, appearing to inspect a tire.

His sagging pants were so low to the point of displaying the whole of his boxers, white with many tiny images of cannabis leaves randomly scattered about. He shot a malevolent look at the one called Stephen, who understood its meaning, and returned the look in kind.

Stephen strolled cooly over to James' car with one hand hidden behind his back. The corner of his lip curled slightly upward, and with a furtive look, he surveyed the surroundings.

"Well, well, well, if it isn't Spooner," he said balefully. "Slumming are we, or have you come to collect on an old debt?"

"Yeah, my shoulder still hurts from the last time I tried to help you," said James.

"I don't give a damn about your shoulder. And do I look like I need help?" said Stephen maliciously.

"I know what you doing, Stephen!" barked James, even more loudly in order for the others to hear.

"Keep your voice down, fool," he hissed. "Damn man, what the hell is wrong with you? You roll up on me and put me on blast in front of my crew using my gov'ment name. Privileged life gave you a big head Spoon." He now continued with his voice at full volume. “If you weren't my cousin, I'd bust a cap up in your ass RIGHT NOW!”

“Blacky,” James began, now comprehending the full gravity of the situation, lowered his voice so that the others could not hear him, an attempt at appearing less confrontational. “Blacky, my mistake. I —”

“Damn right your mistake.”

“You're right, that was totally disrespectful of me. But we’re family, and I love you, cuz. Now, get your ass in the car,” James this time said in a sharp whisper, adopting the same vernacular in which his cousin spoke.

“Man go head on with that shit. I ain't no kid anymore, Spoon. You don’t impress me like you did when we were youngin’s. You can’t tell me what the hell to do, cuz. So roll out dog... I said... roll out,” he added, looking extremely thunderous.

He was right. Long gone were the days when James could impress or even attempt to man handle Blacky, who was now several inches taller than James and muscle bound from many hours of institutionalized workouts and three square meals a day. If he was going to get his cousin in the car, there was only one thing for James to do. He adopted a stone face and turned away from Blacky, fixed his eyes forward, all emotion drained from his face, and spoke in a cold voice.

“I wonder how my dear aunt Olivia would feel about her precious son Stephen trying to get himself locked back up another seven years for boosting cars. I'm sure that would just break her poor heart. Again,” he added, emphasizing his last word. “After what happened to Max, you of all people should know. But... if you think she is made of sturdier stuff and wouldn't mind her son incarcerated again..."

Blacky looked as though he was struck full in the face with a tire iron. As far as he was concerned, this move by James was way below the belt.

"You had to go there, didn't you?" said Blacky with an incredulous look on his face and contemplating the odds of whether James was sincere or not about his veiled threat. "Damn," he added, punctuating his thoughts.

"Wha-up, B," one of his cronies called from behind.

"Finnah bounce, yo," said Blacky.

This announcement of his intention to leave irritated his gang.

"Man get your punk ass out of here," said another, as the others scoffed at him with equal disdain.

Blacky opened the passenger door of James' car and reluctantly got in. He cast James a dark look out of the corners of his eyes and readjusted the seat so that he slumped far back, perhaps away from the sight of those outside who would catch a glimpse of him, undoubtedly looking a little too sheepish for his taste.

"Blacky, I got to ask."

"Here we go again. You ain't changed a bit. Damn man, I'm in the car ain't I?"

"Are you carrying any weapons, drugs, drug paraphernalia, unlabeled medication, and or prescribed medication that is not in its original container? And, are you at present wanted by the law?" James plowed on, ignoring Blacky's protest.

"No Spooner, I'm not holding, just drive," he growled threw clenched teeth. "I swear, it's like signing a damn contract getting in your car."

James drove away, suppressing a small grin with some difficulty, immensely enjoying Blacky's irritated state.

Several minutes in silence passed before Blacky spoke. He cast around for the right words, perhaps feeling slightly out of his element.

"Spooner I —— I really didn't mean —— you know —— about shooting you," he said apologetically, dropping his street vernacular. "It's just you embarrassed me, man. You know how important your street cred is, got to maintain it."

"No, I don't."

"Oh, but you will," he said sagely.

"I don't live in that world, and I don't need to know," James said, tempering his tone, trying not to sound exceedingly arrogant.

Had he lived a privileged life as he was told? Even the name Spooner, short for silver spooner, was affectionately given to him by his cousins on his father's side as a joke that stuck like glue, implying that he was born into money. Even the neighborhood children called him that. It was not his fault his parents were well-off. In addition, this newly discovered information about his adoption, made him feel like an outsider. But he was not such an outsider that he could not relate to Blacky. It was this last thought that usurped the others, offering him some bit of comfort, and he clung to it.

"It's okay cuz, I know you had to man up in front of your boys, and I don't hold that against you."

"Yeah, cause you're Spooner, bad ass," joked Blacky, as he rummaged through the glove compartment. "Dead Prez?" he said stunned, extricating a CD from the jumbled mess of papers accompanied with a clear plastic covered cell phone, that was in mint condition, along with James' identification. "So there is a deep side to you after all. I didn't know you had it in you. I made you out to be a Dido, Yanni, or some European artist fan."

James shot a surreptitious glance at the radio, checking to make sure it was turned off and grinned.

"Yeah, I know a little something. And you're the wise master Yoda of the streets. Now get your crusty mitts out my stuff," he said, noticing an Om symbol tattooed on the forearm of Blacky's outstretched arm, yet made no mention of it.

Their disagreement was dissolved by laughter, and an old familiar bond resurrected between the pair like a soothing balm.

"All joking aside, you know Steph —— Blacky," James corrected himself. "I never really liked —— I mean, I have always been uncomfortable using the name *Blacky*. It seemed —— seems derogatory."

"Damn, cuz, you're a bona-fide buzz-kill. But you know what, you still look like new money. Let me hold some," he said, attempting to lighten James' mood.

When James did not smile, Blacky looked at him and his expression became solemn.

"That's because you live in two worlds, and one is fighting the other. Don't fight it. Embrace it. The answers will come. Trust me. It will all make sense."

James felt this was such an inadequate reply to his awkwardness with the use of the name *Blacky*. He could spend what little time they had debating the finer points of the acceptance of negative labels and stereotypes with his cousin, but what would that accomplish. James instead invited Blacky to accompany him for a bite to eat.

They drove pass a woman walking down a long stretch of highway, and James was suddenly struck with a brilliant idea.

"See that woman there walking?"

"Yeah," said Blacky, craning his neck in time to get a look.

"Okay, remember her. Now let's get a bite to eat."

Blacky supposed there would be something in this singling out of the woman, but James was silent. And Blacky, although curious, remained reticent.

They stopped at Restaurant Siam, located in Ghent, an older and quieted part of the city that most often mistakenly referred to as a separate city within itself. Its very old colonial style homes and spotless cobble streets were well preserved by its many affluent and slightly well-to-do inhabitants. Many residents of Ghent could often be seen jogging early mornings in pairs and some on foot headed towards the local college carrying book sacks and back packs and others just out for a stroll with leash-less dogs. The small urban area had a general air of ease and cordiality. This was James' part of town, but he was keen to make no mention of this superfluous fact.

They proceeded inside, James opening the door for the pair of them and trailing behind. A bell issued from overhead, alerting the host inside. The proprietor, who was a small statue of a man with dark black hair and narrow almond shaped eyes, stood behind the bar and appeared to be taken aback by their sudden entry into the vacant and quieted establishment. The door shut behind them with the jingle of the bell followed immediately by a thud.

The restaurant had that all too pleasant and familiar scent of oriental spices emanating from the back kitchen; its aroma thickened the air. The subdued light issuing through the bamboo shaded windows, sparkled in the many bottles that sat atop the mantle in front of a spotted and streaked mirror mounted on the wall behind the bar. Their shimmering contents that bounce off the mirror, reflected a spectrum of colors onto the walls, reciprocating and complementing the ambient light. The tables and chairs centered in the restaurant were mahogany, and the booths along the walls were semi-enclosed with great high back leather cushions that seemed to reach for the colorful brocade paper lanterns over head.

“Didn't know this place was here,” said Blacky, taking in the overall atmosphere of the establishment.

James had in some way expected that Blacky did not ventured often into his part of town. He ascertained by his tone that Blacky felt a little out of his element, yet all the same very please to have come. James motioned expectantly with a raised head to the host.

“Good afternoon sir,” he said, drawing closer to the gentleman, who was now abandoning his post behind the bar, with several menus in hand. “I have frequented your establishment on several occasions with my lady and found the food here to be exquisitely superb. Your vegetable medley is to die for. And,” he added, looking round and absolutely beaming with appreciation, “my cousin and I would, if you please, like to place an order to go.”

Such enthusiasm caught the manager off guard, causing his apprehension to instantly dissolve.

“May I take your order please sirs?” he said, clearly now eager to serve them.

After settling on what dishes they thought would be the most delicious, according to their individual taste, James ordered for the both. Shortly there after, their food was wrapped and paid for, and they were on their way with an invitation from the manager to soon return.

"What did you think of the service?" asked James, as they seated themselves in the car, obviously with a point to make.

“He seemed like he didn't want to help us,” grumbled Blacky.

CHAPTER EIGHT

"Okay... Now, remember that woman I pointed out to you earlier?"

Blacky nodded reluctantly, knowing that this is where James makes his point.

"Indulge me, tell me your impression of her."

Then with the rapidity of a prepared statement, Blacky proceeded, "A strong Black woman, who's well put together and holding down her own. Fine, takes good care of herself, and —"

"Alright, stop there," said James, cutting across Blacky as if he had heard this a thousand times. "Let me tell you what I saw. I saw a woman walking along a considerable stretch. She was wearing carpet slippers. Her clothes did not fit her well: They hung loose in some places and oddly tight in others. Something about her hair said she was not completely done, and she looked careworn. And, let's not forget the bags that she was carrying. Do you see my point?"

"Yeah, you're too hard on the sisters, Spooner."

James ignored Blacky's implication and continued.

"We all view the world with prejudice eyes: Her appearance... my perception. If that's what you find attractive, then by all means, knock yourself out. I'm not saying what you saw was right or wrong. Just understand, it is our appearance that plays a vital part in the formulation of people's opinions of us, their perception. The way we judged that woman just now, is the same way we were judged by the restaurant manager. That's why the gentleman seemed apprehensive at first in helping us. He was confused. He saw you enter the place with your hip dragging, oversize baggy pants, football jersey, and a do-rag —— wave cap or what ever you call it —— laid, not tied on your head. Yeah, like tying that thing tight around your head would make a difference," he added sarcastically. "He thought you were going to rob the place until he saw me enter. And still he was apprehensive, until I spoke. Bear in mind, we are always dealing with perceptions. Choose how you want people to view you. Your life may depend on it."

Upon saying that, James was reminded of the gentleman shot by the police the night before and considered it for a brief moment, then decided against mentioning it, realizing it would be overstating his point.

"I hear you, cuz. Deep... deep," he said, apparently lost in thought.

"From you Blacky, that's a real comple —— What? Why do you keep looking out of the side mirror?" said James, interrupting his own train of thought and realizing that what he believed as contemplation on Blacky's part, was nothing more than being distracted.

He figured Blacky probably did not hear half of what he had said.

"See, the streets got you paranoid. You can't even relax for a moment."

"You never know, Spooner. You never know. Now drop me off here at the corner."

CHAPTER EIGHT

With his meal laden styrofoam container in hand, he stepped out of the car, gave his surroundings a furtive glance and leaned into the passenger's window.

"I like the name *Blacky*. It's a strong name, a strong street name with a rep. You feel me? And though we teased you when we were children, cuz, *Spooner* is also a strong name, a strong street name which you're going to need, if you keep showing up in places you shouldn't," he added darkly. "Now be safe."

After another surreptitious glance of the streets, and adopting a dark scowl, Blacky strolled away in his cool swagger, leaving James utterly astonished and simultaneously oddly proud to have Blacky as a cousin.

9

Sticks and Stones

S*pooner, spooner, you're just a silver spooner*, a singsong chant echoed in the back of James' mind across the intervening years. Seeing his cousin had raised old childhood memories, and he pushed them aside to contemplate his encounter with Blacky. James mulled over their conversation and admitted to himself that it did not go at all as he planned.

"It's a strong name, a strong street name which you are going to need, if you keep showing up in places you shouldn't." Blacky's words retraced themselves, etching their meaning in his head, and seeing no way around them, he resolved himself to the possibility that Blacky was an authority on all things street wise. James had only meant to express his discomfort in referring to his cousin as *Blacky*, and being such a deep dark shade of brown and calling himself that, James felt his cousin had internalized a negative description of himself. It painfully reminded James of

how his own light skin tone seemed to be a more pleasantly accepted hue, particularly amongst other African Americans.

"Yeah, you're too hard on the sisters, Spooner." Why would he even conjure such a statement? Indeed, the love of his life was not African American. But that did not make him color stricken: He never dated exclusively on the grounds of race. How complicated it seemed at times to be with someone outside your culture. Was Blacky aware of his and Veronica's relationship? James remember never mentioning Veronica to Blacky. And what does it matter anyway? Like James' father always said: *Love needs no excuse, it is its own license.* This very last thought was paramount to the others, because his love for Veronica needed no explanation, nor did his love for Blacky. And his love for Blacky was the reason he was *"in the wrong place,"* interfering. His love for Blacky was the reason he found it hard to call him by any other name than Stephen. Blacky was more than some cousin to him, he was a brother; he was family, and that was all to it.

James thought that maybe his parents needed no excuse as to why they told him not of his adoption. Odd how this recent turn of events bestowed him this inexplicable feeling of separation that he could not even begin to accurately describe. He presently could see how his parents love protected him, as a child, from feeling detached or alienated, and his resentment for their reticence abated.

He wondered who were his biological parents and if they were still together. And had they children that were not given up for adoption as he was? Perhaps they left him because of some enormous tragedy such as death or an act of love by one parent who had not the means to care for him and desired, therefore, a good life for him. Indeed, for the most part, he had a wonderful childhood. But why hadn't either one of his biological parents by now shown themselves? Why did his father feel the need to tell him this, and why now? He continuously posed these shopworn questions to himself. Because James now knew this scrap of information regarding himself, he felt compelled to find out more. Perhaps the letters from his father would yield more. So he made himself a promise to read what his father had written as soon as he returned home. Also, if clever enough, he will scan the letters and try to glean what information he desired from them.

"Now there's an idea," he congratulated himself aloud.

"*Spooner, spooner, you're just a silver spooner*," again the singsong chant of children voices forced their way, this time to the forefront of his mind, and he escaped into the past, where he was eleven years of age and standing before a small group of children with playful smiles on their faces, taunting him.

"You talk funny. Why you talk like that?" asked Anita Forman, who was a dark skinny girl with long brown braids and multi-color beads attached at their ends.

"'Cause he's a *spooner*, rich kid. Thinks he's better," came another kids voice from the group.

"Were you born daft or do you have to work hard —"

CHAPTER NINE

"See, what I tell you. All them *spooners* think they better than us," said a rough looking and stocky built boy by the name of Robert Lee. "Ain't that right, spooner boy," he continued loudly, speaking over James' retort.

His hair was coarse and black. Its dull and dusty look gave the impression of dirty hair that had not been washed for quite some time. Robert, who was carrying an old toilet plunger stick he had found laying about some rubbish, scowled menacingly when he spoke. It frightened most of the kids into submission when any found themselves at odds with him.

"I think he's cute. Say something else in English," said a girl by the name of Rosa-Ann Elizabeth Dalton.

She had fair skin and silky curls that soften her tomboyish appearance of baggy jeans and bulky sneakers. And in her left hand, she held a small piece of sheet rock from a torn down neighboring building, which she used as chalk to draw sidewalk art and hop-scotch on the coarse pavement.

"Cheerios chap," said Floyd Lee, the largest of the group and elder brother to Robert. "Why you guys always talking about cereal? You hungry all the time?"

The other children laughed.

"Is you hungry, Spooner?" he jeer in a mocked baby voice.

"No you git. I sound like this," said James, framing his words with finger quotes in the air, "because I have a proper upbringing, and you lot ——"

"Wo cuz, best not to insult people right off the bat today," a voice issued from behind him.

Stephen had approached unnoticed, and the group at large fell quiet.

"Hey Steph," said Rosa first in melodic tones, absolutely beaming at him.

"Oh, hi Red," he replied with far less enthusiasm.

"Why you call me Red, Steph?"

"'Cause you a redbone. Red to the bone," piped up Floyd.

James thought to himself how she looked nothing like a hound dog.

"Your mama named you Red, I'm a call you Red," said Alfred Clark, the cousin of Floyd and Robert Lee, who was a stick figure of a boy with an enormous afro that seemed to trap every fly and gnat that flew into its sphere.

"My name is Rosa-Ann —"

"Now, if you are done talking to these geniuses," said Stephen, speaking over Rosa's continuing pitch, "got to show you something."

They separated themselves from the rest of the group, and the chatter of idle conversation diminished in the distance with every step taken. And James could hear Rosa's small voice still in protest, tailed away in the murmur with the others.

"Steph," James began, "what's all this codswallop about her bones being red?"

"Cods what?" he ejaculated half laughing. "Listen, Spooner my man, you got to stop talking like that or you will get both our asses kicked. If you must know, that saying originally came from an old Louisiana description, meaning the bones are so light that they are transparent and you can see the blood in the veins running threw them. Well," he added, "that's what I read."

It was obvious, by the puzzled and confused look James bore upon his face, that this explanation was wholly inadequate.

"See, a redbone," he began to explain in detail, "is a person who is *light-skinned* or mixed with something... like you, but... you're not all that light. Matter of fact, can hardly tell your mom's white, and you got that long cool ass tied back dread lock look. The girls be loving that," he finished, sounding slightly envious.

Indeed, as a child, James was very good looking and had grown the most interesting hair that year, drawing the attention of many of the older girls, who spent their leisure time indoors in groups, on porches and leaning out of bedroom window frames, boy gazing. And whenever he would visit his cousins, the older girls made it a point to speak to James as soon as he stepped out of the car or if he was just simply sauntering by on foot. They loved the way he would say in his British accent:

"And good afternoon to you too, ladies."

"Man, and you're a mac-daddy with that *double-O-7* voice," said Stephen, who was now strolling in the middle of the street along with James.

"Excuse me?"

"Never mind," said Stephen. "Just... use your powers wisely, young Jedi."

"Now don't you O'Neil boys go getting yourselves into trouble," said Mrs. Freeman, an ever watchful and unusual elderly woman, who sat all day on her porch, reminding children as they passed to behave.

She wore a large, faded and outlandishly multi-color floral dress that covered the whole of her rocking chair and ballooned like a tent when she stood there in her carpet slippers, peering over her glasses and constantly readjusting her grey wig. Mrs. Freeman had been watching the pair's progress up the street with growing interest.

"Yes Mrs. Freeman," they said, grinning with ill-disguised mischief and doing their best imitation of perfect angels.

"A bit off her rocker isn't she, mate?" said James speaking out the corner of his mouth.

"Yeah, and crazy too," said Stephen loudly, caring less if she could hear them.

"Hey, what's all the fascination with skin color and —"

"Later for that, Bob Marley," he said dismissively. "This is what I want to show you."

They rounded the corner, and there it stood, an incredible structure of architectural wonder. It was an adventurous boy's dream. Its many dark and dirty broken windows were set high in rust colored bricks, and the doors were boarded with large planks of wood that appeared to stretch seamlessly around its massive girth. It was heavy with graffiti, and every part of its wooden surface was tattooed with handbills advertising some product or event. Wild grass reached from beneath the cracked pavement, and grew along the bottom edge of the boarded structure. The grass became thicker and much taller near an unkempt tree growing next to the abandoned building, and it framed the building as if drawing a line in the dirt, where broken breeze blocks, glass, rocks, and other demolished construction material lay strewn outside its perimeter.

"Absolutely bloody brilliant," said James, looking thoroughly awestruck.

"Word —— yeah —— what you say," said Stephen, not at all sure of what James had meant; however, judging by James' glowing facial expression, he interpreted this as being pleased. "See the last window, seventh up and fourth over to the right, in the second group?" said Stephen, picking up a large smooth stone from one of the enormous piles of the rubble on the ground.

James nodded excitedly as Stephen turned the stone over several times in his hand, feeling the surface of it.

"I never miss."

"Never... ever?"

"Never."

And without taking aim, he hurled the smooth stone upward with blinding speed. A fraction of a second later the pane broke, and the ping pong sounds made by the stone bouncing off objects from the inside could be heard.

"Brilliant," said James impressed, bending down and reaching for ammunition of his own.

"We ain't allowed inside, but we can see in from the top," Stephen said, running over to the large tree. "What, you gonna stand there all day and count clouds?"

James laughed at this odd yet familiar comment and tossed his rock at a broken window.

"Wouldn't miss this for the world, just like *blades of death*," he said to himself, hurtling toward the tree on the heels of Stephen.

The tree was huge. Its trunk and limbs were massive at the bottom, and the much smaller ones at the top were surprisingly sturdy. Taking advantage of this, the two scampered to the top with the incredible agility of spider monkeys. They stepped off of a branch onto the roof, and the gravel and warm tar sunk slightly beneath their feet.

James was once again awestruck. He could not believe what he saw. It was like looking down from high upon the top of the world. Many buildings could be seen for miles around, and the sun cast its magnificent light upon glass structures in the distance like precious jewels. In addition, he could hear the noises clearer than ever before, rising up from the streets. What an absolutely wondrous thing to behold.

"Over here, this is where you can look in," said Stephen, knelt down at the far side of the roof with his back to James, peering with absorbing interest into what was apparently a hole. "Don't be such a tourist and come take a —"

Crash! The roof beneath Stephen suddenly gave, and he attempted to lay himself flat to disperse his weight, but to no avail. His foot had broken through the rotten wood, and the rest of the roof below him disappeared, leaving him nothing but pieces of splintering wood and loosening shingles to hang on to. The loud sound had startled James out of his mild daydream. He cast around and saw Stephen in imminent peril.

"A little help here!" bellowed Stephen in desperation.

One of his hands had slipped, and he was holding on for dear life with the other. Without hesitation, James sprinted over to Stephen. And realizing the roof must be weak around the area Stephen was hanging, he did an incredible baseball slide, kicking up gravel as he past the hole. Then with an extended arm, he snatched Stephen's wrist the moment his hand lost its grip.

"Gotcha!" he said, jerking to an abrupt stop and nearly pulling his own arm out of its socket.

"Damn, Batman —— took you long enough," said Stephen, panting hard and clasping the fingers of his free hand tightly around James' wrist.

"I —— was —— taking — in —— the view —— You mind?" strained James. "Now climb —— before —— I lose —— my ——"

And with stupendous effort, James tugged for all he was worth, while Stephen simultaneously climb back up, utilizing James' arm as a human rope.

"...grip," finished James, out of breath and pulling Stephen as far away from the hole in the roof that his small and trembling muscles could manage.

"Thanks, cuz —— You saved my life —— I —— I owe you one," breathed Stephen, trying to steady his breath. "You're bad ass —— ain't you?"

"A kamikaze move," panted James. "It means *divine wind* in Japanese." he added, in answer to the quizzical look on Stephen's face.

"Thanks, I'll remember that."

"Had enough adventure for the day then?" asked James, nursing a very sore shoulder.

"Yeah," Stephen said, spitting dirt and gravel out of his mouth. "That'll do it for me."

And the pair of them lay there on the tar patched roof, utterly sapped, panting and laughing.

10

Between the Lines

"What the hell were we thinking? Ah, to feel invincible again," James thought presently, chuckling in his car parked outside his home. Mr. Berchmier, his curious neighbor from across the street (who claims pretentiously to once worked for the FBI five years ago and now retired) was pushing a spreader, sprinkling tiny fertilizer pellets onto his well manicured lawn, when his eyes fell upon James having a laugh. James caught sight of his neighbor's suspicious look. Then feeling a bit embarrassed, he pulled himself together, stifling his laughter. He grabbed his attaché case supporting his styrofoam container of food, sitting precariously on top and proceeded to exit his car. When he raised himself to his fullest height, he was met by a man holding a badge and identification in hand.

"What the —"

"Detective Lee Matlock," he said, then snatched his badge from James' face with a flick of his wrist.

Detective Matlock was a corpulent man. His overall appearance was careworn to the extent of commanding no authority. He looked as though he had been slumbering in his clothes all night. His wrinkled dingy white shirt was slovenly tucked into his trousers which hung low on his waist, obviously a compromise for his vast midriff, and the button holes of his shirt were expanding beneath his brown dark stained tie, exposing small portions of his pale flesh. His breath, a heavy pungent oder of coffee (no doubt from wolfing down substantial amounts of heavily caffeinated brews) wafted in James' direction, causing his stomach to turn. He smelt of unbathed armpits, and his greasy dark hair was combed over to his left, in an attempt to de-emphasize his balding pate.

"What's this all about officer?" asked a surprised James, absentmindedly activating his car alarm.

"It's detective," he grumbled. "Do you know Stephen Octavius O'Neil aka ——"

"Blacky," finished James. "Yeah, he's my cousin. What about him? Is Blacky okay?"

"Your car fits the description of one reported leaving the scene of a crime today," Detective Matlock plowed on indifferently, treating James' answer and concern for Blacky as superfluous.

"What?" said James astonished. "What crime? I was just with him. There must be some sort of mis——"

"Murder," he said surlily. "It's still a crime in this state you know."

CHAPTER TEN

James said nothing to this. He held his tongue with great difficulty and had a feeling the officer was trying to goat him into some action he would later regret.

"And," he continued. "he had three other accomplices. Somehow you checked out clean, but the others... records long as my arm... very dangerous. Mr. Blacky," he said the name with disdain, "was seen getting in your vehicle and driving off around the time a man was shot for trying to run scum away from his —"

"There must be some mistake," began James once more, determined to finish his previous pitch. "I was passing by and offered a ride to my cousin, who by the way, was walking along and minding his own business."

James never saw much use in lying. He would, however, in this case make an exception as to what kind of business Blacky was actually minding. He did not appreciate Detective Matlock's tone, and it caused him very little discomfort to tell Matlock what he felt was a harmless untruth.

"Once a criminal, always a criminal," he said gruffly. "It's in your people's blood or something. Y'all just do whatever the hell you want to do."

James resentment for this last comment drained all cordiality from his face, and rage swelled inside his chest. He refused to allow Matlock to tar Blacky with the same brush that most people who did not really know him would. Let alone the fact he just insulted his entire family and perhaps, if he wasn't mistaken, his race.

"Now see here officer —"

Just then, Matlock's mobile phone rang.

"Yes sir," he answered almost immediately. "I have his cousin the driver here. No, but —— yes but ——" he spluttered, turning his back to James, lowering his voice. "I don't understand sir," his voice now more strained. "Yes sir —— Sir I —— Yes sir, Capt. Mahony. Damn," he finished, ending his call and turning back around to face James.

"Problem officer? said James with awful smugness.

"That's detective," he snapped. "And I'll be keeping an eye on you Mr. O'Neil. I don't know what kind of pull you and that scum of a cousin you hang with got, but I'm going to get to the bottom of it."

"Yeah you do that," said James derisively. "Good day officer."

And at that, James greeted Mr. Berchmier with a wave, turned on his heel and proceeded up the garden path to his front door, with a smile of immense satisfaction creasing his face.

When James found himself inside his home, away from the resentful glower of Detective Matlock, he placed his things on the kitchen table, walk over to the large bay window of the living room, then cast outside and saw Matlock presently sitting in his car, undoubtedly attempting to ascertain why he was instructed to abandon his endeavors.

"Git," mumbled James with considerable disdain, the word popping out of his mouth as if abandoning restraint then made a tut that sounded something like, "tchuh."

CHAPTER TEN

For now, the reason why he was instructed to leave the both of them alone did not matter to James. The fact that he and Blacky were safe and completely innocent of the said crime, although horrible in itself, was all that mattered. He watched as the detective drove away in a rickety black car with two hubcaps missing from the driver's side, and a faded weather worn top, all of which James could not help but notice. James thought how wrong he was in his choice of words, then corrected himself.

"My bad... wanka."

His breath fogged the window from its close proximity, and he found himself laughing out loud at the sound of the word. And although it fell oddly on his tongue, he felt for the moment thoroughly vindicated.

He could no sooner respect a man like Detective Matlock or even give him the time of day. James saw people like him as weak, people who believed life dealt them a poor hand, which gave them the right to be vituperative to others. James thought he must have had poor rearing. *An impoverished mind creates a poorly under nourished spirit, and poor spirits breed poverty.* That is what his father would say. James considered perhaps there is something true to this high-minded notion.

He gave Mr. Berchmier, who was eyeing him presently from the other side of the pane with growing interest, a cheerful two finger salute then turned and walked over to the phone. He picked it up and began to dial, all the while mumbling to himself irritatedly.

"Saved his butt again. Trouble follows him. Got to talk to him about that. What in the world was he thinking, hanging out with dangerous riffraff."

"*W'sup, yo. You know what to do*," a familiar voice on the other end of the line said, followed by:

"Beep."

"I see you got the po-po looking for you now. Good thing we went to get lunch, 'cause your crew is off the chain. Do me a favor, Blacky. Stay out of trouble."

He hung the phone up then checked his messages. Nothing. Not even one message from William. It was most unlike him to say he would show and then not. Once again James picked up the receiver. He dialed Williams number, and when it rang for quite a while, he finally gave it up as a bad job. Where in the world was William? Had not he realized most of the day was getting away? That was not, however, the immediate matter now pressing. He could no longer wait; his stomach was putting up an enormous protest for lack of food, and he also wanted to dive right into the letters straight away. James therefore made himself comfortable at the kitchen table with his letters and food close at hand. He scanned the letters each in turn and found all were concluded in the same manner. As far as pertinent information to glean, there was none. Admittedly, he had done a shabby job at glancing over the letters and concluded what he needed to know must be somewhere written between the lines. James therefore abdicated himself to thoroughly reading the letters. He opened the next one in sequential order and began to read.

CHAPTER TEN

My Dear Son;

I hope this letter finds you thriving in the best of health. Apparently, you have not yet read my letter or perhaps now find yourself presently without words. No doubt, it would have shock anyone with the strongest resolve into a towering response of incredulity. I know my last letter lend itself a bit much for anyone to suddenly absorb. And again, do forgive me for waiting so long to tell you this. Please do not hold it against your mother. She worries you would look upon her with different eyes once you knew the truth. This you may have worked out already from the argument you walked in on so many years ago. We never thought it important to tell you; however, that day I felt the need, and that remains part of what your mother and I disagree on. You know already that love needs no excuse; it needs no explanation of why we kept it from you. One truth presses on me that I must relinquish (the other part of the argument you see), the truth about another woman and a child being born. The woman existed; however, a sibling of yours did not. You have no brother or sister out there.

"Well... that answers one question," said James aloud, then continued reading.

I will explain what your mother meant by her choice of words. Again, I ask you for a little patience.

For many years, your mother and I tried to get pregnant, but it just seemed nearly impossible. Until one day I came home from work and found her stretched out on the kitchen floor, unconscious in a blood soaked apron. She had fainted at the sight of so much of her own blood and must have hit her head against the counter as she passed out. Naturally, I feared the worst. I managed to put her into the car and rushed her to St. Agnes Hospital. The doctor told me that she had an ectopic pregnancy. And because of extensive damage to her ovary, it would like the other, need removing. It would make it impossible to again conceive. She would need plenty of rest. This news devastated the both of us, and in the following months, your mother drifted into a deep depression. And we began to drift apart. I don't remember who blamed who or did self pity on my part cause the downward spiral of our relationship. I do know that your mother and I wanted a baby, and that would never happen.

I will write you again soon.

Live and love with all your heart; moments in the sun belong(s) to you, my son.

Love,
Dad.

"There it is again, written on this one as well as the others," he thought, mouthing the words *moments in the sun belong(s) to you.* He contemplated them for a moment, then decided to abandon Veronica's hypothesis.

"Okay, let's see. I'm adopted because they could not have their own. No brother or sister out there, and there was a woman. Oh yeah, that really helps," James said sardonically. "I'm glad we cleared that up."

He threw the letter onto the table with the others and started jabbing at his food, all along muttering to himself, stuffing a fork laden with noodles and vegetables into his mouth. It was frustratingly obvious that James would have to waive the rest of the day, pouring over his father's letters, trying to find something, anything as to who his birth parents were. Perhaps he would find the name of an adoption agency or why his birth parents had given him up. What was least of all important to him was the identity of the woman his mother and father quarreled about, for he was sure it had nothing to do with his adoption. The importance of his father's infidelity diminished in the wake of his own new found family status. Sure he was disappointed in his father for many years; however, presently his illicit relationship with Veronica made him a bit more sympathetic, and at times felt somewhat hypocritical for judging his father far too harshly. And what of this *moments in the sun belong(s) to you* curiously written at the end of all his father's letters? For all its intent, however, it was grammatically flawed. Or was it? Try as he may, he could no longer dismiss Veronica's theory.

The sun diligently made its way along the September sky, painted with stratus clouds magnificently stretched out across its face and infused with an orange, red and yellowish glow. Although its magnitude was no longer at its highest, and now found a resting place beyond the horizon of the distant cityscape, it nonetheless left a warm glow upon all beneath the heaven. Its radiance seeped into James' living room where he sat, still pouring over his father's letters. He paused, remembering what Veronica had read in the book store.

"I find moments in the sun..." he recited pensively.

It was truly splendid in all its brevity, hauntingly beautiful. It expressed far more longing than he had ever put pen to paper. Perhaps it was because he spent more time at his present employment correcting and dismantling works instead of composing, and somehow in his endeavors, lost the beauty in the words and between the lines. His heart sank, and he found himself feeling lonely, thinking of Veronica and how she inspired him to write again. She was his beautiful and awe-inspiring muse and made him feel as though he could accomplish anything. And at that moment of realization, James finalized his decision. His heart began to feel lighter. It was what he had desired since his youth. He will resign his position at Quill Ink And Parchment Books as an editor and devote his time and effort in publishing his own; however, this he will do after his vacation was done.

James lifted the phone receiver and dialed Veronica's mobile. He was excited at the prospect of writing and wanted to share it with her. She answered the phone, sounding as if she had been crying.

"Hi, love. Are you okay?"

"I —— I am fine," she said unconvincingly, attempting to sound brighter.

James had a feeling that Uri —— her husband of whom he understood to be some sort of unforthcoming businessman that travels often to different countries, trading artifacts that he would not disclose to Veronica, which led James to express to her how very dodgy it all seemed —— had something to do with her somber mood. He had been both physically and verbally abusive in the four years of their failed marriage. For the life of James, he could not understand why she had not left a man whose name she would not even take. In addition to his bewilderment, James wondered what was taking her so long to leave Uri, now that she was obviously happy with him. But he would not pressure her to leave. No pressure, that is what he had promised her. However painful it was for him, he would stick to it, for she had more than her share of stress. To deal with her anxiety, she would at times consume an entire bottle of Merlot before turning in. And tonight, like many others, she confessed to an attentive James that she had been drinking to relax.

"I am all the wine you'll ever need," he said, coming very close to breaching his promise of no pressure.

All he wanted was for her to be happy. Although selfish it may seem, he preferred her to be happy with him.

"I meant to tell you earlier," redirected James brightly, "that I've decided to write my own book or even books, and it's all thanks to you."

"Really?" she said, her voice coming alive. "You're a very talented writer. I know you will be successful with it. But how am I to take credit for that?"

"You inspire me to be what I'm becoming."

"You are what you're becoming."

And he detected a note of melancholy in her voice.

"Thank you my sweet. Oh, I saw my cousin again today," he added quickly, as if announcing it before his memory failed. "You know, the one called Blacky."

He then recounted the day's events, including the encounter with Detective Matlock and his abrupt departure after a call from his superior.

The latter part of the night was drawing to a close, and they had been carrying on at length discussing James' day. James did not know what next he was going to speak of. He just wanted to keep talking until he was absolutely sure that Veronica was okay. But the night was wearing on the pair of them, and a sleepy haze fogged their brains which made it nearly impossible to continue their exchange of sweet nothings. They stifled yawns each in turn, which indicated the cessation of the night's conversation was at hand.

"Okay baby," said Veronica, stifling another yawn. "Let me get some sleep, I want to be well rested for tomorrow."

"What's happening tomorrow?"

"Your mother's invitation. Remember?"

"Oh yeah, that's right."

"Thank you for calling, Jamie. I love you, baby."

"I love you too, Veronica."

"Night," they said together, then ended the call.

The wide screen television affixed to the bedroom wall presently played the news quietly in the background, reflecting the day's events. James cast his sleepy eyes upward and gave the volume button on the remote a few prods. He listened as the reporter described in detail what now has become a recent outbreak of car thefts and related murders in the Beach Area. He went on in reporting several witnesses, whose names police authorities are not at liberty to release, saying that Mr. Robert St. John of 274 42nd Street, was killed trying to fin off several gang members from his car. He was shot by one, and another removed the keys to his vehicle and his wallet from his pocket. Witnesses had also said that all three men had gotten into the car and drove away, leaving Mr. St. John in the street to die. Paramedics and police officers arrived on the scene shortly thereafter and had found him dead. The reporter went on, but James was not in the mood to listen to more horror stories, particularly one that would have very well been the cause of Blacky's return to prison. So he gave the controller another prod, and the screen went black.

The silence was incredibly loud, and it pressed against his ears and on him like an invisible force weighing him down. Veronica filled his slumbering thoughts. And to keep from worrying about her, James thought he would brave another one of his father's letters. He opened the next in sequential order. The soft pillows propped up between the headboard of James' bed and his back cradled him. It felt as though the last bit of energy he had was siphoned from him, and he slumped lifeless. He began to read and found his father's disembodied voice issuing from the letter.

"You do understand me, don't you, son?" his voice floated in James' head serenely.

CHAPTER TEN

"Leave him alone Alex, he's too young to know," his mother's unearthly voice said.

Then James was dreaming he was his father arguing with his mother, and then he was his mother, arguing with his father. His father was telling James that his mother did not want to be touched by him any more, and he was lonely, ever so lonely. James was now his father, and he was sitting in a café with a beautiful dark head woman. He was explaining that his wife no longer loved him and begged the woman to run away with him, to leave her husband. Then the woman turned into Veronica, and the pair of them were on a beach, the sun in their faces and the smell of the ocean all around them.

"See Jamie, this is why I love the beach. All the voices here are carried away by the sound of the ocean. No one can hear us," she said, her voice clearly buffered by the waves over the voices of others nearby. "The sun feels so good today," she added, stretching her arms upward and running her fingers through her hair.

She was all aglow, which made James' heart filled with such longing. Next they were kissing, and the beach fell away, enclosing them in a room. Veronica's back was up against a wall, James' body pressed against hers. Their hands were groping every part of each other, stripping away layers of clothing. He lifted her up off the floor; she wrapped her legs around him.

"Woof-woof woof-woof!"

James was suddenly awakened by the neighbor's barking dog. His heart was pounding in his entire body, and his breathing was intensely labored. Half disoriented, he reached over while fumbling across his alarm clock and knocking his father letters to the floor. He pulled from the drawer of his night stand a note pad and pen, then began to scribble by the unexpectedly brilliant morning light that stole through the bedroom window.

i penned my inspiration to the door
and locked it
so that her sweet words breathed into me
would go uninterrupted

i painted kisses of our love
here and there
of prophesies yet to come
and when i was done
i left these words
upon her lips
with my finger tips

i... love... you.

He ended with a hard punctuation, nearly ripping the page. "Damn dog. And that was getting good too."

11

Sexy in Red

Sunday morning came sooner than expected, accompanied with sonorous barks from Mrs. Hawthorne's German Shepherd, which for some odd reason James noticed had recently taken to throwing a towering fit at sunrise. It sardonically put James in mind of a bizarre offspring of two species, one half rooster and the rest a loud barking head. He remained in good spirits, nonetheless, and hoped to share last night's or rather this morning's very interesting dream with Veronica, later in the afternoon. Today was the day she would meet his mother, and that was in itself a bit unnerving. She was presently committed, and James would prefer his mother not know that spot of information, for it was quite soon in the relationship for either of them to become acquainted with parents. But the past seven months made it impossible for James to think of being with anyone else other than Veronica. James was absolutely certain he wanted to spend the rest of his life with her. He had several other relationships in the past, all of which he was also seriously committed to, but none like Veronica. It was because of this, he made an exception of introduction.

❦

Two o'clock in the afternoon found Veronica and James enjoying a long drive in the country. James recounted the letters he had read the night before and the odd dream admixed with his father's retelling of his relationship with James' mother. Veronica found the correlation between the dream, the letters, and also her relationship with James fascinating.

"Sigmund Freud would have a field day," she said.

She had been listening carefully to James the entire time and found her thoughts dwelling on how his father was willing to drop everything and run away with the woman he loved, and she suspected James was not far from the same actions. She was exhilarated and equally frighten of what she knew must surely be on James' mind. There was a moment of silence between the pair. She looked at him, and after a few more moments, her gaze turned hungry, and she reached over and groped his inner thigh.

"Mmhmm... Sop you up with a biscuit," she said with her best caricatured southern accent.

The pair of them laughed, James more hardily than Veronica. He was caught off guard by her sauciness and laughed so hard that he nearly choked, causing her to immediately thump him on the back of the neck with her open palm rather exuberantly. This action, however, increased his laughter.

CHAPTER ELEVEN

"Do you mind?" coughed James still laughing. "I'm driving here."

Her aim was poor, and she apologized for whacking him so hard. The pair again broke out in contagious laughter.

"Would you like me to smack you again?" she chuckled.

"That kinky stuff is too advance for me girl," he joked out of breath. "That's enough for me... baby steps."

Their chortling subsided, and James finally caught his breath. Veronica placed her hand on his head, stroking it tenderly, and admiring how long his locks were. Her eyes fell upon her purse resting on the back seat behind James, and she ceased her caresses then pulled the heavy bag into her lap. She extricated a book out of her enormous canvas purse and turned to a bookmarked page. And without preamble, she began to read.

Come what may moments when all shall ask:
Does it matter?
Is it possible to discard the formless
the wordless
my thoughts
the why of which?
What is it I'm reaching for
an unassailable truth?
What am I in my futile attempts to construct?
Do the pieces hold the light?

Do... the pieces... hold... the light?

"So, you brought one of my dad's books with you," he began suspiciously. Then in tones that threaten sarcasm, he added, "Yeah, always the deep one. He was all about introspection."

"Well, you know it is the first step towards positive change and knowing yourself. Listen to this one. It's a long one. Okay?"

"We have nothing but time," he said with a forced smile. "I'm all ears."

children of a lesser god
swallowed by the sea
whose cries are heard as distant pleas
and blood that covers a multitude of sins
have you——

"Wait a second. This is one hell of a long poem. It's like a dissertation or something. You can't be serious."

"Oh come on Jamie. It's not that bad. It's a favorite of mine. Just one. I'll read only one long one. Okay?"

"Wow," he said surprised. "You are a fan. Okay, I'm listening."

"Now where was I...? Oh."

have you tossed your faith into the winds
like autumn trees whose fallen leaves

CHAPTER ELEVEN

dispensed into effusive breeze
a salute to a god of yesteryear

and where is your god now
does it reside in pockets and purses
empty promises
instead of hearts (and kisses)
and can you still kiss
and not expect any in return
or hoard them all in hopes to make
a profit

and where is moses
and the promise of dry land
has he broken his staff
or lost it in the down pour of apathy
the slow fullness of bureaucracy
the chains and images of psychological slavery
or drowned in the flood of complacency

today there are no birds in the sky
and all the clouds have turned to tears
land creatures forced to be aquatic
there is water everywhere
and not a drop
to drink

where is the relief aid
to the mother cried the baby
i have long forgotten how to suckle
and you
have forgotten me
for all your store houses and supplies
lay beneath a rivered city
and your statesmen atop a mountain safe
waiting
behind the curtain of a human levee

all those souls that lay afloat
to never wake from their slumber
are as the living dead
unaware and set adrift
amassing in great numbers
in the current of currents
a prelude to an aftermath to come

they said she would come
but no one believed she would come so soon
they said she would be powerful
but no one believed that she would bring the monsoons
they said she would extinguish the light
but no one believed she would reveal the truth

CHAPTER ELEVEN

and she has come
bringing with her the reality
of what we truly are
wretched
insignificant in the grand scheme of things
when all we need is love

i am not a beatle
but i understand the necessity for such a thing
and such a thing we have done far too long without

from this day forth
love shall be the ship set sail
in search of survivors
carrying life rafts for all
the deserving
the undeserving
and love shall be the food for thought
feeding the hungry
the deprived
it shall dry the drenched
the crying eyes
and forgive the unforgivable
make possible the impossible
and unveil the inevitable

SEXY IN RED

a beauty of which we are becoming

so
baptize me in katrina's tears
release me from the lies and fears
weather up my children the sky is falling
third world families across the sands are walking
shelter me from the coming storm
10 thousand voices crying beneath a superdome
bureaucratic and periodical ballyhoo
a burning bush that knows no truth
they called it aid relief from suffering
red crosses tattooed on empty busses
my sweet country tis of thee
inundated with refugees
and i have no more tears to weep

attics filled with corpses
military forces
cholera and e.coli
and i am sure that more will die
pointing fingers in the rain
through the eyes of hurricanes
born through the solar womb
a sunrise beneath a blood red moon
but

CHAPTER ELEVEN

i am something wonderfully becoming
said the butterfly
to the cocoon.

"My goodness, this is you," she said with a look of dawning admiration. "There's no question that the both of you are so very much alike. I know what you are going to say, Jamie. There's no point denying it. There are certain connections and ties that bind, created and maintained without the aid of DNA. He sounds just like you when you get all fired up and philosophical like. Which by the way, is very sexy when *you* do it," she added matter-of-factly, then continued. "And the more I read him, the more I see you. It's incredible."

"Veronica ——"

"Now before you get all huffy," she interjected, forestalling James' counter argument. "I am going to read a very short one to you, and you tell me if you see any parts of yourself or not."

"Okay?"

"Okay."

She flipped the pages with the rapidity of a bank teller counting money. Then locating the poem, she began.

this longing for your lips
brings them no closer
to me
across this arid void of no you

days go by in agonizing protraction

in your absence
i take your kisses
and stretch them from one moment to the next
to sustain me.

She turned and looked at him with watery eyes. She bore a slight expression that implied to James that there was no denying she was right. He could not say a word. His heart sank. He knew all too well what his father had been feeling when he penned the poem. He could see in her eyes for the first time her pain coupled with her longing to be with him. Or, was it James saw this because it was how he felt.

“Did I tell you I love you today?” he said, breathing deeply the clean country air.

“You say it with your eyes every time you look at me, Jamie. If the words never part your lips again, I would still hear them. I would always know.”

She stroked his beard stubbled face with the back of her hand.

“I hope you don’t mind me saying this.”

“Okay. Go on,” he said bracing himself for the worst.

"I understand your father more clearly now... his passion.”

“Me too,” he agreed, wondering if Veronica was about to make a correlation between his passion and that of his father’s.

CHAPTER ELEVEN

"I wonder whatever happen to that woman, the woman in your father's letters. She must be one in the same to whom he has written many pieces like this for."

Upon hearing that, James again remembered with crystal clarity his mother's angry words the day his father left. *"You shagged some bloody posh bitch and had a child, knowing how much I wanted one. Now that you are a big time author and all that tosh, you want to move back to England and take the only thing that I have left. No Alex, Jamie stays with me."*

"I don't care," James said presently in an effort to repress the memory.

"I don't mean to upset you, Jamie. But she is probably responsible for some of the most beautiful pieces I have ever read that were written by your father."

"It's okay. Sorry, I don't mean to be short, Veronica. It's just... Well, she came between my parents."

"Are you sure that's the reason their relationship failed?"

"There was something I didn't tell you at the bookstore."

He recounted painfully the argument his parents had leading up to his father's unceremonious departure.

"And all he had left me with was that," he finished, indicating with his index finger the ornate necklace hanging from the rear view mirror.

"I see. It's very beautiful craftsmanship. It looks like a family crest."

"It's nothing special, just a fancy necklace."

How old were you, Jamie, when this happened?" she asked, ignoring his indifference.

"I was 17 years old."

"Nearly of age, weren't you? And it seems like your mother didn't want to go with him. I would hazard a guess that your father didn't want to rip you and your mother apart. I would go anywhere with you, Jamie. Anywhere," she said, breathing the last word into his ears and sending electric shocks through his body. "Sometimes, what's light to others can be very heavy for us to carry."

"You say that because...?" said James slightly bemused yet still beaming from her remark of going anywhere with him.

"Maybe you've been carrying something belonging to your mother for so long."

"And that would be...?"

"Her anger. Her shame. Her resentment. Or maybe I'm mistaken. I have made a few doozies in my time," she said with a smile.

But she was not wrong. In fact, what she had said made more sense than he cared to admit. He remembered a portion of one of his father's letters, how he had decided to let go of the pain.

Although we wanted a baby, we drifted apart even further. Sometimes, I think your mother thought that there existed something wrong with herself. I no longer cared. After a while, we no longer shared the same bed. She withdrew from my touch, and I grew tired of trying. Son, sometimes people never recover from certain traumas. It doesn't mean you shouldn't give it your best effort, just know when to move on and when to let go. I thought we would always find a way. Your mother found a way in a bottle. That worked for her. And I found it in the company of a another woman.

He recited it word perfect, watching Veronica's facial expression and nods of understanding. Sometimes it seemed as if she could read his mind. She now seemed to have a firm understanding of what James' father was feeling. Or was it his mother that she understood so well? Was it because of the comfort they both found in distilled spirits? And it was at this moment he decided to question his mother about his adoption.

"And yes, you should speak with your mother," she said, as if reading his thoughts. "I love it out here Jamie, it's peaceful," she added at an enormously transparent attempt to change the subject. "It reminds me of where I grew up, in Messina, near a river. There was a big tree with this one enormous branch that hung low with a swing attached. I called it the swinging tree. Oh, and there were butterflies in the spring by the thousands in this wide field of tall dandelions and wild flowers. And in the summer, a million fireflies would come out at night and flicker on and off as if communicating with one another through light. We'd chase and capture them in our cupped hands and watch them glow through small openings in our grips. Sometimes the boys would use old jam jars with holes punched in the lids, making jar lamps of them. Afterwards we'd set them free."

Her efforts did not go unnoticed. And James, who had been feeling a bit put upon over the subject of his mother and father's relationship, thankfully and with great alacrity acquiesced.

"Sounds like a wonderful place for a child to grow up."

"It is. I would like to return there someday."

"My father chose to live far away from the noise of the city. It's perfect for writing. I believe this is where he did his best work, out here. My mother loves it because... well she feels comfortable away from people. Now that I've mentioned it, people seem to irritate her. Some feel that she is not at all amiable, but the longer you know her, the better you grow in understand her disposition. I have to warn you —"

"Not to worry Jamie, I'll be just fine."

"This is it," James said pointing at the road sign that read *O'Neil Lane.*

"Oh," said Veronica raising both her eyebrows and adopting an expression that indicated she was quite impressed.

He pulled off the main highway onto a road that lead to large overgrown hedges and trees on either side of an enormous automatic wrought-iron gate. They then found themselves at the beginning of a long path flanked with forty towering trees or more, ushering them towards a massive Elizabethan style home.

CHAPTER ELEVEN

"Okay, this is not at all what I envisioned. You didn't tell me your family was this rich."

"Yeah, got a lot of ridicule from it when I was a kid," he said, forcing himself to ignore the memory of children's sing song taunts. "You're sure?" he went on jokingly. "We can turn back around and enjoy the ride back, just you and I and the country side."

"Always the poet, I'm okay, love," she beamed. "Let's go in."

They got out of the car, James opening the door for Veronica, and the pair of them proceeded up the walk way, Veronica slightly nervous with stomach butterflies. She cast over to their right and saw a small cottage along a path set off a short distance away and a car parked near-by.

"What's that, the servants quarters?" Veronica said, attempting to throw a little humor upon an increasingly suspenseful moment."

"No, it's the guest house," laughed James. "formerly where I use to stay."

"Wow, that's some large guest house."

"Yeah, and I've never seen that car parked there before. She must have bought a new one."

They climbed half circular courthouse steps and stood there upon a welcome mat, which was an enormous burnish brass metal plate set into the marble landing. Its embossed lettering were flushed with the surface that encased it, and the size of it could accommodate four adults standing upon it. They stood there looking at each other, James with his hands in his pocket, beaming at Veronica.

"Are you going to ring the door or knock?" she asked, slightly nonplussed at James' lack of interest in continuing on. "Or we can stand here and smile at each other all day," she added flirtatiously.

"Oh, sorry, the brass welcome plaque is pressure sensitive," he said looking down upon it. "It acts as a doorbell. So we won't be getting much smiling time in, but we can always get in a quickie."

Veronica blushed slightly, and just as her face began to color up, the heavy mahogany door with high carved windows, swung slowly open, and a lovely silver headed woman dressed in all white appeared from behind.

"Jamie," she said smiling.

"Hello mother," he said rather stiffly, now with his hands behind his back.

"Jamie, don't be so formal. Come inside," she said testily. "Now give your mother a hug," she added, pulling him into an embrace. "You could have let yourself in."

"I no longer live here, mother," he began, returning a perfunctory hug, "so it would be inappropriate —"

"Enough of that tosh, Jamie. You have a key, darling; this is still your home. Now you must be the one Jamie fancies," she said, addressing Veronica, "And with good reason. It's about time he pays court to someone, and you are quite fetching. Welcome."

"This is Veronica, mother."

CHAPTER ELEVEN

"Thank you Mrs. O'Neil," she said, endeavoring to recover her complexion while extending her hand in greeting.

But before she got her own entire name out, Veronica realized that she had called James' mother possibly by a name that Elizabeth no longer used. This, however, mattered not; she just plowed on.

"Call me Elizabeth," she said, shaking Veronica's proffered hand. "And James, you can continue calling me mother."

Veronica did not know what to make of this. Elizabeth turned on her heel, sweeping the air with her thin layered dress billowing, and glided away across the great circular foyer.

"Do follow me into the drawing room. There is someone here I would like you to meet," she said, her voice carrying in the enormous space.

Its ceiling was high and supported a massive crystal chandelier from its center that cast sparkles of light upon plinths lined along the walls with bust of statues and glass encased artifacts from many different cultures around the world. The staircase curved in a crescent from left to right. Its ivory bannister curled at the beginning like a tight fist and continued upward and around, following magnificent paintings hung on white walls and rooms with doors shut until it found its end nearly 360 degrees above the entrance where James and Veronica stood.

"It's an ambush," whispered James, thinking of the unknown owner of the car parked outside the guest house. "How much you want to bet it's my father in the other room."

"I can hear you, Jamie," said Elizabeth.

And the pair snickered like teens caught in the middle of some adolescent mischief.

Veronica made a soft shushing sound and silently mouthed, "Stop making me laugh."

James playfully squeezed her buttocks, and her eyes widen as she stifled a squeal. Elizabeth turned around and smiled at the pair of them, each adopting innocent faces. She motioned with her opened hand at the drawing room and they entered.

"Please, do make yourselves comfortable. I'll knock something up. Would you like some tea?" she said.

"Yes, thank you," they replied.

"Red," said Elizabeth.

"No, just regular tea," said Veronica automatically.

"Red?" said James with his jaw slightly dropped in shock.

It was a moment before Veronica took in James' expression and turned around to see what he had been gaping at. There stood a tall beautiful woman in a scarlet dress, her slender form impressively framed in the entrance way. She walked with immense self-assuredness across the room. It was almost as if she was gliding. Her gait elegantly oozed sensuality.

"Rosa-Annabella Elizabeth Dalton," he said in disbelief.

"Come now Spooner, you and I go back too far for such formalities. You can still call me Red," she said, walking very close up on him and giving him a great bosomy hug. "I still remember. Happy belated," she whispered into his ear then kissed him on the cheek.

CHAPTER ELEVEN

Her lips were soft and her breath upon his skin was as intoxicating as the perfume she wore. She smelt like some exotic essential oil, ensnaring his senses. His heart pounded out of his chest and he became aware of the sudden rise in room temperature, hoping his body did not betray him. This sudden arrival of Red took James completely by surprise, and he found himself without words, just standing there looking utterly dumbfounded. Elizabeth stood off to the side enjoying the awkward moment, her eyes moving excitedly from Red, Veronica, and then to James. Veronica's cheeks began to color up from indignation.

"Spooner?" said Veronica, betraying a hint of irritation.

"And who is your lovely friend, Spooner?" said Red, her embrace lingering moments longer than it should, her hands now gliding off his body like silk.

"This is..." he said, still flabbergasted by Red's appearance and disarmed by her close proximity, "ah... ahem," he cleared his throat.

"Veronica Thealcey," said Veronica curtly, when James failed to effect an introduction.

She, now peeved at him for his lapse of memory, threw him a very cross look as if to say, *you are so in trouble, mister.*

12

Princess Sophie

Spooner and I go way back," she said to the room at large, her sultry voice filling it like song. "Don't we? It's what we called him when we were kids," she added in response to Veronica's bemused look. "Apparently he has chosen to omit that interesting detail of his life," continued Red, her eyes overtly flirting with James. "Back then, he was so cute when he spoke, sounded like an English gentleman. All the little girls loved it."

"I see," said Veronica, now staring appraisingly at Red.

She was no more beautiful than Veronica, both were exquisite in equal measure. There was, however, something about Red that implied she was accustom to having every man she pursued, and perhaps James was one of her conquered. In addition, it was this sensual confidence she bore so well that Veronica found a bit unnerving.

"We also dated for a while. Let me see," she said tilting her head slightly upward to the right, as if conjuring her thoughts out of thin air and blowing away a large dark curl that fell in her face. "About seven years ago."

CHAPTER TWELVE

"Well... not exactly," said James in an attempt to gain some footing in an increasingly embarrassing one-sided conversation.

"You're right. We skipped a lot of steps. Didn't we?" she said with a slight wink. "My dear Veronica, we Spooner women should get to know one another."

"I bet," said Veronica, glancing over at an ever increasingly livid James, her suspicions now confirmed.

"Oh come on, Spooner, don't get so defensive. Loosen up." said Red. "You're always so intense."

Veronica was now even more curious of who this woman was. She seemed to know a great deal about James that Veronica knew and perhaps much more.

"Come Veronica, my dear. Help me with the tea," said Elizabeth. "Let those two catch up while we chat a bit. No need to worry, We'll have you back before the good part."

Veronica could only wonder what in the world could she have meant by that. For the sake of affability, she reluctantly joined Elizabeth, and James could hear emanating from the hall, his mother complementing Veronica on her hair and asking who did her nails for her. Their footsteps and voices tailed away in the distance, and James found himself alone with Red.

"When did you get back?"

"Friday," she said brightly. "When we stopped by on the way into town to visit Anita Forman, Elizabeth insisted on us staying in the guesthouse. Bless her."

"Yeah, that's my mom, the saint," said James sarcastically. *"She is up to something, and I can tell,"* he finished the last comment in his head. "After all this time, why did you come —— Wait a minute, where is the rest of your party? You did say *we*. Did you not?"

"Twenty-seven, twenty-eight, twenty-nine..." came a tiny voice a short distance away, growing louder. "Thirty, thirty-one..."

"Do you hear that," said James, taken by surprise yet again.

"Yes, I have someone you should meet. Sophie," she called.

"Forty, forty-one, forty-two," she ended, walking into the drawing room with here eyes on her feet, obviously counting footsteps. "Yes mommy?"

"Mommy?" said James. "When did you ——"

"Yes, this is my daughter Sophia,"

"Hi there, that's a very pretty dress," said James, stooping to her level, his bright expression hiding his trepidation.

"Thank you. My name is Sophia S. Dalton, but you can call me Princess Sophie," she said in a delightfully small voice that made James' heart feel light. "And what's your name?"

"My name is James. And that's quite a title you have there young lady. She's beautiful," he added, standing up and addressing Red while Sophie continued about her happy way, counting the square patters on the floor. "How old is she?"

"Thank you. She's a joy. And... she's seven years old."

"What!" exclaimed James, after quickly doing the simple math in his head, his worries finding ground to stand. 'But ——"

He was interrupted by Veronica and Elizabeth both returning with tea kettle, cups, and saucers atop a matching porcelain platter, all of which were etched with matching floral design. Veronica nearly dropped the platter at the sight of Sophie. Elizabeth, catching the bottom of the platter in support, looked utterly pleased.

"Good thing we had forgone on that honey," she said.

Veronica stood there, slightly in shock.

"My word, let me take those refreshments before we have an accident," Elizabeth said, then added under her breath to Veronica while taking the silver platter, "Yes, resembles James a great deal, no?"

"Mommy can I go out back and play on the swing?"

"Okay, but be careful and no acrobatics," said Red, stroking Sophie's head.

She set off skipping, disappearing in the corridor towards the side door leading out onto the play area, and the sound of the glass sliding door could be heard opening, then closing with a loud thud.

The room in which they stood had a general air of immaculacy about it. James and Veronica made themselves comfortable on one of two very long Roman style brown leather sofas that were perpendicular to one another in the center of the room, surrounded by an impressive library consisting of very ancient looking books. And above it all was a very large golden blade fan which hung from the ceiling, turning slowly. James looked up at it, and a slight smile creased his face.

"Remind me to tell you later," he whispered, in answer to Veronica's curious look.

He then peered at Elizabeth, who stood over in the light of a large mullion window with her back to them, preparing the tea. She poured it into the small porcelain cups that sat upon the tiny matching saucers. She turned her head for a moment, peering out of the window and smiling at Sophie, quite at her enjoyment playing on the swing, then continued pouring the tea.

"She is absolutely adorable," Veronica said to James. "She kind of looks like you, James. Is there something you need to tell me?"

"I think I need to ask Red that question, 'cause I am at a lost as well."

"Cream, sugar?" said Elizabeth.

"Two cubes please. Thank you." said Veronica.

"Straight," said James.

The pair of them watched Sophie though the large window. Her swing rose higher as she stood in it, pumping her legs for all she was worth. Red was conversing with Elizabeth in a low whisper then turned to join the two, who were sitting in silence with an air of polite interest. Red handed the pair in waiting their cups of tea with saucers and sat adjacently across from them.

"Thank you," they said.

"I'm a coffee drinker," Red said to their inquiring looks at her absences of tea in hand.

"Mother," James said, wasting no time in realizing Red was about to make things, at the very least, extremely uncomfortable for him. "I have been reading father's letters, and he told me."

"Told you, did he?" she said, turning around to face them and taking a seat next to Red. "Well my preference was to the contrary."

She stirred the swirls of cream in her tea with a tiny spoon, then tapped it once on the edge of the cup.

"And I saw no urgent need for such a disclosure that was sure to cause you undue disquiet," she concluded with perfect indifference. "My dear," she redirected, now addressing Veronica, "fancy a look at some of James' childhood photos?"

"Yes," said both Veronica and Red with much enthusiasm.

They looked at each other smiling. Veronica smiled, realizing there was after all something Red did not know about James. And Red realized that under cover of displaying old family photos, Elizabeth may have cleverly and successfully skirted the issue of adoption. Placing her tea cup and saucer on the corner table, Elizabeth stood up and walked over to the massive book shelf and extricated a photo album that resembled the rest of the leather bound literary works, all in perfect symmetry. She handed it to Veronica, who promptly freed her hands of her tea cup and saucer by shoving it into James' half clumsy digits.

"No, not the photo album, mother," he said exasperatingly, casting outside the window at Sophie's growing progress, higher and higher. "Must we do this now? I'm trying to —"

"Of course, Jamie," she interrupted, taking a seat in front of them and smiling.

"Oh look, there you are with — Is that your dad?" asked Veronica.

"No, it's my uncle Octavius. We called him Otty. He and my father looked very much alike, a strong family resemblance. And standing next to him is my aunt, his sister Madeline. Aunt Maddy is quite a character. She tends to show up at weddings and funerals with all the latest gossip on every member of the family, no matter how distant the relation. Don't let her get to drinking. Goodness, I see why she never married. And uncle Otty," continued James warming up to his audience. "He died from a stroke a while back. And his wife, my aunt Olivia, here in this picture," he indicated an old sepia photo below, "had to raise Paul, Maximilian, and Stephen alone. There he is Stephen."

He pointed to the right at Blacky standing in a picture. A skinny young boy with an air of supreme coolness was posing next to his two older brothers.

"Man, did I want to be like him. He was tested as highly gifted back then, but after his brother Max died, he wasn't the same anymore. He saw him die that night, you know. He seemed so —"

He broke off, glancing over at Sophie, who was now sitting in full swing and at the apex of both her backward and forward trajectories. He remembered as a child what it felt like to fly so high, to move as fast as the wind, and he allowed himself a tiny moment of indulgence. He pulled himself back from his reverie.

"Well... Paul, the oldest, presently lives in Rome with his family. We correspond often through phone messages and e-mail for lack of time on both our parts. His job as a research manager for some major European company keeps him on the go. They visit when they can, most times on holidays such as Christmas. As I mentioned, the second oldest, Max, died. He was killed running with a very dangerous element in the streets. They never found out who killed him, just filed as another drug related crime. The family rarely speaks of it, because it nearly destroyed my aunt Olivia with a nervous-breakdown. She worried constantly about Stephen. And although, like I said, gifted, was a rambunctious teen and ultimately fell in with the very same crowd his brother did. And there are my parents before I was born," he indicated with his index finger.

Now that James realized it, for the first time his parents did look a bit somber in the picture, he nevertheless continued on.

"Here's a picture of me and my best friend William when we lived in London. We kept in contact for years. I had spoken so highly of the U.S. that he could not wait to come when he was of age, and we've been hanging ever since. And that's my eleventh birthday party. I had it in a park just outside the neighborhood where my cousins lived. My father insisted," he said, indicating another picture to his right.

"There I am," said Red standing and taking a seat on the other side of James, "and Anita Forman, Robert and Floyd Lee and their cousin Alfred Clark, Paul and Max." Wow, we were so tiny compared to Paul and Max. Those were the days huh, Spooner?"

But James was distracted and had again glance out the large window. He saw Sophie travel so high in the air; she looked as though she was attempting to wrap the swing around the top pole in one complete turn. Then out of nowhere on her return swing, she soared into the air, flipping backwards and landing neatly onto her feet. She returned to her swing laughing, no doubt to give the nerve racking act another go.

"Yeah," replied James, a little shaken yet impressed all the same at what he alone had just witnessed. "And Max's little cronies Two-Pound, Ray-Ray, Nukey, and Polo tried to crashed the party and somehow managed to get into the picture. You see there," he pointed to the right of the photo, behind the main group of children at the said boys, off in the distance sitting on a picnic table smoking. "Max was furious with them," he chuckled, "told them not to ruin my party and to get the hell out. He had a good heart, and we all miss him."

"And that one," began Veronica.

"Yes, that's my father, the writer, the philosopher, the... Well, you know.

"See Jamie," Elizabeth said softly, "this is your family. No different than any other family and no less connected. It is our history that binds us together, not so much the blood. We are all family."

James saw Veronica was wearing a slightly smug look, and he became somewhat indifferent. Just then, the phone on the desk next to the window rang.

"Save by the bell mother."

"Jamie," said Veronica in shock and disbelief of his haughty attitude.

CHAPTER TWELVE

Elizabeth sat there for a moment staring at her son in silence. The phone continued to ring. After a moment which seemed to stretch on for hours, he broke the silence.

"Shall I get that mother?"

"No sweetie, you're always so thoughtful of others. I wouldn't want you to strain yourself. I'll get it," she said, standing up, smiling and gently patting him on the knee twice patronizingly.

"Hello? Well, speak of the devil. If it isn't Mr. Honesty himself," she said in polite tones. "No... Not yet, but he's here," she added then cupped the phone and mouth the words to James, *"It's your father."*

James shook his head adamantly. He just did not know what to say.

"Maybe next time, he's a bit engaged at the moment," said Elizabeth. "Okay... Yes... I will Alex... I assure you; I will," she added emphatically. "Chat later, take care."

She hung the phone and turned to look at James, her expression unfathomable.

"My word, at times that man can be insufferable."

"What? What's happened?" asked James.

She walked over to her seat, took it, and looked James full in the eyes.

"I am sorry to be the bearer of bad tidings, Jamie. But, it's your friend.

James' heart leapt with fear.

"William?"

"Yes, it's William. He's been shot."

13

Broken

A long awkward silence stretched across the intervening country miles, and the rhythm of steel belted tires passing over the masonry line breaks in the road was a steady heartbeat beneath the car, ebbing its passengers unspoken thoughts to the surface. Besides James' apparent preoccupation for William's well being, he was not at all confident the visit to his parents' home was productive or wise. In all honesty, he felt it was disastrous and had not gone as well as he planned. His mother, upon meeting Veronica, was to become completely enamored with her, thereby giving her blessings with request of many grand children. However, he now realized this was optimistic to the point of foolishness. Why did he let his mother talk him into it? It all seemed a set-up. Why hadn't he payed more attention to the phone message? *"Also, I heard from Red. She is in town,"* he recalled.

Indeed she had spoken to Red, and her matter of fact tone in the message was deceptively precise, leaving out crucial information James felt was pertinent. What an uncomfortable visit that was. He could only imagine how it would have been if his father were there. He relaxed the thought for a moment with a great breath of relief. At this abatement, however, an agitated voice to his right spoke.

"And you know," Veronica began out of the blue, plainly as though the pair of them had been carrying on the conversation in her head at great lengths and now aloud, "she asked me if I were still married."

"She what?" said James astonished, his voice raspy from lack of use. "How did she —"

"She said I twiddle my thumb and ring finger. Actually," amended Veronica. "her exact words were..."

And she did a crude imitation of Elizabeth's accent.

"*If you are at present espoused and possess every intent on having a life with my son, it would be prudent to consider someone may get hurt in the process. And if you are to keep your failed marriage a secret, you should start by not twiddling your thumb and naked ring finger* — Like this," added Veronica in her own voice.

She held her hand up and demonstrated exaggeratedly the movements with her fingers.

"How presumptuous of her."

Indeed, Veronica had a tendency of touching her left ring finger with her thumb as if unconsciously straightening an invisible ring, which stone inset was rotating underneath or too lose to remain stationary. But he did not want to enlarge the issue any further and was sure it would soon become an abandoned inclination, now that she was painfully aware of it. He therefore steered clear of the subject.

"So, what did you tell her?" he said, trying to keep his voice even and casual.

"I told her that I'm separated and intend on being divorced very soon."

"And what did she say to that?" said James, excited at this possibility of which they have never spoken.

"She said..."

Veronica seemed caught between telling the truth and hurting James or not saying anything at all, which was pointless, now that the cat was nearly out of the bag.

"Come on, spit it out. I will love you no less."

"She said you are just like your father," said Veronica speaking very fast, hoping to diminish the impact her words might have.

He fell silent again. But when it seemed to stretch on for far too long, or Veronica could no longer hold hers, she broke the silence.

"You never told me about Red."

Her words seemed to force themselves out of her mouth without her volition, as if held back for too long, and James thought he could here the slightest bit of resentment in her voice.

"Oh lord, here it comes," he thought. "I never considered," he began aloud, "that I would have —— I mean, it

never came up —— I'm sure eventually it would have. She's here visiting for a short while and —— It was a long time ago, Veronica," he said exasperatingly, trying to make some sense out of his word vomit.

"Yeah, about, hum, let me see," she began in tones of sarcasm. "How old is little Sophie?"

"Seven, and like I said, I didn't know about her. If she were my daughter, I think Red would have told me so."

"If she were? You didn't ask her."

"Well, she would have said so; I think. Don't you?" he added hopefully.

"And why after all this time has she come back into town?" she said, ignoring the question. "I think she is back for you, Jamie. I saw how she overtly flirted with you. *Spooner and I go way back.* And the affect she had on you when she came into the room with that," she paused, trying to contain her sarcasm, "bright red dress on."

She said the last few words with as much contempt she would allow herself and gave him a reproachful look as though he had committed some unforgivable act.

"What was that, fire engine red? How tasteless," she finished, her arms folded tightly cross one another in contained outrage. "You want her too, don't you?" she started back up again. "I can tell, *Spooner*," she said the name in an exaggerated mocked sultry voice of Red. "Well, go for it. I don't care."

"You are making much more of it than what it is." he said slightly irritated, slightly tickled and oddly flattered all the same. "She means nothing to me. Nothing. She and I were over long before you and I met, Veronica. I'm sure she is here visiting Anita Forman like she said. My mother is just being meddlesome from want of something to do."

"But why does she have to stay with your mother, Jamie? Your mother."

He recounted the conversation he had with Red while Veronica and Elizabeth were getting refreshments and hoped this explanation would suffice. Veronica, however, did not look entirely convinced. She therefore remained stone silent, arms crossed with her face increasingly coloring up.

James as well was not entirely convinced of his mother's innocence in the matter nor was he of Red's intentions. He also could not help but wondered if Sophie was his child. There was such a strong family resemblance. Curiosity was getting the better of him, and he needed to find out whether or not it was true and soon. He thought perhaps once he has dropped Veronica home and had a chance to see William — Yes William, he reminded himself, the reason why they concluded their visit so abruptly — he would double back without Veronica, for he had been uncomfortable enough during their first visit, then try to get some straight answers about his father's letters from Elizabeth. Hopefully he would have some success coaxing the truth of Sophie's parentage out of Red as well. James decided it was not yet too late in the evening to put his plan into action.

CHAPTER THIRTEEN

An hour and a half later, James became aware of the sound of his own foot fall echoing in the long sterile corridor, and the faint noise of blips and heavy respiration from medical machinery met James' ears while sidling by rooms with doors slightly ajar. He tried, and with great difficulty and trepidation, however, not to gape at bedfast occupants whose conditions seem to worsen the farther he proceeded down the corridor, stealing furtive glances and casting disturbed expressions ahead again and again, forcing himself to keep his gaze directed forward. He became weak kneed and sick to his stomach from the general antiseptic smell of the quiet ward, and his affliction increased at the approach of room 742. James steadied himself for a moment, listening, then rounded the room and found its sounds amplified in the entrance where he stood absolutely thunderstruck. His eyes fell upon William lying there, seemingly immobilized by large body bandages and several different colored wires (held in place by miniature clips), some tethering his arms to intravenous drips and others stretched from beneath covers and bandages, attaching themselves to monitors and sophisticated equipment that James had no knowledge of. A tube that reached into William's mouth and judging by the sound of it, down into his throat, connected itself at the other end to a transparent cylindrical container that had a small bellow which rose and fell, expanding and contracting like an accordion with William's labored breath. And James feeling a bit rueful, thought absurdly of Darth Vader at this.

James became suddenly stricken with sadness, and he rapidly blinked back watery eyes and convinced himself that the cause of such was the abrupt adjustment to the sunlight that flooded the room via the window. A sudden wave of rage and resentment came upon him, and a morose expression shadowed his face.

"Damn *animals*," he whisper through gritted teeth.

He walked over to the other side of Williams bed and stood there. A muted television that sat high and to the right of the room played to no one in particular. To his back, was a very large window that took up the whole of one side of the room, framing a magnificently soon to set sun. Its warmth penetrated, soothed and relaxed him with an embrace that made him feel safe, secure. Its amber glow that had fallen upon William moments ago was presently eclipsed by James' shadow. Realizing this, James took the empty seat next to William's bed, making its tight brown leather groaned at his weight. A lump formed in his throat and the room's dry air seemed to siphon what little moisture left in his mouth. His lips were sapped; he swallowed hard.

"I see why you like this spot," he said raspingly, appreciating the sun's warmth. "The things you'd do to get my attention. Sorry I wasn't there to catch you, like you were there for me. Please don't die... please." he mumbled his last words, burying his face in the palms of his hands.

Childhood memories were racing with each other through his mind, and he found himself in a tug-of-war of boyhood moments.

CHAPTER THIRTEEN

"Think happy thoughts... *happy* thoughts," he encouraged himself.

His mind rested on one of many lazy Spring days, and the pair of them were laying on the lawn of a London preparatory school, looking up into the endless sky and making shapes of passing clouds, something they had become quite proficient at.

"I'm going to be a rock star some day and live in a castle like Sting or my family, 'cause my mum says we are from royalty. All my mates will be invited over everyday to have ice cream and cake," said William, adjusting his book sack on which he rested his head.

"Yeah, now that one looks like a fish dancing with a bowler hat and cane," James said, still staring up at the clouds in deep thought and brushing his long black curly hair from his face. "What? What was that Will?" he added, coming out of his reverie and readjusting his book sack as well.

"What do you want to be when you grow into a right proper bloke? Because I am going to be a rich rocker and own a castle, a big one. And all my mates and I will have cake and ice cream and gum drops and taffy and pop and —"

"I'm going to be a writer like my dad," said James speaking over William's litany of treats. "And I am going to write just like him, in different styles, and all the girls will say *"ooh you write so pretty,"* and they will all fancy me."

"Why would you want to chat up some girls? Don't get me wrong mate, I'm not trying to take a mickey out, but I prefer the ice cream and cake. Wouldn't you? The girls ruin everything. They don't know how to have fun. Besides, if you have cake and ice cream and other sweets, the girls will come anyway. But if that's what you want."

"Yeah, I suppose you are right," replied James, slipping back into his reverie.

And the pair of them lay there beneath a cottony sky, making shapes out of clouds while the sound of schoolmates' feet shuffled off in the distance, signaling the end of another school day.

James sat there presently at the side of William's bed smiling. He continued, now reminiscing a few years later, when he and William were ten. He could smell the delicious aroma of blueberry scones wafting upstairs from the kitchen. They were standing in the middle of James' father's almost empty study, where once full book shelves that reached from the floor to the ceiling, nearly spanning the entire area of the room, were now bare. Boxes of books sat in the middle of the floor, forming a sort of cardboard mountain with nooks to squeeze in and some to sit on. They were trying to resist the urge to disobey the orders of James' mother, to keep their feet on the floor and hands to themselves while in the study. And like most little boys their age, they found themselves hard put to follow adult instruction.

"Here, help me climb to the ceiling fan."

"It's still on, James. But if you going to give it a go, I can turn the switch off first."

"No, leave it. This is far more exciting. Better than counting clouds, isn't it? Now steady that box for me," he said, climbing onto a second one that gave slightly at his weight.

"And what will you do when you reach the top?"

"I will calculate the velocity of the fan blades, and by doing that, I will match it with that of my own and then grab the blades and proceed to ride them," he said in his most deep and heroic voice, standing with one foot atop a box and his tightened fists upon his hips, posing like a super hero.

"Sounds like a plan to me," encouraged William with a great deal of excitement. "Then I'll have a go."

"Now, once I'm high enough, I need you to stand in the doorway as a look-out for my mum, 'cause she will do her nut if she catches us. And my dad, well let's not even go there.

"Right," agreed William. "Okay, up you get."

He steadied the boxes on which James trampled, one by one, higher and higher, until his hands were inches away from the fan blades. William slid over to the doorway at a run and halted by gripping its frame then leaned out into the corridor and peered around the corner and down the stair case. He nodded to James.

"Now, on to the blades... the blades... the blades of death... death... death," he added in a mocked echoing voice that reverberated off the empty shelved walls.

James shook his hands, loosening his fingers up. He concentrated on the fan blades and found a spot in its rotation which appeared to slow down with the intensity of his gaze. Then with lightening speed, he thrust his hands upward. Bang! A searing pain shot through his hands, and he was thrown back on his heels, boxes yanked from beneath him, and he was toppling backwards, every moment suspended in time. William saw him falling and sprinted over to the center of the room, in time only to throw himself beneath James and breaking his fall.

"Umph," came the pair landing with a thud beneath the toppling boxes.

"Change my mind, mate, said William. "I think I will pass on the blades of death."

And they both sat there laughing beneath the fan's settling dust, James wincing from the pain that shot through his hands.

"Ouch, what the — ?" complained William, pulling a leather bound book from beneath himself.

Its cover was black, smooth, and an ornate symbol in the middle stood in sharp relief against an embossed shield.

"Moments In the Sun," William read, opening the journal. "Is this one of your dad's books? Brilliant penmanship, mate."

"Yeah, that's how he starts them, then he has them typed up and made all fancy like this children's book," said James, liberating a book from a pile of many others that had toppled in the kerfuffle, and he held it up. "Like this children's book my dad used to read to me all the time. It has a cover, you see, *The Adventures of Argile and The Missing Socks*."

"Oh, I get it. This one here is the original. Nice bookmark," he added, pulling a silver necklace from between the pages.

CHAPTER THIRTEEN

"Jamie!" an approaching voice from below in a distant part of the house called out. "What's all that ruckus?"

"Blimey, it's your mum, mate."

"Quick, put that back, and help me tidy up this mess."

And somewhere between lying on the plush green field of the school yard and climbing cardboard boxes, James presently, nodded off to sleep.

14

The Weak and the Dead

A dark menacing figure with a loping swagger slowly made his way down a damp and dimly lit alley way. He pulled his black leather gloves snugly over his fingers, and they groan by the sound of his clinching fists. Loud voices accompanied with heavily bass music that buzzed the ears and drowned out the sound of his foot steps, emanated from the back of many apartments along the ally. This was it. He had come too far now to turn back. The present circumstance he had found himself in made it impractical for him to manage his affairs. After tonight, there will be no question of who he is. His name will be spoken with caution and his orders followed to the letter. He stopped outside of a wood rotten door that hung lopsidedly on its hinges and quickly checked the silencer and safety on his firearm beneath his leather jacket. The man in black adopted a dark scowl on his face then quietly uttered to himself the word *kamikaze*. He banged the door three time with thunderous force.

"Who the fuck is it?" A man's voice on the other side of the door boomed.

CHAPTER FOURTEEN

"It's me," said the caller.

"Who?"

"Open this goddamn door!" the man in black commanded with such force that his very words seemed to shake the door.

Then with screeching and wood filing effort, the backdoor to the rundown building was forced open.

"Damn, my bad, didn't recognize," said an apologetic six foot tall, bald and muscle bound doorman, whose body mass was equally comparable to the caller.

He was slightly intimidated by the man in black, but quickly gathered his resolve. Fear had no place in their world. If any man showed fear, it was a sign of weakness, and weakness was synonymous with death. He cleared his throat.

"He's been waiting for you and the list... in the back."

"Has he now?" he said darkly.

The doorman bit back the retort on the tip of his tongue and did not dare to respond. He realized this was not the time to challenge a man who could, with the mere sound of his voice, shout down a door when he is angered. He therefore resumed his post, standing sentinel at the back door in silence as the man in black turned on his heel and proceeded down the hall.

The corridor was small, dank and as dimly lit as the alley way. The floor creaked under the weight of his foot steps, and the distinctive pungent odor of mildew from the walls and peeling paper that swayed in his wake was strong in his nose. The man in black stood there silently at the opening of a smoke filled room of five people chatting lazily, unaware of his presence.

Dirty cream colored drapes, that set in contrast to a musty burgundy threadbare sofa, were pulled shut in rebuff of all that was visible from the outside. A small coffee table with a tiny mound of white powdery substance, a razor and several curled bills that sat upon its inlaid mirror, stood between the man in black and the sofa. A bottle of Wild Irish Rose wine and several dirty glasses rested upon the table. A few moments passed before he was noticed, and when his presence became apparent, the room at large fell silent.

"Would you look at what the muthu-fuckin' cat dragged in," said the first gentleman in a deep slow drawl, seated at the sofa.

Upon this, there was derisive jeering from the other two men on either side of the room, who each had a woman joined to them, pawing like lower primates engaged in some bazaar grooming ritual. The man in black was disgusted at both women's behavior and cheap appearances.

"Send the bitches away," he said gesturing with a dismissive nod of the head toward the other door across the room.

"Now you trippin', B," said the first gentleman, still supported with laughter by the other two men and their companions, lounging in their tattered love seats.

"Get the fuck out," said the black clad gentleman in his most dangerous voice yet.

The women took flight, fleeing the room like swallows avoiding a deadly prey. The two men on both side stood up, and the first gentleman sitting on the sofa raised his hand, forestalling an attack. He spoke again, this time more shrewdly.

CHAPTER FOURTEEN

"What the hell you do that for, B? Them bitches cost money. I ain't get no ass either. Oh you gonna come out of pocket."

"I told you, Ray, no women and no killin'. Y'all asses bona-fide fuck-ups. That shit you pulled is all over the damn news. Got the po-po on my ass, harassing my family and —"

"Harassing? Aren't you an articulate muthu-fuckuh," said the second gentleman, who was standing to the left of the room.

He surveyed him and sneered contemptuously, cracking his knuckles and neck.

"Bitch!" roared Ray, "You don't run this *shit,*" he added nastily, his arms wide and his eye brows narrowed menacingly in an attempt at disguising his pointed ineptitudes. "Who the fuck died and made *you* God, B? "Nuke!" he called to the second gentleman to the right of the room."

"Yeah Ray."

"You hear this shit?"

"Huh, best recognize B," said Nuke, his eyes growing wide, looking crazed.

"You gotten soft, B. You know what? Fuck all the talkin'!" barked Ray. "Polo," he said, speaking to the third gentleman standing to his right. "put a couple hot ones in his ass."

Then several things happened in quick succession. A wine bottle was broken over the forehead of Polo as he reached for his gun. The neck of Nuke was opened up by the jagged end of the broken bottle. And he grasped at his throat in a desperate attempt to stanch the blood gushing from it, forcing its way from between his tighten fingers. He fell, slumping over like a marionette puppet, whose strings were unexpectedly severed. Polo bellowed in anger, his eyes burning and face scarlet, yet still managing to free his weapon from its holster. This, however, was met with deadly force. Several bullets found his head, and he was thrown back into the wall and crashed onto a nearby folding table, landing finally with a thud, face down and motionless on the hard wood floor.

Ray had hesitated a moment too long, and now found the gun was trained on him. He sneered and sucked his teeth, unimpressed.

"Yeah, I did it," said Ray with awful coldness. "Did your punk ass brother too," he added while under cover of his bravado, attempted slowly to extricate something from beneath one of the sofa pillows. "Like you, he didn't fit. High minded, always givin' a shit. What the *fuck* you waiting for!" And he spat. "Wha-up nig—"

There were two small pops, and he was rocked back on the sofa, lifeless, a pistol in his slackening grip.

"That was for Max you piece of —"

He broke off, remembering the doorman.

"Yo, Two! Get your ass in here quick!"

"What? What happened?" said the doorman in the near distance, bounding down the hall, entering the room and presently finding a gun pressed to his temple.

CHAPTER FOURTEEN

"This is what happens when we have a religious disagreement," said Blacky, cocking his pistol in the ear of Two-Pound. "Are we clear?"

"As a bell," he said, with his arms held in capitulation.

"Then step," said Blacky.

And keen to vacate the room, Two set off, his heavy footfall trailing away in some distant part of the premises. The sound of the front door slammed, signaling his final departure from the macabre scene. Blacky safetied his weapon and neatly stowed it beneath his coat then pulled out his mobile and began dialing. He was incredibly calm in the mist of the carnage while bearing an air of perfect indifference.

"Yeah," answered a deep voice on the other end of the phone.

"It's taken care of," said Blacky. "Send someone to clean up."

15

Exposed

Many miles away, the last of the sun's glow that traveled beyond the landscape of distant rundown neighborhoods, faded into nothingness. Towering buildings that had scraped the afternoon's brilliantly blue sky hours ago, with bustling city goers moving in and out and about their fixed positions, acquiesced to the night casting its dark velvety and starry canopy over the sleepy city. And as if the night drifted into the window of room 742 and announced its presence, James woke with a sudden start, wondering the time, his lungs fully inflating with air from his apparent doze. He had been drooling in his sleep, and he half groggily wiped the corners of his mouth with the palm of his hand. It was several minutes, or so it would seem, before the recollection of his slumber informed his present mind of his excursion down memory lane.

"Those were the days, mate," he said, smiling over at William, who remained starkly immobilized. "Wait a second," he added with a look of rising comprehension brightening his eyes. "Moments In The Sun, I remember. It's like Veronica said, a journal, and you had it in your hand. Remember? How could I've been so thick. Okay, this is good. But where is it? You wouldn't know, would you, Will? I guess not."

He did not expect William to respond, but was somehow comforted just talking with him. James sat there pensively for a moment, examining the bandages with absorbing interest, noticing how unrecognizable William was under the many strips of closely wrapped mesh cloth to the head and torso. It gave him the bazaar appearance of an archeologist's amalgamated half unwrapped recent find and some pet projects of Dr. Frankenstein. And although half mummified, he seemed vulnerable, lonely, and most of all, exposed.

"You know," he began, "I found out I'm adopted. My father told me."

And James regaled to an immobilized William, how he had been saving his father's letters. How after reading them, they explained he was adopted, leaving to his great annoyance, however, many unanswered questions.

"Yeah," he said, after concluding his recount of the visit to his parents' home and thoroughly elaborating on Elizabeth's and Red's subterfuge. "We saw it you know... What happened... Veronica and I," he now whispered in a cracked voice, his heart pounding from mental images replaying themselves. "You got to stop dressing like these kids, man. I didn't even recognize you. You know it's far too easy to mistake you for a drug dealer, a thug or something like that. Perception, Will, we've often talked about this."

He paused.

"Sorry man, I didn't mean to say it like an *I told you so*. After all, if I hadn't asked you to come to the states, this never would have happened to you. I was going to tell you, when you came around the house, that I'd decided to give up my job as an editor and just write. I have enough money to do that, you know. I also have letters with me from my father. But I'll read them to you when you get better. Huh," he tittered, "I need to read them all myself."

"I think he'd fancy that, James," came a soft woman's voice emanating from the room's entrance.

James was taken aback by this sudden intrusion and whipped his head around to find a lovely and elegantly dressed middle-aged woman, who William bore a striking resemblance to, now walking closer. Shafts of light from the ceiling recessed fixtures fell upon her beauty as she moved in and out of shadows.

"The pair of you have always been like brothers. You might as well be. By the way, the receptionist told me that William's brother or rather my son was here. Imagine to my pleasant surprise to hear this. I instantly knew it was you."

James returned her smile with a wide grin. Indeed, he had lied to the front desk in order to gain entry. How would they know that he and William, with their obviously distinctive physical differences, were not brothers. He was sure stranger things had happened in the hospital, and his hunch paid off.

"Oh, Mrs. Barinard," he said with surprise in his voice. "I didn't hear you come in. You're here... I mean you're *here*, *in town*. Please," he added, standing up and gesturing to his now empty seat.

Although she was smiling, William's mother had obviously endured a trip across the Pacific Ocean from England and looked every bit of tired and drained of life that her grueling ordeal had cost her. Perhaps it was that she had been up all day and night since William's misfortune and found herself at present running on coffee, snacks and inadequate nourishment the hospital cafe had to offer. And as true as James felt his assumption might be, it nonetheless did not detract from her beauty.

"No, please sit. And yes, I've been here for several days with William," she said moving closer to the bed while James reseated himself.

She leaned over and touched William's bandaged head ever so slightly with the back of her hand, bestowing a look upon him that only a concerned mother for her child's well-being would.

An ornate necklace that hung low around her neck and between her ample bosom, swung loosely and dazzled in the room's recessed ceiling lights. It caught James' eye. And to his great astonishment, it resembled the very one his father had given him many years ago, which presently hung around the rear view mirror in his car. He averted his eyes from the necklace and felt slightly uncomfortable for taking notice of what nature had so richly endowed her, and he inwardly reprimanded himself for staring. He thought, now was not the time to ask about something as trivial as a necklace. However, the necklace brought to mine the curious matter of how is father, who is at present living in London, came to know of William's dilemma before he did. And while she continued to speak, he maintained eye contact with absolute interest.

"I received word from the head physician, Dr. Bell, that William was here at DePaul, then came on the first flight from London. The doctor informed me he was doing far better than what was expected. He'll be fine. He's a fighter," she added reassuringly, trying not to betray a hint of trepidation in her voice. "And how have you been, James?"

James had a feeling, that possibly, she had been standing in the doorway longer than he cared to imagine, and she appeared pleased to see him, perhaps in such a sappy state over his best friend. He felt himself, however, a stronger man, and such men don't have sappy moments of tenderness, at least with their best friends. And for the second time within the span of five minutes, he found himself ill-at-ease but did his best to ignore this uncomfortable moment, clearing his throat and straightening his back in his seat.

"I'm fine, can't complain really."

"Always appreciative of what you have. So much your father's son," she said. "You know, you look very like him."

Again, here was another person bent on perpetuating the lie of how he and his father were so much alike. James, however, did not argue the point. Obviously she had not been standing in the doorway long enough to hear him convey to William the matter of his adoption. And what if she had? He did not care to think.

"Yes. That's what everyone tells me. Thank you, Mrs. Barinard. How did my father know William was here? Was it you who informed him? We learned of William's condition via a phone call from him. And as you know, he's at present residing in London —"

"You know, there is this lovely doctor," she paused to collect her thoughts, possibly ignoring his question, "by the name of... Forman. That's her. She has taken quite an interest in the well being of William. I always feel a great deal of assurance when she is here. I must say, Forman is quite *the lady with the lamp.* She takes such good care of him. If you stay a while, you both will have a chance to meet. Her shift I believe, is about to start."

She broke off, casting her eyes upward at the muted television perched high upon a metallic shelf that was extended by a mechanical arm tilted downward. She shook her head reprovingly at the crawling banner across the bottom of the screen that read: *Om Gang Wars: Three suspects from car-jacking of Mr. Robert St. John found dead.* The aftermath of the car-jacking scene was shown, outlined in chalk where Mr. Robert St. John had lain. Then the scene cut to an old rundown apartment building where the three men, identified as the assailants who had stolen Robert St. John's vehicle a day earlier, were televised as three bodies carried out in great black teflon bags that zipped from one end to the other and flopped heavily when stowed in black and white station wagons marked CORONER'S OFFICE. Also on the scene were two female witnesses who looked extremely lowbrow to James. They were highly animated, flailing their arms and mouthing words unheard. Their lips continuously framed a word that stood out from the others as their faces pulled in constant disdained expressions.

"Blacky," murmured James through clinched teeth, peering up at the muted television as well and lip reading one of the women's report, then once again standing, this time patting his pockets, apparently for some hidden content. "Mrs. Barinard, it's..." he paused, half distracted. "It's really good to see you again. I have to leave, but I'll be back tomorrow. I —— um —— let me give you my number."

And locating the object he was searching for, he reached into his back pocket and extracted a thin silver tin, opened it and handed her his business card, then stowed the metal container back into his pocket.

"My home number is listed there. So please," he said earnestly, "if there's any change in his condition before I return, any ——"

"No worries, my dear boy. I'll keep you informed," she said, in a soft and reassuring voice.

She accompanied him to the door of the room and gave him a great motherly embrace. James' heart went out to her, in light of what she was enduring. He therefore reiterated that he would return. This moment of concern, however, did not negate the fact that she had purposely skirted the issue of his father's act of omniscience regarding William. They exchanged air kisses cheek to cheek, then James set off, curious of Blacky's predicament, yet more determined to obtain some answers from his mother Elizabeth and ex-girlfriend Red.

16

Naked

An hour later or so, after a trip home and a steaming hot shower, James had changed into gray athletic sweats that sagged terribly in the crotch. Its hemline covered nearly the whole of his gray and white tennis shoes, which were nonetheless fashionably paired with a matching top that was overlong at the waist. He did not particularly like dressing scruffily. It made him feel as though he appeared unrefined. It was, however, much too late to fuss about looking dapper, and he felt the less attractive he appeared, the more information he would be able to coax out of Red and not entice her otherwise. On the other hand, his mother would not approve of his bedraggled look. James also felt he might gain some satisfaction in his appearance possibly irritating her, and this sardonic notion shadowed his face and parted a grin. He decided to check his phone messages one last time before he was off. And as he did, he swallowed a pill with the aid of warm bottled distilled water that sat nearby, then pushed the play button of his machine.

"You have one new message," the machine droned mechanically. "Message one, beep."

Hi Jamie, yes it's your mother. I know you must think I am a horrid person to have kept something like that from you. I will, however, share what I know. I only know the name of the woman who we adopted you from. We never met her, but your father managed to wheedle it out of someone at the adoption agency. Imagine that. Don't ask me how. I don't know. Her name was or is Marie Bar of London. That's all I know. You have every right to know your birth parents personally, if you choose. Pray you, Jamie my dear boy, let this rest. Remember to take your medicine. Love you... Night sweetie.

"Beep," finished the answering machine.

"Finally," thought James. *"Now we're getting somewhere, but I am not done with you yet. I still have a few questions for you."*

He picked up the phone and dialed his cousin Paul. Surely if anyone was able find out more information on Marie Bar, he could. Paul had an entire research department at his disposal and could easily investigate the most obscure of topics, pulling droves of information from many sources. And although James deemed this idea capital, he refrain from congratulating himself too heartily, for he had no idea how long it would take Paul to find Marie Bar or if it was against some foreign law to do so. Nonetheless, he remained hopeful and outlined his situation as briefly as he could into a message machine thousands of miles away on the other end of the phone.

❦

The night wore on, and the last of the street lights that flittered feebly hours long after the brightest ones, flickered themselves into bright incandescent glows and hovered on either side of the road as if something out of an H. G. Wells' *War Of The Worlds*. The road stretched long into a vanishing point beneath the canopy of haze. And James, after a fashion, found himself again in front of his parents' home, this time knocking rather forcibly on the great mahogany door.

After several unsuccessful attempts to gain entry into his parents' home, for his mother must have by now turned in for the night, James noticed a light emanating from the guest house accompanied with distorted silhouettes moving behind the curtains. It was so dark outside that James could only see the lit windows and a path that was illuminated by miniature lights recessed into the cobble paving. He wondered why on earth hadn't she turned the porch light on? Then thought perhaps it was to keep the countless bugs, that hovered in the night's sultry air, from gathering about the front door.

He approached quietly, taking in the scent of the dwarf gardenia shrubs on either side of the front entrance. He knocked. Red answered the door straight away and seemed upset, then rather quickly gathered her resolve and became the flirtatious vixen she had been earlier.

"Oh Spooner, what a pleasant surprise. Do come inside," she said, her words dripping sensual innuendoes. "I love this look on you. It looks so... dangerous."

He closed the door behind and adopted a business like air.

"Sorry, I don't have time to —— Were you expecting someone else?" said James, changing tact in mid-thought and picking up on her fleetingly disappointed look.

"Nonsense, who but you would be visiting this late hour," she said with a coy smile, allowing her lavender chiffon lingerie top to open slightly upon her release and revealing much more than cleavage as she turned away.

James could see through her gown that her delineation was perfect as ever. The lamp lights on the other side of the room casted their glows beneath her garment and illuminated her nearly naked body, causing James' heart to jump into his throat and his temperature to rise. She turned back towards him, her top opening even more, the areolae of her breast now barely covered, and a purple lace thong that could be seen through the thin fabric, was now in full frontal view beneath her smooth and firm midriff.

"Why Spooner, your making me blush," she said with a shy smile and no apparent inclination, however, to cover up.

"Pull yourself together," thought James, blinking hard and long once as if to clear his mind. And he marshaled every bit of his concentration, now maintaining only eye contact.

"Red ——"

CHAPTER SIXTEEN

"Yes Spooner?"

She looked longingly up into his eyes.

"I come to ask you about Sophie," he said as if forcing himself to remember the words.

And she stepped forward, moistening her lips with a tuck, her soft perfume becoming stronger in his nostrils. She was intoxicating. Her eyes were a hungry deep brown that seemed to plea with him, *take me.* James felt his palms begin to moisten, and his heart hammered in his throat.

"Mommy, is that daddy?" said a little voice entering the room.

Red snatched her top closed in surprise and turned around to face Sophie, who was still groggy, stumbling slightly as she walked and rubbing her eyes with one hand, her stuffed bear dragging low on the floor in the other.

"No sweetie," she said bending down, giving James an eye full of her naked backside. "It's just Spooner, now go back to —"

"Spooner!" she yelled, dropping her stuffed bear and running around Red and hurling herself into James, bestowing upon him a tight hug. "Mommy said I should call you Spooner instead of James."

"That's perfectly fine, Princess Sophie," said James, kneeling to her level, his heart filling with joy, yet still managing to cast Red a *you've been busted* look.

"Now off to bed with you Sophie," said Red.

"I don't want to. I'm not sleepy."

And she conjured a frown.

"Listen you little actress —"

"How about," interrupted James still knelt, Sophie now upon one of his knees, "if I read you a story. Would you like that?"

"But —" began Red.

However, it was too late. Sophie had dashed off into her room, and in what seemed no time at all, returned with an old and familiar looking book. She handed him the book and took him by the hand, leading him to her bedroom.

"Okay," began James, taking tiny steps behind her as to not trample over her while keeping himself at a respectable height, comparable to the length of her little arms. "I will read you one story, then nighty night with you. Okay?"

"Yea!" she said elated, executing ballerina turns in her pink flowery night gown then jumping into bed and pulling the covers high, finally plopping her arms on the outside and interlocking her tiny fingers together like an angel in waiting. And James slightly tickled, grinned widely and took a small chair next to Sophie's bed and opened the book.

"The Expressions of Muntu: by Alexander Frederick, a C.M.B. Royal House Publishing," he read to himself then began aloud. *"Long long ago before, men had forgotten their true worth in the world and understood that they were but an extension of something greater than themselves, a power that created all that is ..."*

"Yeah, an extension like the wind," said Sophie bright eyed. "I like this one."

"Yes," said James impressed, "like the wind."

He continued the story.

"...there lived a little princess who challenged the sun morning and night. She was of the belief that the power to command the elements was hers if she kept at it long enough. So she would rise every morning to command the sun to set and waited evenings to tell the sun to rise. She believed whole heartedly that her attempts were possible because man was named Bantu, which is a smaller form of the greater Muntu, the all powerful."

"And one day it came to past that the clever little princess, after much painstaking effort engaging the sun, came to her father and posed this question.

"Father, we are Bantu are we not?"

"And her father, being wise and understanding answered, certainly we are, my princess. But you are already aware of this. What is it that you have been working out in that clever little head of yours?"

"And the little girl said, if we are Bantu, the expression of Muntu, then we have the same power as Muntu. We are Muntu as well. Are we not?"

"Yes my child, we are, said her father"

"Then we can command the wind to blow and the sun to stop shining."

"And her father laughed at this and said, I see, you have given this much thought. Let me help you, for there is no doubt you have put this theory to test and found something is not adding like it should. We are Muntu in quality but not quantity. We are made from the same stuff, power or force that created us, but we are not the force itself that has created all things. Although we may command the sun to rise when it should set or set when it should rise, a greater Muntu has set it into the sky, on its course and told it never to depart from it, so all under the heaven will know when it is time to sleep. And all creatures, even the sun, moon and stars, are bound by the wishes of the Great Muntu."

"And so the little princess —"

James broke off. He looked up from the book and saw that Sophie had fallen asleep somewhere in the telling of the story. He smiled at her peaceful form and remembered how this story had lull him to sleep many years ago. Back then, the child was a prince instead of a princess, which he had on the spot cleverly altered the wording. And now the story has found a new place in another child's heart, and since he was older and perhaps a little wiser, its meaning for him was a bit more esoteric.

"Very nicely read," whispered Red. "Your father is a wonderful story teller and his son also."

CHAPTER SIXTEEN

"Actually," began James. "It's a story told by my grand father and passed down to his children. My father put it into this children's book of African stories like many others my grand father had told him. Am I correct in assuming that Princess Sophie has heard the story before?" asked James.

"Yes," she said with another coy smile. "It's time I turn in as well. You know, it's a long drive back and there is enough room here, if you wish, for another," she added while slyly nodding her head in the direction of the other bedroom,

Her fingers trailed away on the edges of the door frame, disappearing after the rest of her alluring form.

"She's hot for me and way too sexy not to — What the hell I'm I doing here? I got what I've come for," he thought to himself. "Sophie is not my child," mumbled James with a sigh of relief and finally appreciating the magnitude of his present situation. *"But she's offering more, perhaps a once more in a life time opportunity to just... And Veronica said earlier 'You want her too, don't you. I can tell Jamie. Well, go for it. I don't care'."*

James stood up, his loins full, urging him on to partake in a night of wild carnal frenzy. He marched straight down the short corridor for the door with absolute determination, opened it, stepped across the threshold and yelled goodnight as he shut the front door behind himself and disappeared, striding into the deep, the black and capacious night.

Now that the matter of Sophie's parentage was settled, who then was the father? And why was Red so evasive every time the subject would remotely present itself? This train of thought passed through James' mind several times. He felt, however, a strange sense of relief coupled with a peculiar feeling of lost. He had gotten the information he needed and was after all not the father; yet, some part of his heart sank. Possibly because he loved and wanted children and for a moment entertained the notion that Sophie was his own. He had often imagine Veronica and himself with a child who was just as beautiful and just a loving and vivacious as Sophie. His heart ached, and he tried to put the insisting images out of his mind.

On the upswing, his mother had surprised him by being forthcoming with the name of the woman from whom James was adopted. James' spirits lighten at the thought. He felt again as though he was getting somewhere, and soon Paul will have called him with more information on his birth mother and perhaps even who his father was or if the pair of them are still alive.

Then suddenly without any warning, a brilliant and blinding light from out of nowhere inundated the car. To his enormous irritation, James could see in his rearview mirror, intensifying the flashing blue and red lights from behind, that he was being pulled over. For what reason, he had no idea.

"What in the —"

But his question was answered before he could ask it.

CHAPTER SIXTEEN

"This is the police!" an amplified and metallic voice boomed. "Stephen Octavius O'Neil, turn your car off and place your hands outside the window."

"What the hell has he now gotten me in?" said James, his mind racing to resolve this misunderstanding without fatal consequence.

But he could not resolve. All he could think was what had happened to William, and now he has found himself in the same predicament, pulled over for something he believed his idiot cousin's reputation was responsible for. He fumbled in the glove compartment, sifting through its content of crumpled pieces of paper, an envelope that read *the list,* a brand new mobile phone, several business cards, old candy wrappings, and a jewel case containing a Dead Prez CD, only to finally locate his identification in the very back beneath the clutter. And peering out of the rearview mirror, he could see the police officers now drawing their firearms.

"Great, just great," he said through gritted teeth, his fear rising. "Now the guns. Damn-it Blacky."

He closed his eyes and took deep breaths in an effort to master himself. He took one breath, another and then another long one, holding the last in his lungs at full capacity then releasing it slowly. The solution came to him from a most unlikely source.

"That's because you live in two worlds, and one is fighting the other. Don't fight it. Embrace it. The answers

will come. Trust me. It will all make sense," came Blacky's voice from the depths of James' arrested mind.

"That's it," said James, turning his car off, sticking his identification in his mouth for safe keeping and unbuckling himself.

But first he will try something else less risky. He extricated the business card from the glove compartment that read, FRANK NEFER, The Law Office Of McNeal and Nefer along with his seldom used mobile phone then dialed Veronica's number. He did not expect her to answer, but to his enormous relief, she did.

"Jamie?" she whispered. "You're still up? I'm having a glass of wine. I know I sounded a bit jealous earlier and —"

"It's okay Veronica," he said, removing his identification from his mouth. "I need you to —"

"Where are you Jamie? It's rare that you use your cell phone."

"Sweetie, I need you to listen and not interrupt me. I'm at the corner of," he said peering up a the street sign, "Bellevue and Atlantic. I've been stopped by the police and they think I'm Blacky for some reason. And they have guns drawn."

She gasped, but he continued on.

"Please call Frank Nefer of the law office of McNeal and Nefer and explain to him that I am about to be arrested *(or more than likely shot)*," he said, finishing the last part in his head. "He doesn't know me, but he dinged my car the other day outside the book store where you and I met. He left his card on my windshield. I need you to call him as soon as I hang up. Okay?"

"Okay, baby, I will. What's the —— ?"

But they were cut off. James' phone had gone dead from lack of charging, or for that matter, lack of use.

Why didn't he use his phone more often? He inwardly cursed himself, throwing his mobile back into the glove compartment and replacing his identification between his lips. His second option, a historic shoot out in Oakland again came to mind, and he acted as swiftly as humanly possible in the small and constricted space allowed him.

From the outside of the rocking car, James' silhouette could be seen through tinted windows, contorting and twisting about. When his writhing had ceased, he rolled down his window and stuck his hands out slowly. He followed the officer's additional bellowed instructions, carefully opening the door. James' bare feet were the first to be seen. They touched road, and he stepped away from the car, hands raised high and his identification still held firmly between his lips. And like his feet, the rest of him bore not a stitch. He was stripped completely naked.

Arrested

The night air was a sauna in contrast to the cool interior of James' car. It felt as if it clung to his impressively sculpted nude form and caused his body to immediately exude an inordinate amount of perspiration. He was an adonis, glistening in the headlights and street lamps beneath the midnight blue canopy's winking stars. Passersby slowed their cars and screwed their eyes in awe and disbelief. Several admirers, both men and women wolf whistled at his all together birthday suit.

"Ooh goddamn Mandingo," whooped the loudest woman from a car filled with women oglers. "Hung like a gov'ment mule ain'tchah? Can I get some of that?"

"Yah mon!" yelled another. "He's a Rastah, au naturel!"

"Officer... officer!" called a red head admirer in the group, "Leave him be. He ain't done nothing. It's hot out here. I would take my clothes off too, but I don't want every man in the vicinity sprung. Put your hands down, baby. Come get in this car. Mamma's got something forya!"

CHAPTER SEVENTEEN

"Oh, you not even gonna look in our direction huh? Saving it for the vanilla girls? You best recognize!" screamed the driver of the group, honking her horn several times in an attempt to catch James' eye.

James had a strong inclination to cover up; however, he did not want to give the officers further reason to be any more alarmed than what he believed their present expressions must now betray behind the brilliant wall of light shining in his eyes. He therefore hung his head in the blaring lights and hoped he would immediately be arrested and saved from his extreme mortification. But the humiliation continued. They were all now yelling at the same time. And James thought he could make out a few more colorful comments.

"Come gorilla this vanilla."

"I know that's right, white girl," said another.

"Who you callin' white girl? I'm ——"

But when James afforded them no recognition what so ever, they drove away jeering loudly and bantering with one another.

"You aught to be ashamed with your nasty self," quivered the high pitched voice of a very irate grizzled woman driving a well preserved 1974 Oldsmobile, who like the other late night revelers before her, slowed down to take a closer look. "Lock that pervert up officer," she added with an air of incredulity yet managing a quick examination of James' state of undress.

"Give me a break, lady," mumbled James half irritatedly and half despairingly, his identification nearly slipping from his mouth. "I'm trying to get arrested here. Damn, just arrest me already."

"Playah, you're straight buck to the wild!" bellowed an old tramp wearing a dirty jacket with ripped dog-eared pockets, several tattered pairs of pants, a scull cap, and laceless boots.

He was pushing a broken-down shopping cart filled with empty grimy bottles, aluminum cans, and some other rubbish James could not make out.

"Yeah, yeah, yeah," said James.

He thought for a moment, he should had taken Red up on her offer. At the very least it would have been a private and pleasurably alternative to this absolutely humiliating public display of nudity combined with jeering and critiques that made him feel incredibly diminished.

"Boy, what in tarnation," blustered the first officer after the shock of James' state of undress wore off. "Oh you're one of them smart ass nig——"

"Easy, Frank," said the other officer. "Looks like a 10-64 now."

"Alright *Triple-X*, get your ass on the ground, face down, spread eagle —"

"You have got to be kidding me," shot back James this time indignantly, his identification finally falling out of his mouth.

"Now Frank, we wouldn't want him to scratch that *perdy* skin of his," said the other officer in mocked concern.

And both officers, seeing that there was no immediate threat they could somehow misconstrued, stowed their weapons.

CHAPTER SEVENTEEN

"Alright then, Mac," said Officer Frank. "Let's see what *Triple-X* dropped out of his mouth. You there —— *freak nasty* —— hands on the car!"

James acquiesced. He did so, however, grudgingly and took care as not to tread on any sharp objects strewn on the tar smoothed pavement. It was hot beneath his feet, something he had not given a second thought until now. The car shook oddly as though someone was in it, but James felt it was not worth considering. He would have a mechanic take a look at it later, once he has gotten out of this most unfortunate circumstance. And now that he had the presence of mind to consider his x-rated status, he wondered how long would it be before someone who knew him drove by and witnessed his state. Or worse, someone with a video capable phone, who would —— like so many opportunists in the past —— take full advantage of his situations. He imagined himself standing there in all his glory on the morning and evening news. Even worse, he would become an overnight internet sensation on one of those well known sites dedicated to amateur video postings. He felt technology was such an inconvenience at times, and if this were to get out, his reputation would be ruin beyond retrieve. How would he explain this to his family and friends. These thoughts careened themselves back and forth, yet all he could do was to hope one day he would be able to look back on this and somehow find it all laughable.

Officer Frank recovered James' identification from the pavement while the other officer reached into the window of

James' car and extracted a bundle of clothes. He threw them at James.

"Here, get dressed."

James eagerly dressed himself. And no sooner did he finish, he was wincing from Officer Mac slapping the hand-cuffs tightly around his wrists.

"What's your name son?"

"O'Neil. I'm James O'Neil."

"You got that hoity-toity air about you, James O'Neil."

"Yeah, Mac. I hear it too. Where you from, boy?"

"Excuse me?" said James a little taken aback by the use of the word *boy*.

"You heard me. Where you from, boy?"

James' face drained of all emotion, and he thought it would not help his situation if he demonstrated any contempt by engaging in an exchange of words or disclosing the fact he grew up in London to a pair of ill-mannered police officers.

Over the years he had done everything he could to fit in by masking that articulate sound in his voice. Although James lacked the talent to master the African American vernacular, which his best friend William had accomplish almost immediately after his arrival in the U.S., he felt his own attempts at sounding flat was sufficient enough. His refined childhood rearing, however, never parted from him. He thought ruefully that some things will always remain the same, no matter how much effort put into altering them.

CHAPTER SEVENTEEN

"I'm from here," he said politely, catching his balance as he put on a sock and trying to sound as less foreign and more unlettered as possible.

"You sound like you come from a well-to-do family," said Mac. "Tell you what. I am going to go easy on you. Got to take you downtown though. You showed your goodies to the public, and that's a Class 1 Misdemeanor."

"Should make you ride downtown in the buff," said Officer Frank scowling at James. "But we can't have your black ass sticking to the back seat."

James, however, paid this comment no attention, for he was nearly fully dressed and thought it ludicrous to even suggest such a thing. His attention was focused on an all too familiar rickety black car with two hubcaps missing from the driver's side and a faded weather worn top that stood off in the distance. He riffled through his brain, wondered where he had seen that car before. But no sooner had he clothed himself, Officer Frank tugged on the hand-cuffs and marshaled him rather forcefully into the cramp doorway of the squad car before James could get a proper look at the driver inside. His head bumped the door frame, whereupon Frank cautioned him after the fact, but James made no mention of it. He figured, the less he complained, the faster the ordeal would pass.

The other officer walked over to the rickety black car and bent over into its window, and his backside obstructed James view. James thought, if he could just get a look at who was in the car. He peered though the windows, shifting left and right uncomfortably, yet could not catch a clear view of who Officer Mac was talking to. After a fashion, he returned to the car where both he and Officer Frank got in and stowed their night sticks upon exchanging whispers.

"Yeah," said Mac speaking in low tones, yet was heard through the thick wire-meshed fiber glass that segregated the front seats from the back. "It's just a 10-64. I thought this guy was suppose to be dangerous. He's not even the one they're looking for. Remind me not to follow a lead by Matlock again."

"Matlock," whispered James, wincing uncomfortably from the tight cuffs. "I knew it."

18

What's in a Name

Why was Officer Matlock there? Had he been following James all this time, hoping to catch Blacky with him in some nefarious act? What dangerous business did Blacky get the both of them mixed up in? Sure the pair of eye witnesses on the news accorded Blacky with the killings, but James refused to believe it. And why, why does this guy want Blacky so badly? These questions were racing each other through James' mind, only to be interrupted by a searing pain.

"Sss —"

James hissed inaudibly, wincing from the hand-cuffs tightening around his wrist. He leaned to one side to take the pressure off his bound wrists and thought he saw the driver cast him a furtive look in the rear view mirror, no doubt in James' mind, to see if the rough ride was causing him any discomfort. And when James remained tight-lipped, the driver seemed to become more determined to drive around the city, taking care as to run over every bump and maneuver hard turns when the opportunity presented itself.

"Why don't you turn around. I believe you missed a few potholes," James murmured under his breath.

He thought of William and the ride he would have had if he had only kept his hands where they could have been seen and wondered why did William go through all that trouble tugging at his belt. Then it came to him as quick as the flickering lights that darted through the windows of the squad car.

It was many years ago when the pair of them worked for Acorn Super. James had entered the dairy cooler that day looking for William and walked in on him and another coworker both in the middle of a very explicit act. The woman had run out of the cooler, thoroughly embarrassed at what James had witness, never to be seen at work again. William, however, just stood there with his pants down around his ankles complaining about the interruption and the opened cooler door. James had stood there, all the while astonished by Williams unabashed behavior, then pointed out to him —— in an effort to remain casual and make light of a situation which was far too awkward in itself —— that he was disappointed William did not wear any underwear. The pair laughed, James much more uncomfortable than William, for it had been a test of their friendship that James, standing there before his bold as brass childhood mate, did not betray any hint of disgust.

"Yeah, I like raw-dogging it, keeps them cool," James presently remembered him saying. He therefore concluded that William was probably not wearing any underwear the night of the

shooting, just as he did on that day long ago but had now become reserved with age and did not want to share naked facts with the public. It would explain his tugging at his belt. He had worn pants that were too large in the waist and was attempting to keep his pants from falling around his ankles. If only William was as bold as he was when they were young, he might not be convalescing at De'Paul Hospital right now. At this thought, James was sure he had made the right choice to strip before an audience of police officers and oglers.

"Do not complain," thought James to himself. *"You're still in control of what's happening to you. You are still in control."*

He kept repeating it to himself over and again as if a mantra and hoped Veronica managed to contact Frank Nefer or someone who would bail him out as soon as he reached the precinct.

A half an hour later or so, on the other side of town, a brick building rose from the darkness on the corner of MacArthur and Fruitvale, illuminating an entire block, due to its vastness. The lights from precinct 23 flooded the early morning fog that made the humidity even more stifling as the morning progressed. James had lost track of time. He thought disappointedly of all the good his watch he was sitting on in his pocket would do, even if it was on his wrist. He assumed therefore that it was very late in the night or as it should be properly noted, early in the morning.

"Here we are *Triple X*," began the officer called Frank, pulling James out of the car and onto his feet, "home sweet home, which you will be enjoying for quite a while."

"Not if I can help it," thought James.

The officer named Mac waited in the car, and James was marshaled through the doors of precinct 23 with his hands still bounded behind his back. The station's closed scent of musk filled his nostrils and interrupted his steady breathing. It smelt slightly of a locker room and some unknown pungent odor, and James found himself taking short breaths in order to tolerate the smell. His preoccupation with less than favorable clean air was eclipsed by an ominous cry. Somewhere in the building a distant voice called out, barely audible beneath the bustling noise. James' stomach writhed and turned nervously. No sooner did this occur, James was rushed into the section for fingerprinting and processing before he could properly identify the haunting sound or take in his surroundings. He was drained from his long day and would give anything to just sit on one of the crowded benches lining the walls and drift of into blissful sleep. But his brief reverie was quickly dashed by hands groping in his pockets.

"Don't take this personally," said Officer Frank, turning James' pockets inside out and removing his identification and keys, including the watch Veronica gave him for his birthday.

"Sorry Frank," said a surly officer who looked thoroughly overwhelmed and steeped in paperwork. "We just have too many to process. Put him in the tank with the rest until we can get to him. Jeesh, must be a full moon or something."

"Well," began Frank slyly, "this might be your lucky day. If by some miracle you are sprung by someone on high before you are processed, your record will remain clean, unless you have priors we are not yet aware of. But the chances of that happening this morning are zero to none. So let's get you a nice comfortable cell, *Mr. McNasty.*"

"Yeah, right," shot back James.

James was now marched up a hall of several doors, one of which read INFIRMARY, and he laughed silently to himself at this odd phenomenon, thinking absurdly how a place filled with guns and bullets would need more than a nurses office. While gaining their way up the corridor, James became aware of the linoleum making slight crackling sounds beneath his feet. And just as his mind began to wonder when was it the last time the floors were retiled, Frank tugged suddenly on the cuffs and James was wheeled to his left before a half door that was opened at the top. Frank tossed James' belongings through the door, and they slid across the counter of the bottom half before they were halted by the quick hands of an officer manning the cupboard. This gave James cause for concern of his property. He would preferred his things were taken better care of than what Officer Frank had just so callously demonstrated.

"We have here *Mr. McNasty,*" he said gruffly. "The name's on the license."

"You'll get your things back after you are released," said the officer behind the enclosed counter, sealing James' belongings in a very large manila envelop, writing his name on it and filing it away behind him in an enormous bin.

James was handed off to another officer standing nearby and ushered down a poorly ventilated hall, which was painted green and reeked strongly of the faint scent James detected earlier. Now that he was well shut of Officer Frank, he did not mind the increasing stagnated air as much. However, his trepidation grew with the ever approaching scream. The man's voice James heard earlier became louder and more distinct as they rounded a narrow corridor, only to be in the company of more guards. James could see through a barrier of bars the gentleman whose voice filled the entire floor. He spoke with a gruff voice and wore a matted beard and had dreaded hair that was massive, giving him the look of a very bad tempered lion out of the *Wizard of Oz*. And the screaming coupled with his appearance made James felt as though the gentleman must have taken full leave of his senses.

"What you gonna do when I come for you!" he bellowed over and again. "Hey, big man... big man," he now directed his hostility to the largest of the guard escorts in the area, "what you gone do when I come for you!"

"Spank that ass you silly *wabbit*," said the corpulent guard. "Now BACK the hell off the bars!" he added with much disdain.

"Oh, you got jokes, pudgy."

CHAPTER EIGHTEEN

"You get one call... one call," the guard said curtly to James.

He slid open the bars which frame was bolted to one side of a wall, forming a passageway that connected to a larger cell farther off where detainees were corralled, undoubtedly awaiting further processing. James caught sight of a phone mounted onto the wall, and the bars behind him slammed shut with an enormous clank that unnerved him. He grabbed the receiver of the phone with trembling hands. Trying to steady his nerves, he and began to dial, praying Veronica would answer her phone and at the same time cursing himself for not memorizing Frank Nefer's number.

He thought oddly of what his father, Alexander Frederick O'Neil in his youth, was told by his own father Rufus. *"You go out there and get arrested if you want. When they call me or come to the house for money to bail you out, I don't know you."* That was his grandfather's way of keeping his sons Alexander and Octavius in line. And it appeared to have worked, or perhaps it was that his sons had not the inclination for breaking the law and steered clear of behavior worthy of incarceration. It was sure enough a hard pill for James' father to swallow, and he wondered if his father would come to his aid if he called. But James was not in the least bit interested in contacting Alexander, and he felt that calling his mother was absolutely out of the question. All he needed was Veronica. As illogical as it may seem, he felt if he could just talk with her, everything would be all right. He would be all right.

"Come on, pick up," he whispered desperately, his hopeful expectation deflating with every unanswered ring. "Where are you?"

He hung the phone up, sorely disappointed and dare not a second attempt at calling for help. The bars slid open to the larger holding area and James was instructed by the guard to continue through. With great reluctance, however, he stepped through, joining other detainees.

The man who was creating a disturbance was still yelling at the top of his lungs, and James found this now oddly amusing, but betrayed no hint of it.

"What you gonna do when I come for you! Hey, big man... what you gonna do when I come for you!"

"Why don't you shut the hell up!" roared the corpulent guard.

He approached the side of the cell where his challenger stood, then ran something that looked like a small leather baton across the bars, causing the rowdy man to quickly release them in indignation and taking several steps backwards. He threw the guard, who was now returning to his station, a nasty look and continued his verbal assault.

"Why don't you jog your fat ass around the block a few times!"

The other detainees jeered at this last comment. James, in an effort to comport himself, stifled a snicker under his breath. He could not believe the chaos he had found himself in. What sort of people was this motley bunch? What on earth had each committed to place themselves here? And what, what on this good green earth, in each of their lives, made it so easy to be entertained under such condition? Sure it was sardonically humorous to James, but he felt he was unable, as they did, to take as much delight in their own impertinence, not to mention the general air of griminess the place exuded. He surveyed his surroundings and eyed a very filthy looking toilet to the back right corner of the room and hoped to himself he would never find the necessity of its use. He then walked over to the center of the cell and took a seat on a metallic bench that was as long as picnic tables he had in the past witnessed merry-goers make happy use of in public parks. It felt cold to the touch and even less inviting than it appeared, almost indifferent. It was bolted to the grimy concrete floor that seemed to perspire with the windowless walls.

"Man," began the loudest of the detainees again, taking another shot at the guard returning to his post, "would you look at the chee-chees on that one."

The hilarity mounted, fifteen detainees or more laughing at the top of their lungs, some banging the bars and other shouting a few choice descriptions, undoubtedly to express disdain for their jailer and revel in his discomfort. However, there was one who had not joined in the festivities; he just sat there staring from a corner at James. And when the ruckus subsided, James became ill-at-ease with the hulking gentleman's stares. He, however, dare not to try and stare him down. So he nodded politely in the gentleman's direction.

"That's my seat," said a skinny man who looked very hang-dogged, catching James off-guard and dividing his attention.

"Excuse me?"

"That's my damn seat playah. I don't like pretty muthu-fuckuhs like you sitting in my seat."

And wanting no trouble from a man who James felt was obviously no match for him, James slid over, but not by much. He was as close as would allow himself to be near another man to his right, who appeared stricken with withdrawal symptoms from some narcotic that James could only guess at. The twitching man was complaining to himself ardently in low murmurs about how hot it was.

The silence fell.

"Damn," said the lion mane detainee, "Here we go again."

"That's my seat too bitch," came the skinny man again. "Who the fuck are you to roll up in my spot and just sit where ever the hell you want?"

If James told him his name was Blacky, then he would never have to worry about defending himself against anyone else in the cell. He could not, however, take a chance that this pitiable excuse of a man would know Blacky. But whatever he say now, it must work for the group at large. And for the second time in a span of several hours, James again remembered something Blacky had said.

CHAPTER EIGHTEEN

"'Spooner' is also a strong name, a strong street name which you are going to need, if you keep showing up in places you shouldn't."

He thought, wasn't this the very type of place Blacky was talking about? James felt he was not like the rest of the detainee. He could not be like them. Sure he was dressed like most of them, but appearances have a tendency of being deceptive; he did not come from a depraved background. No, he was not like these cons that surrounded him at present, not one bit. He consoled himself with these thoughts knowing deep inside he was being judgmental without any supporting evidence, just like Detective Matlock had been with him and Blacky. However, no matter their backgrounds, he must become, for the time being, one of them, by embracing the moment to survive.

"You hear me talking to you bitch?" taunted the skinny man, now in a towering temper. "Who the fuck are you!" he bellowed again, now positively hostile and leaning into James' face, close enough for James to feel his spittle and breath.

"Spooner," James said calmly into his adversary's face, which now turned from vituperate to fearful.

"That's all you had to say, man," he said, backing away thoroughly shook. "If there's anything you need to make your stay pleasant, Mr. Spooner, just call on me. Diddy-Bop."

This timid response caught James totally by surprise, but he recovered without notice.

"Yeah, get the fuck out my face," he said with an incredible impersonation of Blacky's nastiest mood, and thought to himself sardonically, *"Diddy-Bop, what a ridiculous name."*

"Sit your punk ass down," said the scruffy lion mane detainee to general whooping and guffaws,

He did not even bothered to turn in their direction to acknowledge their appreciative outburst, but continued to peer out between the bars in the direction of the guards, undoubtedly to seize upon his next opportune moment of provocation.

"Heard of you," said the hulking man in the corner, whose arms were tattooed with barbwire and tribal art that matched the markings on his bald head.

"You have?" said James a little too surprisingly and simultaneously regretting the momentary lapse of his tough guy facade. "Really now?" he added adversely, attempting to camouflage his astonishment.

"Indeed," he said, presently eyeing James with some suspicion. "That's unusual."

"Excuse me?"

"You don't look like a killer."

He studied James for a few moments, apparently deliberating on the validity of James' facade.

"No matter. What's in a name? They call me Rock. When I first heard of you, it was about seven years ago in the state pen. Me and an associate by the name of Smoke, who owes more than a debt of gratitude to this brother we met, were told by him a story about some bad-ass he use to roll with who saved his life."

He paused for another moment, wiping his bald head as if slowly sweeping hair away from his face. As he raised his arm, James noticed a tattoo on Rock's forearm that was one in the same with that of Blacky's, but was quite sure it would not be wise to inquire about it; so he made no mention.

"Said they got in a scuffle with some guys on the streets over territory, and his partner picked up a rusty spoon off the ground and stabbed some soldier from another crew with it and proceeded to cut out a vital organ. That was an incredible story that many came to believe, including myself. Sometimes when I hear the story on the streets, I hear it was the liver. Some say it was the heart. And, others say it was just an eye. Odd how it is that no one seems to really know. So you tell me which was it."

"Does it matter?"

"Now either you are that urban legend," said Rock, his voice turning icy, "or you are a dumb ass liar to use that name up in here. So I'm going to ask you one time. What set you roll with?"

It took James a few moments to realize what he was being asked. And he cast around the cell and saw the rest of the detainees, including the lion mane gentleman, were listening attentively.

"I don't roll with nobody."

"Really?" said Rock, his voice obviously inflected in a manner suggesting his disbelief, coupled with a sardonic tone that threaten harm in every way.

James boldly raised a finger, forestalling Rock's next observation, and marshaled his thoughts as quickly as possible.

"One person. I trust only one person, and that's Blacky," he said with perfect confidence.

"I see," said Rock nodding his head in approval.

And James breathed an undetectable sigh of relief.

"That very man I was talking about is Blacky. He was an odd and unpredictable soldier, preferred to assault the guards and spend most of his time in solitary confinement. Odd thing is, the more they put him in there, the more invigorated he seemed to be when he came out. It was like a holiday for him. He gained much respect from the yard. No one, and I mean no one messed with him."

Just then, the twitching man sitting next to James stood high on the metal bench and started pealing layers of cloths off, until he was stripped down in his underpants to an astonished James.

"I can't take it. I just can't take it. It's too hot in here," he said wild eyed.

And just as suddenly as he stripped away his layers, he dove off the bench, head first into the concrete floor as if into a pool of water. There was an awful crunching sound as the man folded under impact. James employed a great deal of comportment yet winced slightly at the horrible account. He had never witness anyone behave as if they had taken full leave of their senses. He could not wipe the look of shock and astonishment steadily growing on his face as the man lay there bloody and unconscious. The detainees were once again in an uproar.

CHAPTER EIGHTEEN

"Guard!" bellowed the entire lot, deploying an enormous clamor of harsh, colorful and none too flattering insults to their jailers, who apparently did not respond quick enough to their liking.

"Everyone," bark the corpulent guard over the tumult, "move back along the walls. Now!" he added with a threatening tone of finality.

The fifteen or so detainees moved from the bars and away from the broken man upon the concrete floor, James included. One guard and a male nurse stood before the bars; however, not in front of the part that corrals them one by one, but rather the largest portion of which the lion mane gentleman stood moments before. Two other guards approached and got into a pre-rehearsed stance. And to James surprise, the entire broad side of the cell slid open to one side.

"Ladies," said the corpulent guard standing next the nurse, "moving you to another cell. So follow me."

"Man I was just getting comfortable," joked one of the detainees. "Five star accommodations and a pool in the room. Hey, can I take a dip too before we leave?"

The laughter returned, but the guards were stone faced. They marshaled the group out of the great cell in one long cue, following the large guard with another guard half way down the line ushering and another at the point of origin. James peered back to see what had become of the concrete diver. The nurse hovered over him, undoubtedly checking to see if he was still alive. James thought he saw the man move for one brief moment, but his vision was obscured by a corner they had turned, and a tall and distinguished gentleman approached the cue with something in his hand that resembled James' envelope of possessions. The queue came to a halt, and he conversed with the lead guard who nodded, turned and pointed at James.

"Damn," said James, the word coming to his lips as if without his volition.

"They found you, Spooner," said Rock. "See you on the outside."

"You," said the distinguish gentleman, pointing a long finger at James, "come with me."

James pulled himself out of the line and resolved himself to the fact that he was about to be fingerprinted and processed. There was no getting out of this now. He will be here all night long or until someone comes to bail him out. He pleaded desperately to himself for Veronica to come through.

James Benjamin O'Neil?" said the distinguished gentleman with a silver name badge that read, Capt. Mahony.

"Yeah."

James tentatively braced himself for the worst and wished the gentleman had not uttered his name as loudly as he did. He did not wish the inmates to know this bit of information about himself. Nonetheless, his ordeal was near over, and James felt he would never again run into anyone from this lot.

"I'm Capt. Samuel Mahony, and today is your lucky day. You're free to go."

"What?" said James flabbergasted yet simultaneously relieved.

"Let's just call it a case of mistaken identity, and we will not charge you with indecent exposure. I have released your car from the pound, and it's parked out back. Hand this ticket to the person manning the booth to the gated lot.

James took the ticket from Mahony's proffered hand.

"Now, I must warn you about your cousin," he said with a stern face; yet, James detected something more in his voice, something out of the ordinary he could not put his finger on. "Blacky is involved in something way over your head and you need to leave this up to the professionals. Stay clear of him or you will find yourself laid out on a slab. That would cause me a lot of paperwork, and I hate paperwork. Understood?"

He handed James the manila envelope containing his possessions, holding them just out of James' reach.

"Understood?" he asked again, this time more sharply.

"Yes," I understand."

Awkward Moments

Dammit Blacky," said an ill tempered James over the loud barks of Mrs. Hawthorne's dog. It was the following fortnight of his release from incarceration, and the dark wee hours of the morning had passed so quickly into what was apparently now day. He slammed the phone down after speaking with Veronica at length for the umpteenth time over why he was out late the night of his arrest. He had spent much of the very early morning talking with Veronica, which was a feat within itself. They had in the past managed only stolen moments or on several occasion her husband Uri was again off on some secretive business deal that he so often refused to disclose to Veronica.

Veronica had also shared that Uri often took her car when his was functioning perfectly fine, only to give no reason but to stay out of his business affairs. From this, James suspected Uri was undoubtedly mixed up in some illegal or unscrupulous affair of sorts. It therefore did not come as any surprise to James that Veronica felt the need to interrogate him in a matter that lend itself to distrust.

CHAPTER NINETEEN

James could not blame her too much for her suspicions. Veronica's last husband, as told to James one late night during their foray into her past marriages, was overbearing and uncompromising on every account. He had, however, astonished her with his cowardliness the night of a mugging. He had run off, leaving Veronica alone to deal with a mugger, and she could not forgive the act. The husband prior was a violent man whose temper got the better of him during a heated argument. She found herself laying on a pile of glass in the middle of her living room, her coffee table shattered beneath her in a million pieces. It's a wonder, thought James, how she managed to get up the courage to marry again. She did, however, held onto her maiden name. It was proof enough for James that she still reserved some trepidation in the matter of trust.

He did not, however, appreciate being made to feel very like a child caught in some wrong doing. Yet in spite of that, he had explained he could not wait another moment in darkness and needed to know immediately of Sophie's parentage. He thought Veronica would be quite pleased to know that he had gotten to the bottom of it all. She was not so much upset over James' returned visit to his parents home as she was with him seeing Red again in the wee hours. Indeed, the news of Sophie's parentage was well received. He could have chosen, however, to visit during the day or make a simple phone call. And his foray into the wee hours did not bode well with Veronica.

"Men!" she had said disdainfully, "You're always thinking with the wrong head."

"Well someone has to or there wouldn't be any people on the damn planet," which had been James' retort, bringing the conversation to an abrupt end with Veronica hanging up in anger rather loudly in his ear.

"Great," said James irritated with himself. "Nice going, genius."

There had been such a finality in the tone of her voice that James felt beyond a shadow of doubt that it would be a long time before he heard from her again. He wondered, why was he after all this time feeling guilty. Didn't he spend the last two weeks trying to explain? Was it because he had considered it? It was just one moment, one tiny moment of weakness, a mental slip-up. It's not a crime to be turned on by someone. He convinced himself that it was natural. He thought any man who met Red or caught site of her would have to be a Tibetan Monk not to find her desirable, and the practices of Tibetan Monks aren't all that natural. He brewed even more. Hadn't Veronica realized by now how much he loved her? Hadn't she appreciated how long he was willing to wait while she remained indecisive of leaving a man whose skullduggery and abusiveness left her in constant darkness and fear? And why, why on earth was she so afraid of her husband Uri? The more these thoughts raced, the angrier he became. In truth, James had been upset because Veronica did not answer her phone the second time on the night of his arrest. But he thought he understood why. Although she had not manage to contact Frank Nefer, she did, however, leave a detail note with his answering service. He checked himself, and thought no harm was done and realized it was a fair attempt on her part. This left the unanswered question of who was it that actually posted bail for him. And he thought wryly that another unanswered question was all he needed.

It was a beautiful day out, and James resented himself for remaining inside closeted, pacing back and forth in the living room with angry and resentful thoughts. After a fashion, James calmed himself down, only to realize he was blaming the wrong people for his misfortune. Blacky, his ne'er-do-well cousin, who was one of the most brilliant cousins he had grown up with and always tested extremely high and branded gifted as a child, had warned James about showing up in places he should not. James thought perhaps it was after all too late to be out gallivanting, visiting the hospital, his mother and definitely much too late to be out visiting an ex-girlfriend then consequently landing himself in jail for indecent exposure. Indecent exposure, what was he thinking? To add insult to an already taxing night, he was reminded by a Capt. Mahony to keep his nose out of the business of others. He thought maybe not in those exact words, but that is how it appeared to him. It was almost like hearing Blacky tell him to mind his own business, by warning him to stay out of places he did not belong. James thought it was quite strange that Capt. Mahony seemed more peeved with him than with Blacky.

And what about that fantastic story Blacky had put out on the streets about James, or rather Spooner. He had been racking his brains for days and could not figure out why Blacky created such a character and not tell James. What did this mean? Did Blacky have the foresight to predict James would need, what he called, a reputation? Every time James thought of this, he could not stay angry with Blacky, and his curiosity was piqued with his ever increasing confusion.

Nonetheless, one thing was clear, James had to admit to himself that it was he who needed to accept responsibility for his own actions. He did not know, however, why he was so upset. He just felt frustrated that things were not at all going his way since his decision to quit his job and write for himself. His endeavors were to be easily accomplished. He was now, however, somewhat discouraged. Instead of writing, he had been whiling away the wait for his cousin Paul to call, by analyzing the last of his father's letters over and again. James had imagined Paul would soon call with some earth shattering news of his parentage. And to his very great disappointment, he dismissed the prospects of his cousin ever finding any useful material.

He could not dwell on these things for far too long. Now that the sun was high in the sky, he was preparing to visit William, something he had as of late taken to during daylight hours. He had been keeping with his promise to read his father letters to William over the past visits and often running into Mrs. Barinard, who seemed to manage her over seas business quite proficiently from a cell phone when she was not by William's side most of the time.

Upon exiting his house onto the landing, James was greeted by the noon sun dazzling his eyes and the sight of his inquisitive neighbors Mrs. Hawthorne and the loquacious Mr. Berchmier. She was standing there pruning her yellow chrysanthemums and unseasonable red and white roses as she often did this time of day. She was in a purple flowery smock and matching gloves that fit her tiny fingers snugly, allowing her to operate a pair of small sheers in her hand. She had that well styled silvery hair, that looked like something out of an old *Leave It To Beaver Show,* with a slight hint of blue that many elderly women James had in the past witness wearing. And to finish off her ensemble, she wore shoes complementing her smock and gloves.

James supposed she had been standing there talking with Mr. Berchmier about some dubious FBI adventure for quite some time, and James hoped he could sidle by the two unnoticed, or at the most, a cordial wave and brief salutation. By the position of their body language, the pair seemed to be engaged in an intimate conversation, giving no thought to her German Shepherd, which was throwing a towering fit behind the tall wooden fence along the side of her home. James suspected that Fido, as he called it, did not take too kindly to Mr. Berchmier's proximity to Mrs. Hawthorn. And he wondered ironically, if Mr. Berchmier had anything to do with Fido's morning wake-up calls.

"Oh hush Willoughby," she called to her dog. "There you are James. I was just saying to Mr. Berchmier about that police officer that came by your door the other day while you were out."

Great, thought James. The neighbors were already talking about him. He greeted the pair of them with mock surprise while carefully locking his door and noticed that Mr. Berchmier had moved back a step away from Mrs. Hawthorne.

"Asked me all sorts of questions about you. And I told the gentleman —— Willoughby no, now stop all that racket. I tell you, I don't know what's come over him," she digressed, her face coloring up with what James thought was embarrassment. "Now where was I —— ? Oh... And I told him you were a fine young man who kept out of trouble. But he just kept going on and on with the questions until I just told him, no more. I had my scones in the oven, you see, and did not want to ruin them, so I suggest he'd come back at another time, if he wanted to know anything else and talk with you."

Mr. Berchmier, who look as though he were bidden to examining the nearby chrysanthemums said nothing, and continued to look suspiciously uncomfortable. But James' feeling of annoyance was wiped clean by the mere mention of one word, *scones.*

"Did you say scones." said James, his mouth water up and causing him to swallow enormous amounts of saliva.

"Yes my dear boy. It's my grandmother's recipe. Been in the family for a very long time. I use to make them for my husband, rest his soul, but there is no one to share them with. Well... Rupert —— Mr. Berchmier enjoys them. Don't you?"

But James did not hear her. His mind had wandered across the intervening years to a place and time where he was very young, and life was simple. He would enjoy his mother's fresh baked scones on a Monday very like today.

"Willoughby Fitzwilliam," she called out this time much sterner to her extremely exercised canine companion, causing James to snap out of his reverie. "You shush all that fuss this instant, or no doggy treats for you today."

"Well, you two have a wonderful day," he called back to the pair as he set off. "Goodness, the names people give their pets," he added privately to himself.

"Such a nice young man," James heard her say. "But his hair is far too long"

"In my day..." began Mr. Berchmier.

But the rest was lost to James in the distance.

He strode up the remainder of the garden path, entered his car, and drove off to the sound of Willoughby Fitzwilliam barking and the sight of Mrs. Hawthorne and Mr. Berchmier resuming their intimate conversation.

When James later arrived in the doorway of room 742, he was surprised to see Red standing there conversing with the doctor and Mrs. Barinard. Their backs were turned to him, yet he would know the exquisite delineation of Red at any distance.

"Oh, you must come by the guest house Anita," said Red addressing the doctor.

James thought it was absolutely unforgivable the lengths Red would stoop to work her way back into his life. But why were the three carrying on like old friends united again after years apart. This was now way too disturbing for James, and he backed away from the threshold and out of sight, hoping none would be the wiser of his brief appearance. He had gained the corridor midway when a voice behind him called, stopping him dead in h s stride.

"Spooner! I thought that was you. That's the second time you ran out on me. What? You afraid of little-o me?"

"Oh, Red," he spluttered, thoroughly caught off-guard and turning around to face her. "How are you? I was just going to — I was about to —— I left something in the car."

"Sure," said Red in a non-convinced tone. "Anita," she called to the room, and the doctor stepped out into the corridor, beaming at James.

"Anita?" said James surprised, striding back in their direction. "Dr. Anita Forman, wow, you've done alright for yourself."

He gave her a hug.

"See Anita," said Red with one eye brow slightly raised.

"Yes it's me, and thank you, Spooner," said Anita. "My goodness, Red, you're right. He's still fine as ever. I can't believe no one has managed to tie you down by now. Still the playboy as ever?"

CHAPTER NINETEEN

"No," said James with a little embarrassed smile. "That's not my style."

"I told you girl," said Red. "He hasn't changed, so serious all the time."

"Relax, Spooner," said Anita. "Just giving you a hard time. It's good to see you again. And William is pulling through nicely. It's amazing. He's quite lucky no major organs were damaged in the shooting," she added, gesturing with a nod towards the room in which William convalesced. "Now I must continue to make my rounds, but I will be checking up on your friend again later. And if we have the chance later, I would like to catch-up sometime with you and Red. She has invited me over your parents' guest house. Hope to see you there. Take care now."

And she swept from the both of them, leaving a giant pink elephant of an empty space, an awkward silence between the both of them. An uncomfortable few short moments went by, or was it more like several days, and the pair started to speak at the same time.

"Why don't you come on in?" began Red.

"About the other night," began James.

"I'm sorry. What?" asked Red.

"Excuse me?" said the both simultaneously.

"I'll be back later, I have something to take care of," recovered James. "Say hello to Mrs. Barinard for me would you."

And keen to be well shut of Red, James turned suddenly and proceeded down the corridor, leaving Red there absolutely stunned with bemusement.

20

Alfred Clark

It wasn't that James needed to be somewhere in particular. He did not want to find himself explaining to Veronica why he and Red were both visiting William at the same time. At least that is the reason with what he convinced himself. He thought that if he did not want things to get out of hand, then he needed to avoid Red, at least for now and at all cost. He supposed that at some point he would have to share his encounter with Red to Veronica, but he could not bring himself to having another argument with her, no matter how innocent he felt himself. It made him feel terribly lonely to be at odds with her. It was the very thought of her that made his heart soar. He figured he would return later to check on William, and by then, he thought hopefully, Red would have found some other interest and left by then.

Since James had at present no particular place to be, he found himself hard put to heed the warnings of Capt. Mahony. He had restrained himself from setting off in search of Blacky over the past two weeks and now sat there behind the wheel of his car going over the pros and cons of maintaining his distance. But there he was yet again, a half an hour later driving through an old rundown neighborhood by the name of Hunter Heights, which was far more populated than the Colonial Park neighborhood he had driven through weeks ago. It was one of Blacky's old hang-outs and the best place to begin his search.

James was not sure as of who to ask about Blacky. He figured Blacky's name would be a hot button; therefore, the need for caution would be wise. But how was he going to do this. He realized that he could not very well drive up and down the neighborhood streets until he ran into Blacky. And if he asked the wrong person, it could be fatal.

After cruising the neighborhood for a half an hour, passing young men on corners who were casting furtive looks up and down the streets, tossing dice, leaning against store fronts with apparently nothing to do and some trading hidden items stealthily from one man's hand to another. And by the nature of the exchanging, James thought perhaps something illegal. He realized this search method he so duly employed would continue to yield poor results, possibly bringing much more attention to himself than what he intended. He decided therefore to be adventurous and go at it on foot but not too far from his car. And when he stepped out of it, he was met by a scruffy and dirty man asking for money. James assumed he was homeless, because he was pushing an old squeaky wheeled shopping cart that appeared to have all the man's worldly possessions, including tin cans and plastic bottles that teetered on the brink of spilling over onto the ground.

"Sorry, I don't have any money to lend you," James politely said.

"Lend?" said the beggar rather peevishly. "Come on, buck to the wild, I ain't asking you to lend me nothing. Hell, by the looks of you playah, you got money coming out your ass."

"Excuse me?" said James taken aback, remembering he had heard the phrase *buck to the wild* from somewhere.

"Yeah, I saw your little peep show you gave on the street a few weeks back."

The humiliating moments of jeering passersby flooded James' brain, and he combed every moment, trying to place the vagabond's face.

"Reminds me," the man went on, "of the ambush of Eldridge Cleaver and Bobby Hutton by Oakland cops, back in the day. My man Eldridge came out the house butt-ball naked, but Bobby was not. They popped Bobby. But cops won't shoot a butt naked man. Will they?"

"Yeah that's right," said James, now remembering the man and his bedraggled appearance from the other night.

"But you don't even remember me, do you?"

James looked utterly perplexed now. What did he mean by this? Absolutely he remembered him from the other night.

"But I remember you, Spooner. And I know your secret. You're not the man they say you are on the streets."

"What —— ? Who are you? How did you —— ?" stammered James, now even more bemused.

CHAPTER TWENTY

"You're Blacky's cousin, right? That rich kid that use to follow him around. What, don't recognize me yet?"

And he pulled his knitted hat off, exposing his matted hair that was black, thick and coarse. He tugged at it in different places to give it volume, making a lopsided afro, and James thought he may have seen a bud move in his woolly top. And upon sight of this, the memory of a kid with a large afro that seemed to trap every bug that flew in its sphere, James' eyes lit up.

"Al, is that you?" he said. "Alfred Clark, as I live and breathe. It's been ages. Well it's been since we were kids. I'm sorry I did not recognize you."

"Yeah, but I recognized you, Spooner," he said, putting his knitted hat back on.

"Here," said James reaching into his pocket and pulling out a money clip and separating a fifty dollar bill then handing it to Al. "I know this will not solve your problems, but can you find a way to use this to make things at least a little better?"

"I ain't no crack-head," said Al sounding a little offended.

"Then here," said James, none too apologetic. "Take it in payment for information."

"You five-o, Spooner?" he asked suspiciously, snatching the money from James' proffered hand and crumpling it into a tiny ball with one of his crusty and brutish looking fists.

"Hell no Al, I am a writer, not a cop. All I am trying to do is find my cousin Blacky. Can you help me?"

"Blacky rolls with some heavy weights. You can't just go around asking people about them. The last time someone asked about them, they disappeared. And the time before that, an entire family. It's Smoke and Rock that people are scared of, but no one dare not ask about Blacky because he is tight with them. You ask about one, you ask about the others. Smoke is the one with his ears to the ground. He knows everything that goes on in the streets."

"Can you take me to him?"

"Ain't you been listening to me? If you have a death wish, then asking about Smoke or any one of them will do. Do yourself a favor, rich boy. Wait until your cousin finds you. Don't go looking for trouble."

And he turned towards his cart and began to push.

"Wait," James said, removing the thin tin from his pocket and taking out a card, handing it to Al. "If you hear anything, anything at all, please call me."

"All the pay phones are busted around here, Spooner."

"I know, buy a cell phone," said James returning the card holder into his back pocket.

Al took the business card from James and tossed it into the basket of eclectic items, and set out. James watched as he tramped away with his old beat-up shopping cart and wondered how in the world did Al find himself in such an unfortunate state.

21

Wrong Side of Town

The day was incredibly beautiful and in full swing. After leaving the corner in which he had spoken to Al, James felt it would be a perfect opportunity, since he was passing in the direction of the hospital, to stop by as he had planned earlier to revisit William. He hoped Red would have left by now and found himself a little angst dwelling on her subterfuge. He did his best to remove every intrusive thought of her from his mind, but he kept thinking how absurd he must have appeared sneaking off along the corridor without saying not one hello. He wondered why did she get him off his stride so easily. He thought she must have found it extremely entertaining to see him behaving quite dodgy. James felt nonetheless that she had always been the way she is, and it was he who was having trouble readjusting to her sudden appearance after so many years. But that would not last for very long. It was only a matter of time before Red returned back from whence she came. It was this thought he found comforting, and he felt the mounting anxiety drain away.

When James reached room 742, he found it empty, with the exception of a catatonic William. He was, however, now donned with far less bandages than before. His head was unwrapped and fewer tubes were tethered to him. And upon sight of this, James smiled and convinced himself that it was a good sign. He took the seat he had often done when visiting William and pulled out a few of his father's letters.

"I hope you don't mind me reading you these. They say it's good that someone is here to talk with you, but all I have is a series of unfortunate events that I'd prefer not even get into at the moment."

He began to read. After a fashion, James finished the few letters he had brought with him and promised to conclude with the rest upon another visit. He stood and gathered his papers.

"Well, I guess that's all, Will. I'm off to call Veronica and make —"

"Hi Spooner, I thought I'd find you here," said Anita Forman entering the room with Mrs. Barinard and carrying on like before, as if old friends.

"James," said Mrs. Barinard brightly. "I have been talking with this delightful young lady for quite a while now. And up until the other day — of your short visit and hasty exit — I was unaware that the pair of you were already acquainted. It is a small world indeed."

"Yes it is," agreed Anita.

James looked mortified.

CHAPTER TWENTY-ONE

"She is such a fascinating person, Spooner," said Mrs. Barinard using his nick-name in a rather suggestive manner.

"If I did know any better, Mrs. Barinard, I'd think you were trying to fix us up."

"And would that be such a bad thing. Look at her, she's quite fetching."

Indeed, Anita was very beautiful. She was willowy yet shapely, with dark brown skin tone that was smooth as melted chocolate. Her hair was tied up off her shoulders and her eyes seemed to twinkle when she smiled.

"Okay," said Anita grinning widely. "It's one thing to jest with Spooner, but now you're making me blush. I thank you for —"

She was interrupted by her pager vibrating rather vigorously on her hip, and after a quick look at the message, she was off again.

"Upon my word, she will never marry if she's always dashing about like that. And what do you think of that beautiful young lady name Red?"

"Well," James said feeling rather uncomfortable and searching for delicate words to describe his past relationship with Red. "She and I were at one point — were —"

"Oh my heavens, dear boy. The whole affair must indeed be very awkward for you. And she seems to fancy you still. My word, what a pickle... What a pickle."

"Yeah, tell me about it. A very sour one at that," he added privately to himself.

"By the looks of it, you were on your way out, perhaps a rendezvous with some lovely young lady? Am I correct in assuming there is someone out there in the sun waiting for you?"

"Yes, there is someone," said James with a pensive gaze and a smile slowly creasing his face.

"Wonderful!" she said, jarring James a little from his mild revery. "Now off with you. We will have plenty of time in the future for a pleasant catch-up. Now go and enjoy some time in the sun."

And with that, James was on his way and soon to be home, his mind preoccupied with elated thoughts of Veronica. Twenty minutes later, however, he found himself disconcerted and standing before the slightly ajar front door to his home. James pushed open his door slowly. He was sure he did not leave the door unlocked, and he thought it was most curious that someone would have the gull to break-in during daylight and in sight of his inquisitive neighbors. James entered the house with a creep, taking care as to open the door as wide as possible. He then caught sight of his Louisville Slugger propped next to the small table. He reached for the bat, his fingers inches from it and thought sardonically that someone was about to receive a massive head ache. And suddenly there was darkness.

James was awaken by freezing water dousing his entire body. His breath came in great gasps, and an agonizing pain stung his face. His head was throbbing angrily. He was sitting in the middle of a large and dimly lit room that echoed the sound of his gasps and shivers. His arms were pulled taught around the back of the chair with his wrists tightly bound. Another incredible sting licked his face with the dead clap sound of a hand striking skin and reverberating upon the walls of the darkened room. He was painfully disoriented: He ached all over, wondering where he was and how he had gotten there. Someone had struck him; this he was sure of. And before he had the time to consider it any further, he heard an eery scream of horror somewhere in the near distance.

"I tell you, I'm telling the truth. Please," sobbed a frighten man's voice. "No, please. No —"

Bang! What sounded like a single gunshot, echoed in the dark, and terror gripped him. Then James heard someone's footsteps draw near and something metal was place against his already pounding head.

"Who are you?" came a calm, cold and deep voice emanating from the darkest part of the room, behind the goon who had been striking him.

James' head was swimming with jumbled images, and he was trying to collect himself and ascertain his predicament.

"Foot," said the cold voice to the man standing before James, "wake him up."

There was another blow to the left side of James' face, and he tasted blood in his mouth. He swayed in his seat, nearly passing out until he was once again doused in freezing water, finding himself gasping again for air.

"Now," said the cold voice, "I am going to ask you one more time. Who are you?"

"I'm —— I'm ——" said James shivering with agonizing pain, his face bloodied and swollen, "James O'Neil. They call me Spooner," he ended breathlessly.

"Now there's a name I haven't heard in a while," said the voice out of the darkness, his raised hand reaching into a shaft of light, forestalling another assault by the one called Foot. "If it isn't the legendary Spooner."

Foot severed James' bonds around his wrists, and James found the consolation that he once did in invoking the name Spooner. It was like a protective incantation of some sort.

"Where am I? Why am I here?" asked James rubbing his wrists and nursing the bruises.

The one called Foot placed the gun to James' head again, and the comfort he found in invoking the name Spooner, quickly evaporated. He fell silent with fear as the lights turned up to reveal five other men. They were standing in a semi-circle before James in the middle of a large warehouse room, all looking horribly threatening. Their leader, who stood between them drew closer to James and surveyed him dispassionately.

"Tell me, do you want to die? 'Cause when a man goes around my part of town asking about me and my associates and handing out business cards, I got to ask myself if what I'm hearing is a urgent cry for exquisite release."

He was presently walking back and forth with both hands behind his back, professorial like.

CHAPTER TWENTY-ONE

"So, you are not in the position to ask any questions, Spooner. If that's your name. What I would like to know is why you were driving around looking for Blacky?"

"I have some business to talk over with Blacky," said James, desperately trying to keep his voice from shaking with fear and extreme cold.

"I don't think so, Spooner. And you sure as hell not what I expected. You don't look like the type who can kill someone with the aid of a blunt eating utensil. Rumor has it you cut a man's heart out with it, but seeing you now, I find it even harder to believe. Do you know why lions and other large cats don't hunt each other?"

James bore a look of admixed bemusement and trepidation and was unsure as to how to answer the question.

"I will tell you. Because they are at the top of the food chain, and predators recognize other predators. Do you follow?" he said pausing for a moment and drawing closer to James. "And something tells me that you are a pretender," he added in a more deadly voice. "Do you know what we do to pretenders, Spooner?"

James shook his head vigorously.

"Smoke," said Foot with his finger applying more pressure to the trigger, "just say the word."

"Take him out back, don't want to mess up the floor," said Smoke.

"Wait, wait," said James casting around his brain for some leverage in a situation gone terribly wrong. "Om," he said trembling even more with dread.

"What did you say?" said Smoke, betraying for the first time a look of curiosity on his face.

"He said ohm," replied Foot. "The unit of measurement for electrical resistance. One ohm is the resistance in a circuit when one volt maintains a current of one amp. So what?"

James was astonished by Foot's ability to give the definition of ohm on the spot. But quickly qualified his position.

"No, not ohm... Om, you have one on your forearm just like Blacky," said James inclining his head in Smokes direction, whose arms remained hidden behind his back. "There are three of you with that type of Om symbol. It's *the sound of the sun, the sound of light.*"

James knew he was grasping at straws. Why on earth did he say that? But he had nothing else but the truth, and that may not go over well with this lot, he thought.

Smoke looked impressed with James' on the spot trivia, but his face slowly became stricken with tedium.

"Nice try, Spooner."

"Wait, wait, please!" cried James.

Foot snatched him up by the back of his collar from his seat with the gun still pressed against his head, and began marshaling him towards a back door.

"He's my cousin! Blacky's my cousin! I just want to ——"

"Now there's the first thing you said that has any validity," came a familiar voice from behind the group of men and Foot tugged James by the back of his shirt collar and swung him around to face the new voice.

He drew near to the front and smirked.

"I see you had no trouble making bail, James O'Neil."

"Rock," James said surprised, feeling as though he would relieve himself in his pants and simultaneous relieved to see a familiar face. "It's good to see you again."

"You are on the wrong side of town pretty-boy. So I'm going to do Blacky a favor and send your ass back on the other side of the tracks."

"Thank you, thank you, thank you so much."

"Now you have a choice," Smoke said this time. "You can wait until two in the morning on Wednesday and be dropped off Pier 42, or we can drop you home. Pick one."

"I get to live, right?" said James a little worried about being dropped off a pier.

"Pick one."

"Home," said James, keen to back in familiar surroundings.

There was another sharp blow to the back of his neck and once again darkness.

Several hours later, an angry man's voice filled the entire warehouse. He was throwing a towering temper and in no mood to be fussed with.

"Smoke! Smoke! Where is he, Rock? Where the fuck is my cousin?"

His voice echoed impressively in the dark warehouse. Rock stood there in silence, however, unimpressed by Blacky's blustering.

"And good to see you too my old friend," said Rock calmly after a fashion.

"Don't fuckin' play me Rock or ——"

"Or what?" said Smoke entering from one of the doors at the far corner of the warehouse and wiping blood from his hands with a white towel stained with red. "I am disappointed in you Blacky," he added, throwing the bloody cloth into a large metal barrel. "Firstly, you come back from prison and not look up your old comrades, but find yourself in bed with some European black-marketeer trash, who by the way, feels it's his duty in life to snatch and grab as many cars on the streets he can, without any regards as to whose territory he may be encroaching upon."

Blacky was caught off guard and betrayed a fleeting look of surprise then resolved himself once again with a stone face.

"Yes, Blacky," said Smoke, who had not missed Blacky's moment of astonishment. "You forget. I know everything. And you will find out soon enough what else that trash deals in. Secondly, you come busting in my place disrespectful and foul mouth. What's come over you Blacky? I have never seen you come undone like this. But I am going to forget all of that, because I know as of late you have been hanging around those knuckle draggers you called associates. Bear in mind, talented as you are, we will not befall the same fate as your former colleagues. Now, what is your grievance?"

Smoke drew nearer to Blacky until they were a few feet apart. A crisp white towel was handed to Smoke, and he wiped the remainder of the blood from his hands and tossed it back to Foot, who promptly disposed of it by lighting it on fire and tossing it into a large metal barrel. Horror then fury gripped Blacky at the clear sight of blood, and he reached inside his leather jacket, only to be halted dead in motion by seven other men bearing the same tattoo as he on their forearms, with guns of their own drawn moments before he could free his weapon.

"Now Blacky," began Smoke, his voice now icy. "You know I cannot have you whipping out your tool like that. You are going to give me the wrong impression of you."

Blacky repositioned his hand beneath his jacket and slowly withdrew from it a high school graduation picture of James.

"My cousin." he said, holding the photo up. "Word is that you have him."

Rock removed the photo from Blacky's fingers and nodded to Smoke and returned the photo back to Blacky, who made no effort to stow it.

"I have to admit, Blacky," said Smoke. "He was quite brave to come looking for you. Or was it shear stupidity? Now before you get all worked up and we began shooting at one another, let me inform you that he is still alive, only because he is your family."

Blacky breathed an undetectable sigh of relief.

"Did you think I was some animal, Blacky? Come now, we are civilized." he said with tones of indignation, examining the drying blood beneath his fingernails and picking them each in turn.

Blacky remained silent.

"But ——" continued Smoke presently waving an admonitory finger, "make no bones about it my dear old friend, if I see him in this part of town again asking questions about you or anyone of us, it will be the last thing he does."

22

Betrayal

Wednesday night came without Tuesday or for that matter, most of Monday. James had found himself in bed, awaken again by the loud barks of Willoughby, accompanied with a violently splitting head ache and did not care how he had gotten home. All he knew was that he was alive and not dropped off some pier with cement shoes. That was all that mattered. He thought absurdly that Mr. Berchmier must be somewhere near, perhaps having a late night rendezvous with Mrs. Hawthorne, which would account for Willoughby throwing another one of his towering fits. And he laughed at the ridiculous images his mind conjured.

James' stomach was putting up an enormous protest from lack of sustenance for the past few days. He felt at present, however, too done-in to pull himself from the comfortable cradle of his pillows and his bed, of which his weight formed an indentation that nestled him in its center. He had remained there since Monday until present, still dressed in his blood splattered shirt.

And while in bed, James lay there lazily listening, or rather screening his calls.

"Beep."

Hello Jamie. Are you there? Jamie?

"Go away, lady," he said in exasperated tones.

My word, do you ever answer your phone? I spoke with your aunt Olivia today about Stephen, and... well... Please give me a call back as soon as possible."

It was his mother again for the fourth time today, and she seemed to have some urgent matter that James could care less about. He was waiting for Veronica to call, which she often did late at night, just before she turned in. He was feeling very doleful and could care less if the phone rang all night and day, as long as it was Veronica. And at that thought, his answering machine picked up on another call.

"Beep."

Hi baby, I... I don't know what to say or how to say this. Uri is leaving the country... for good I suspect. I just found out. It's not fair. I love it here, and I don't want to leave. But what can I do? I have to go... call you later.

It was Veronica's voice coming from the machine. The shock of this news caused James to hesitated too long before deciding to force himself out of bed to get the phone. But it was too late, and Veronica was gone.

"Damn woman!" he said hotly. "You don't have to do anything you don't want to. What is it with this Uri? Why the hell is she so scared of him? Forget about her James, just let her go," he added to himself. "All this time and no phone call, then this. Note to self: Turn the damn ringer off."

James felt betrayed. All this time he had wasted with this woman when he should have known she was not his to have. It made him feel better to just lash out. So, he lay there brooding for ten minutes or so before another call came in.

"Beep."

Hey cousin, it's me Paul. My mother called me today worried about Stephen. What a head ache. But that's not why I'm calling you. I got your message about the adoption. I'm shocked and don't know what to say. It's so hard to believe. I hope you're okay. Man, you're still my cousin no matter what. And I'm working on your request. Can't say anything definite as of yet. I want to be absolutely sure of what I've found. Call you back soon with more.

The message barely registered in James' head, he was still processing Veronica's message and was presently sitting straight up in the bed. He forced himself out of his mild stupor and thought, finally some good news, or potentially good news. That's what he needed to hear.

"Beep."

Hi James. It's me, your aunt Olivia. I am looking for Stephen. He came in a few days ago and removed your picture from the photo album and stuck it in his jacket. He looked troubled, and when I questioned him on it; he said nothing and stormed out the door. He looks up to you James. Please see if you can contact him somehow and let me know what's going on. Is he alive or ——

Her voice cracked with emotion, and then she hung up. James' heart felt as though it fell into his stomach, which managed sickly to increased his hunger pangs. He thought, not aunt Olivia. She could not stand another shock if something happened to Blacky. And James figured it was a good thing his dear aunt Olivia, who was an avid news watcher, did not know Stephen and Blacky were one in the same. But before he would even consider stepping out into the night, he would have to put something in his stomach.

James felt presently well enough to stir around, possibly make himself a late night hero sandwich. He thought it was ironic, since he had found himself in a compromising position that had very little to do with being a hero. The hard headed hero, that's what he was. He must be the thickest person ever who could not follow simple instructions to stay clear of Blacky. And now against sound advice, he was about to go bumbling around in the dark in search of a person who did not wish to be found.

James cast around his brain for a clue to where Blacky would be. Nothing. He felt it was getting too late in the night to put such demands on his weary brain. Why even bother? Besides, it sounded as if it were about to storm. And if he were so bold as to venture into the night, he might enter the wrong neighborhood again; he just might be tossed off a pier with cement boots. Cement boots, who does that nowadays? And something that Smoke said began to dawn on him.

"Now you have a choice. You can wait until two in the morning on Wednesday and be dropped off Pier 42, or we can drop you home. Pick one."

James wondered, could this be a suggestion by Smoke, a helping hand?

Thunder shook the night's sky, and the ground echoed its sentiments, deeply reverberating its roar amid the earth and sky. It electrified the night's air ominously and casted skewed shadows of buildings along the docks, perhaps a prelude to something more sinister brewing.

In the distance, a driver slowed in his approach to the rundown Pier 42. His headlights, diffused in the darkness by the drizzling rain, were turned off several piers in advance to his approach.

"And the winner of tonight's LOTTO Jackpot is Mr. Clark of —" issued a radio announcer's voice but was abruptly turned off by James' need for silence.

The radio was beginning to irritate him with more of the same back to back commercials coupled with news breaks he so disliked.

James thought this to be the very thing William would love to be a part of. The anticipation, the excitement, it was an aphrodisiac to his heightened senses. Now he would finally find out what was it that Blacky was up to and put an end to the madness his cousin was bringing into the family.

Upon his approach, James noticed the black rickety car with the missing hubcaps and thought about the rude police officer who paid him a visit. And upon closer observation, he was now absolutely positive the car belonged to Detective Matlock. James surmised that he must be following Blacky, perhaps even trying to catch him in the middle of some skullduggery. James felt sure, if Matlock was present, there must be something going down tonight, and an enormous feeling of dread stole over him.

James parked his car well shut of Matlock's view and proceeded on foot a short distance to Pier 42. He tried as much as he could to approach stealthily, but the wet wooden walkway constantly groaned and teetered loosely at times beneath his feet. Its spaced planks were elevated above the ground and were worn from much use by sand-grinding feet and the harsh seasonal weather that blew off the ocean. Abandoned shops, which once bustled with happy tourist, stood adjacent to one another in depiction of some eery ghost town. He made his way through the maze of empty shops and found a courtyard in the center, flanked on all sides by more shops that towered ominously with rickety steps. He caught sight of movement just inside his peripheral and spun around, his heart hammering out of his chest.

"Who's there," he whispered.

CHAPTER TWENTY-TWO

But he found himself speaking only to his dark reflection, roughly ten yards away, casted in a soot covered pane of a storefront.

"Oh, it's just you. Pull yourself together, James."

He proceeded forward into the dilapidated maze and trusted to the loud rumblings of the sky that he would be able to locate his quarry undetected.

And as he rounded the last of the shops, there stood Blacky, just as Smoke had suggested. James was not in the very least shocked to find Blacky standing on a deserted pier late at night. He did, however, realized something peculiar. He had never given much thought to Blacky's resourcefulness. For an individual who had no mode of transportation, he was certainly getting about the town with great ease. He stood there with a silver briefcase in hand and three men in front of him, two of which were hulking, and the third was an average built gentleman who stood between them.

"What the —— ? That's Veronica's car. Damn your thieving ass, Blacky. You've gone too far."

However angry he was to become, his growing curiosity was getting the better of him, and James needed to hear what was going on. He therefore drew closer for a better listen.

"What assurances do I have that you will not back out on the deal," said Blacky.

"Why Mr. Blacky..." said a voice speaking from out of the darkness.

His very enormously build and muscle bound goons towered before him, flanking him in the dim lighting. Their brutish features slid in and out lightening flashes.

"...I am disturbed that you would even consider that my intentions are not... How shall we say? Respectable. After that messy business of yours, killing your own men and starting..." he added, then paused. "Let's see, what did the news call it? Oh yes, a gang war. I believe the question of your loyalties and trust worthiness are far more of an issue than mine. However, if you need assurances, then the fact that you are still in possession of your life should be sufficient enough."

"Yeah," said Blacky, unimpressed by the threat. "If we are done posturing, let's get on with it. Since my former crew — "

"Yes, by the way Mr. Blacky, why did you kill them?"

"We had a religious disagreement."

"I see, one of the oldest reasons. And the issue was?"

"Of the utmost profound and delicate nature. So I taught them one last lesson by giving them a big send off. And you can take that any way you choose."

The voice in the shadow was silent, undoubtedly ascertaining the meaning of Blacky's words. And a stunned James listening, felt he had been a fool all along believing in Blacky's innocence. How could he have killed those people? The Blacky he knew was not a killer. But there it was, the words from Blacky's own mouth. None of it made sense in the brief silence.

Blacky therefore took the silence as an opportunity to recommence with his previous pitch.

CHAPTER TWENTY-TWO

"As I was saying, my former crew attracted too much attention to themselves and made it very difficult to obtain the product."

"Is this the part where I kill you because you are about to inform me that the money I gave you was not payment enough? I urge you now Mr. Blacky, choose your words carefully."

"No. I do by the way have something more than what you expect."

He placed the brief case down to the left of his foot and gave it a kick, sliding it over into the shadows for the others to examine. One of the well dressed cronies stepped out of the dimly lit area and extricated the case from beneath the flickering light of a nearby lamp. The latches on the briefcase issued loud clicks from the shadows, one after the other in immediate succession, and its sounds reverberated in the distance, then was swallowed by the rumbling of the night's sky. The goon held the case up so his superior could examine its contents hung on velvety black hooks.

"Ah, clever indeed, Mr. Blacky. It looks as though you have procured about one hundred or more master keys of some of the most luxurious and highly sought after automobiles on the market. Yes, nice, very nice indeed. And where did you get them?"

"Never you mind how I acquired ——"

"But where is the list of addresses?"

"I have them. And seeing that my men are at the moment permanently incapacitated, I would like to use some of your men. If that's okay with you."

"No, Mr. Blacky. It is not okay. Why would I want to do something foolish like that? All I require from you is the list. And our business is done."

"I don't have it with me."

"No? I think we have some trust issues, Mr. Blacky."

"And if I had it on me, why would —— ? What the hell —— ?" he said, spinning around, staring for a disturbance and whipping his gun out so fast that it appeared to have materialized out of nowhere.

"Blacky, you never change. Do you?" said James thoroughly peeved, walking out of the shadows and stopping before his cousin.

"Damn Spooner, you following me? What the hell did I tell you about being in the wrong place?" he said, trying to keep his voice low and unheard by the others. "I got it under control," he added in an even lower whisper.

"No, you are out of control!"

"Is there a problem, Mr. Blacky?"

"Shit," he said, with a wild searching look on his face, as though he was recalculating his plans on the spot. "No problem," he called back in answer and pointed his gun at James' head. "Never ever," he whispered to James.

"Blacky," said James calmly with a look of understanding. "Don't do this. There's still time to turn back. No one has to know. We can walk away from here, you and I. What you gonna do, Blacky, shoot ——"

CHAPTER TWENTY-TWO

Bang! Blacky discharged his weapon, and James jerked his head backwards and was thrown off his feet.

A gut wrenching scream issued from a short distance away, and a woman came running out of the darkness, stumbling, the heal of her shoe breaking off in one of the spacings between the dock's wet wooden planks. It was Veronica.

"Jamie! Oh my God, Jamie! NO... NO!" she cried, pegging her voice out in a piercing scream, and she threw herself next to James' body lying on the ground and pulled him into her lap, holding his profusely bleeding scull in her trembling hands, trying to stanch its flow.

It seemed as if it came from everywhere. It ran down the side of his face from his temple and copiously down his neck from around the back of his head. Her blood soaked hands were scarlet. Blacky looked at her curiously and pointed his gun in her direction.

"Stupid white girl," he said. "No, I said I got it under control," he added in a inaudible whisper.

"You fucking psycho bastard!" she screamed, spitting at Blacky. "Jamie —— Jamie baby," she sobbed, her anguished voice quivering and cracking with despair. "I'm sorry baby. I'm sorry —— Kill me you!" she redirected, now screaming at Blacky. "Kill me too you piece of shit!"

"I'm sorry too that this had to happen," he said, his gun still pointed at Veronica's head.

"Mr. Blacky," came the voice from across the way, still speaking out of the darkness. "Now that wouldn't be advisable."

The man stepped out from between his goons and into the dim light, his features thrown in sharp relief by the lightening. His hair was dark, wavy and combed back from his face, and he had classic handsome features, yet were diminished by his menacing expression. He was dressed in an expensive designer suit, and the sound of his shoes became louder upon his approach.

"Get up, Veronica."

"You know this woman?" said Blacky.

"You disgust me. Let's go."

She raised her head to see him standing there, and for the first time since knowing James, she did not care. He was gone, taken from her, and she had no one, no one else to love. All her dreams were destroyed in one moment. Why hadn't she left this maniac of a husband long ago? Images of waisted opportunities along with moments of pointless bickering flashed through her mind. And now it was all gone, everything. She had given him too much of her precious time —— time she and James could have spent together —— and now she will not give this man another moment of her life.

"No! Go away," she said, turning her attention back to James and gripping him in a tight embrace, rocking back and forth.

He seized her by her hair none too gently, jerking her face upward into the flashing night sky, and her tear filled eyes looked upon him with extreme loathing.

"Leave me alone Uri."

"You tramp. Very well." he said, and he threw her head back down.

CHAPTER TWENTY-TWO

"Mr. Blacky, this meeting is adjourned. I am going to have to insist you hand over the list."

Then several things happened in very quick succession. A thunderclap lit the sky violently, and the drizzling rain thickened. Veronica renewed screams pierced the night. Blacky whispered again under his breath, *kamikaze*. A siren in the near distance blared, and Blacky with wide eyes spun and trained his gun on Uri and his men, locking eyes with the former.

"Mr. Blacky," said Uri with a calm and deadly tone. "When next we meet, have my list."

Uri turned on his heels and gave his men a curt nod. They receded into the shadows and filed into the waiting car, one crony opening the door for Uri, where he vanished into its dark depths behind tinted windows. And they drove off, leaving Blacky there with his weapon still in hand.

Blacky turned his attention once again to a screaming Veronica and safetied his gun, stowing it beneath his jacket. He stared at her for a moment in strange bemusement and admixed admiration. He seemed to hesitate for a moment. Then with incredible speed, he dashed off, leaving Veronica there, her breath coming in great sobs, clutching James' blood soaked form in the pouring rain and desperately screaming for help.

23

Blacky's Retreat

Above the howl of distant siren echoes, the sound of rapid foot fall pounding rain drenched pavement, paralleled his quickened and labored breath. Blacky was running at top speed. Every instinctual gulp for the night's humid air was suppressed in an effort to keep pace with his enormous strides. He was powerfully built and appeared to move across the land with ease, as if a shadow in changing light. The rain splashed against his face unaffectedly as he hurled himself through beaded curtains showering all around. His jeans, unlike his leather jacket, were thoroughly soaked through, clinging to him like a second skin and making it difficult for him to maintain his speed, causing him to expend more energy than he cared to. It had been nearly two miles back where he began his marathon and presently found his stamina beginning to wane. Blacky caught site of a park and turned into it by way of a patch of trees, then crossed the clearing of a soaked green field and found an enormous concrete barrel for refuge. It was the largest one of three that stood off a short distance from a set of swings hanging ominously, seemingly immobilized by flashes of lightening. Their skewed shadows reached long thin fingers across the quiet playground and curved themselves along the largest of the concrete barrels. The barrel smelt of ammonia, but was thankfully dry. Blacky sat calmly there catching his breath. He could now breathe a little better. His clothes were sodden, dripping and forming a pool beneath the spot in which he rested. His heart was pounding, yet there was no sign of dread. Blacky was a man without fear. He was never afraid. He was, however, at the very least not afraid since he was a young boy that awful day atop the old boarded up building, the day the roof gave way beneath his feet.

He remembered that sinking feeling with vivid detail along with a weightlessness preceded only by the sound of a sudden and enormous crash. He remembered how so afraid he had been for his life that his grip was vice like, clinging to the splintering wood and peeling shingles along the jagged edges of the hole in the roof. His cousin James had slid by his position, kicking dust and gravel in his face, temporarily obscuring his vision. Blacky remembered his grip failing in the dust. Then out of no where, James had caught hold of his arm just in time before he would have plummeted to a most certain death. James had saved him that day, which made Blacky forever in his debt. He sat there presently thinking how ironic it is that we are born with two fears, the fear of loud noises and the fear of falling. The rest we learn on our way.

Although Blacky was an individual with a deadly talent, he worried a little that his aim might have come up short in a time when he needed it the most. He thought anxiously that James has to be all right. He must be all right. He wiped his face and shiny rain flecked bald pate with his hands, wondering what on earth was James doing there. How in the wide world did he know about the meeting? Someone must have leaked it, and he would soon get to the bottom of it. No sooner did this thought cross his mind, a musical sound issued from inside his jacket.

"Yeah," he said now irritated. "What? You're asking me?" he barked into the phone. "I haven't the foggiest idea why they were there. The real question is: How did they come about the information? And why was that over grown walrus of a cop ––?"

Blacky paused in mid thread for a moment to master himself.

"Yes, definitely him," Blacky answered. "I saw him parked on a side street when I took off from the pier, just sitting there. Now, this is how I see it. I'm out covering my end and my own ass, and someone on your end is flapping his trap, trying to get me killed. Don't tell me you don't know why Matlock was there," he added hotly. "You said you'd take care of him, but I'm beginning to think your men can't handle the job, which I might add gives me a bad feeling about this. One more slip-up like that and I'm out. You hear me? I promise you I will walk away."

And with the flip of his wrist, Blacky ended the call highly irritated and stowed the mobile back into his jacket. He could not help but to continue wondering if James was okay. As sinister the act itself appeared, he had meant only to wound James, not to kill him, and Blacky thought that James was sure to understand and would find it in his heart someday to forgive him. He thought simply; that was just how James was wired. However, he then thought grimly that he would be chastised by family members. Once they get wind of what transpired, he may even be excommunicated from the family for his actions. What will they think of him now? And because he could not divulge his plans, he realized that his intentions, no matter all the good it was for, would be gravely weighed, and he would be found wanting.

Blacky's thread of thought returned to its previous, where he found himself once again wondering how on earth did James know where to find him. And why, of all the people in the wide world, did James have to get involve with Uri Sergei's wife? Why was she there as well? Now that he thought of it, he remembered her coming from a different direction other than the car in which Sergei had made his speedy retreat. He figured that was curious enough in itself. Blacky shook his head in disapproval, thinking James could be no more reckless than he was tonight by bringing her along.

What astonished Blacky even more was the anguished look she bore upon her face. He found her desperation hauntingly familiar. The look she gave James was as if her world had fallen apart and all her hopes were dying with him. To add, he was impressed by the way she had stood up to him and Sergei. Blacky wondered if it was love that blinded her to emanate peril or was she simply brave or was it foolhardiness. No, it was love, it had to have been. He thought, that is what love must look like and longed to be love the same.

His mind returned again to the question of how did they know where to find him. If they knew, then anyone with a head on their shoulders could have found out, including Matlock. But, Matlock was a no brainer. And this gave him more pause to reconsider trusting anyone now. He thought perhaps he would contact Smoke for a much deserved favor, somewhere to lay low, because his apartment at present was too hot a spot to even consider. Undoubtedly it must by now be under surveillance by Sergei's men. And the police, they were the least of his worries. Although Smoke had James brutally worked over, Blacky was more than sure Smoke would reciprocate a favor from long ago. Contrary to this, he also considered the fact that Smoke not killing James may have been considered payment enough.

He pulled out his mobile again and dialed, all the while peering outside the cement barrel for any signs of a tail.

"Yeah, it's me," he said still surveying the land. "I know —— I know you are upset with me. I know what I said, but —— will you just listen, Rose. Right now, I can't trust anyone else other than you. Come pick me up at the park," he paused, then added, "Please."

He hung the phone up. Images were once again racing each other through his head. Images of James laying in the lap of Veronica, the look on her face. And then it began to come back to him, a suppressed memory forcing its way to the surface of his consciousness. Instead of Veronica there holding James, it had been Blacky, the little boy Stephen, holding his older brother

Maximilian in his arms. The full account of the traumatic incident exploded in his head with a thunder clap.

Olivia, their mother, worked the night shift at the hospital, trusting in Stephen to comport himself accordingly in her absence and a much more mature Max to watch over him. However, that was not the case. Max, who was prone to late night prowling of the streets, had come home that dreadful night, staggering in the entrance to their small apartment before young Stephen and clutching a horribly bloody wound in his side. Upon Max's collapse, Stephen found himself sitting there on the living room floor, holding a bleeding Max, telling him everything was going to be okay, to save his strength and not to talk. But Max was determined to speak, determined perhaps to right a wrong and many that would possibly follow. Blacky was just a kid and did not understand what Max was trying to tell him then. But now the words had more weight than they once did.

"Keep your heart pure, Steph. And it won't fail you."

And it seemed his heart could no longer keep up with the blood lost. Max closed his eyes and breathed his last breath.

Blacky sat there presently, still drenched in the playground barrel, speaking aloud to the memory of Max.

"Before I was old enough to comprehend the enormity of your actions, the blood stained shirt, the clutching vice of your scarlet slackening grip, you were my hero, Max. Since that day, I am less than what you were to me."

And he loathed the person he had become.

24

Bruised Egos

The highly excited sounds of murmuring voices in the distance rose from the darkness beneath James' heavy eyelids, and he opened them to a blurry figure hovering over him, coming painfully into sharper view. It felt as though the pain shot from the back of his head with a sharp stab, straight through to his watery eyes. And his head felt enormous as a water mellon, pinned down by shear weight of its size.

"Blacky," he groaned, reaching for his temple and finding his entire head wrapped. "Great, just great," he added morosely.

"You smacked your head on the pavement rather hard, gave us quite a turn," said Elizabeth. "So try not to move around so much, Jamie. Okay?"

"How did —— ?"

"The ambulance brought you here early this morning. I received a call from a Capt. Mahony saying you had been shot during a police sting operation involving Stephen. It's an absolute miracle you were not killed. What were the two of you doing out there, Jamie? Were you working with the police?"

CHAPTER TWENTY-FOUR

"Yeah, how about that," came a man's sarcastic voice from the door way.

"Oh, Detective Matlock."

"We've met, mother."

"Indeed, have you? Nonetheless, he was so kind as to stay until you'd awaken."

James could see that Matlock's general appearance of untidiness had not altered one bit since last he saw him outside 427 Redgate Avenue and surmised that the detective, more than likely, smelt of it.

"Just wanted to check to see if he's okay. Did you see who shot you, son? Tell me, I promise you, he's off the streets as fast as I can make the call."

"Yeah, sure," answered James suspiciously. "I'm not talking to anyone but Capt. Mahony," he added, recalling how Mahony once ran interference when Matlock had harassed him in front of his home.

"Well," began Matlock "he is a little busy down town interrogating your little girlfriend, or should I say Uri Sergei's wife. Did you know that he is a very dangerous international criminal, and your cousin Stephen is all tied up with him?"

Elizabeth gasped.

"My word, detective, you did not make plain any involvement my nephew may have had in it. Is he now formally a person of interest in the investigation?"

"Sorry Mrs. O'Neil, I can't tell you much, but he is a key player."

"Officer Matlock," began James.

"Detective," said Matlock through gritted teeth and a counterfeit smile that did not hide his irritation.

"Yeah right," said James curtly. "I appreciate you doing your job. I would rather speak with the captain. Thank you."

"Now don't be cheeky, Jamie."

"No it's okay Mrs. O'Neil," Matlock said, shifting massively in her direction. "He is welcome to cooperate with our ongoing investigation through the captain, if that's what he wishes. By the way," he now addressed James, "how did you get those nasty bruises on your face and those terrible lumps on the back of your head? I can see it's more than just a little bump and scratch from falling. From the looks of it, you look as though you have been worked over. Must hurt something fierce."

"Good day, officer," said James.

Highly irritated, Matlock turned on his heels and headed for the door, only to be greeted by an elegantly dressed Red. She cast Matlock such a nasty look that James thought he had given her provocation to take a swing at him.

"Officer," she sneered.

"It's detective," he snapped, then recollected his counterfeit and cordial manner. "Good day, Mrs. O'Neil," he added then pushed past Red out into the corridor and disappeared from sight.

"More like Officer Humpty Dumpty if you ask me," she murmured, rolling her eyes.

And James smiled at her impertinence and took pleasure in the fact that someone else did not like Matlock's brusque personality.

"I'm so glad that you're okay, Spooner," Red said, hurrying to the other side of the bed. "I don't know what we would do if something happened to you. Thank goodness you're —"

"If you can call laid up in a hospital bed all banged-up with aches and pains okay, then I am doing marvelous."

"Jamie," said Elizabeth with some heat. "What's going on? And don't you give me that stone face you gave the detective. I will have no more cheek from you. You're hiding something. Now out with it."

"Aunt Olivia left a message on my phone. She was worried about Bl— Stephen, so I tried to stop him from ruining his life. This is the thanks I got. He shot me," James finished, pointing at his heavily bandaged head indignantly.

"Is that it?" said Red incredulously. "Come now, Spooner."

"Jamie," gasped Elizabeth with a look of shock and incredulity of her own.

"Okay, okay there's more."

His head was now thundering with pain, and he checked himself then gathered his patience to retell the event.

"I heard them talking over some deal involving stolen cars, but they had only master keys and no cars. Stephen asked to use Uri's men, because he killed his own gang, which by the way was the same one that Max use to hang out with."

"You mean —"

"Yes, Red, the very same friends, all dead. I didn't want to believe it myself, but it's true. I popped out, then Stephen shot me. Well... I asked him to walk away from the deal first, then he shot me."

"I can't believe it. Little Stephen."

"Believe it mother."

James felt betrayed. He lay there propped up in bed, his face falling in deep disappointment, wondering how Blacky could do such a thing.

"I saw that fat cop," began Red, "on the first floor at the information desk. He asked me a ton of questions, none of which I answered, but he did let slip your Veronica was there at the scene. She even road in the ambulance here with you, but was swept away by police to give full account of what had transpired. Did she go there with you, Spooner?"

"No, I didn't see her there at all. That's odd."

"The police found her holding you in her arms."

"Really now?" said James slightly indifferent.

"Yes, Spooner sweetie, she was there."

"I told Veronica, Jamie," began Elizabeth hotly, "that someone could get hurt —"

"Mom, it's not her fault —"

"But she was there, Spooner," said Red again. "And nobody knows why."

James did not care why Veronica was there. He just did not want to hear anymore of it. His head was smarting more than ever, and his ego was thoroughly bruised.

CHAPTER TWENTY-FOUR

"Okay," came the voice of Dr. Anita Forman from across the room. "Look who's up and stirring," she added as she drew near, taking a tiny flash light out of the pocket of her white jacket and examining James' eyes. "I spoke to Capt. Mahony earlier —– you're doing far better than what we thought you would —– and he told me that he would not need to speak with you just yet; however, do not plan on making any trips until he has done so."

She smiled, stowed her flash light and grasped his wrist to take his pulse.

"You'll live," said Anita after a few moments of calculative silence, "but with a really big head ache to go with your big head, Spooner."

She released his wrist.

"You look as though you have been struck in the back of the head several times. They look like old wounds, which appear to have been opened from the fall. I should keep you here for a few days of observation, but you are surrounded by so many people who love you. And your x-rays show no cracks in that thick skull of yours. So I'm going to write you a prescription for antibiotics and let you go home as long as someone is watching you. Since you have a concussion, you will need to be awaken every four hours for the next twenty-four hours, which means someone will have to watch you during that time."

"I will," piped up Red.

"And no over exertion of any kind," said Anita. "Any kind," she repeated, casting a knowing look at Red. "Are we clear?"

"Yes Anita," said Red, her face flushed with embarrassment.

And James thought undoubtedly that at some point in time, the pair must have shared some provocative girl talk about him.

"I'll be fine over mother's place," he said, hoping to add a third party buffer between himself and Red.

"Nonsense, Jamie. It's much too long of a drive to the manor. Sometimes I just don't know where you've placed your head. You're better off at your place. Red will take good care of you, and I will pop in from time to time and check up on you both."

"But ——"

"And that's all to it. I simply will hear no more on the matter."

"Okay then," Red said brightly, placing her hand on James' shoulder and beaming down at him. "It's settled."

"Great," said Anita. "Take as much time you need getting yourself together. I will have your release papers at the desk down the hall for you to sign."

And she swept from the room, glancing at her pager and looking very hurried.

"Wonderful. Just wonderful," groaned James.

He cast a curious look at Red.

"Where is Sophie?"

"She's..." she said pausing. "She's, for the moment, with a sitter. I didn't want her to see you in this condition. So let's get on with it so that I can get back to her."

And after a great deal of complaining and dogged determination, for James was in a surly mood after finding his set of keys missing, he agreed to calm down and instead use

Elizabeth's copy of his key in order to enter his home. He signed himself out at the desk and gave reassurance, to a busy Anita in passing, that he would not exert himself in any form and promised to go home straight away. His hopes of visiting William, who was coincidentally in the same hospital, were dashed by Anita's insistence that he leave for home immediately or return to the hospital bed. They therefore set off to his place by way of Red's car while following Elizabeth's in hers.

The both were tight lipped most of the way, until Red decided to break the uncomfortable silence that seemed to stretch on for what felt like hours. She was checking to see if James was sleeping. His eyes were closed, and he did not answer when she called his name. She therefore seized upon the moment.

"I'm sorry about long ago, Spooner. I didn't mean to hurt you. You were always a good guy, a real boy scout. I see that hasn't changed one bit."

She paused for a moment, casting an even graver look at James.

"For some stupid reason I didn't want to be — I mean — be with someone whose life I would eventually ruin. I had a problem settling down. You were ready, and I wasn't. The truth is, I was afraid. Lord knows I've missed you, Spooner. I still love you, and I hope you can one day forgive me."

"Isn't that rich," said James, who had been feigning sleep.

He did not rightly know where his anger was stemming from. Perhaps he was irritable, or maybe it was bitterness from long ago when he and Red were considered an item. Then one day without preamble, she disappeared without so much as a goodbye. James had received a call from her after several day of constant worry —— not unlike the brief one Veronica left him on his answering service —— offering her sincerest apologies for her unceremonious departure. He had always known that she was wild in manner and suffered everyone who had the pleasure of her brazen behavior. But that was the appeal he had so enjoyed about her and thought she would someday settled down, perhaps with him. But he had been mistaken and did not understand what he had done wrong to cause her to leave. He presently sat slumped in the car, anger rising.

"You were off with one of your bad-boy type then found yourself pregnant with no man. Why do you all go for the bad boy? You can't change them. And if you manage to do the impossible, you would never be satisfied, because one day you will look at him and say he is nothing like the man he use to be. You'd then think less of him. You're no different than the female primates who are smitten with the loudest ape in the group."

"That's not fair, Spooner," said Red, her face beginning to color up.

She blinked rapidly, maintaining her dignified composure. Her eyes watered. She was silent for a moment, her head steadily forward. James knew he had hurt her and found some perverse pleasure in it, thinking she could use a dose of her own medicine. Then regret came over him like an enormous invisible weight pressing against his chest.

"Red ——"

CHAPTER TWENTY-FOUR

"Are you sure your talking about me, Spooner?"

Her voice broke, yet she maintained a calm air. She was not the woman James remembered. Sure she was incredibly sexy and a flirt, but there was such a dignified matureness about her he had not taken time to consider. He wondered if he had been misjudging her the entire time. The old Red would have let him have it, pulled over and kicked him out of the car or perhaps even snapped his head off and thrown it out the window and damned to hell the doctor's orders. But she was calm and vulnerable.

"I'm ——" began James once more apologetically.

"Sorry," cut in Red. "I'm not to get you worked up, I promised Anita. Besides, we're here," she added, her voice sharp and bordering on indifference.

They parked near the front of James' home behind Elizabeth, and to James' enormous surprise, there in front of his house was his car.

"Oh, there it is," said James sardonically. "I forgot I left my car and keys home that night and went for a nice little stroll. What the hell is going on!"

Red reach over and touched his hand, smiling.

"We'll go in and find out. Okay?" she said calmly.

After carefully aiding James out of the car, Elizabeth and Red slowly proceeded up the walk with him, all the while offering encouraging words.

"That's it Jamie," said Elizabeth. "Almost there. A few more steps and ——"

The door was suddenly flung open, and to their surprise, there stood Veronica.

25

Veronica's Choice

The trio stood there in utter surprise for what seemed an eternity. Veronica took in James' pitiable state. He stood there supported by both women who seemed to struggle with his weight.

"Oh, Jamie baby," said Veronica, standing there in an apron and James' large house shoes. "I'm so sorry, I didn't know —"

"Yes, yes... although it's a fine day to teary long over door steps, I fear we may give the neighbors something to speak of if we linger any longer," said Elizabeth dropping her arms to her side and immediately righting her disheveled appearance.

This removed all support in which she reluctantly gave, causing James to slump over onto Red.

"What she meant to say was, let us in," said Red with far less sophistication than Elizabeth.

"Oh please, do come in," said Veronica, coming to Red's aid yet shooting her a suspicious look.

"Upon my word," began Elizabeth in tones of indignation, "you have afforded yourself the comforts of my son's home.

House shoes?" she added, looking down at Veronica's feet and the slippers in which they stood, then stepped over the threshold and adopted an air of a home inspector who was about to give the property a white glove assessment.

"Mother, please," groaned James.

"Yeah, how about that," said Red sarcastically, struggling with James' weight, then addressed him. "You need to put some of these muscles that you have developed all these years to good use and help me get your bulky self to the bed."

And after what seemed to James a long journey from the front door, through the foyer and into the living room, with the aid of Veronica and Red, he could go no farther and was plopped down onto the sofa.

"Smooth ladies, real smooth," he said, feeling sickly dizzy and on the verge of loosing consciousness.

James did not know whether he should pass out or throw up.

"Now everyone out. Go home."

"I promised Anita that I would take care of you, watch over you for the next twenty-four hours," said Red.

The color in Veronica's face began to rise and she looked thoroughly indignant.

"Excuse me?"

"Yes, that's why I'm here," said Red, threatening contempt in every word uttered. "Don't you have a husband you should be hiding out with?"

"My place is here with Jamie."

"He would not be in this ——"

"Are you saying this is my fault!"

"Finally caught on, did you?"

"He wouldn't be in this condition if it weren't for that nut-job of a cousin Bl——"

"You hold your peace," said Red, speaking over Veronica and looking extremely venomous. "This is family business. No one invited you. And for that matter, why are you really here?"

"Who the devil is Blacky?" cut in Elizabeth. "Not little Stephen. I remember you referring to someone by the name of Blacky. What is this?"

"Yeah, it's a name he goes by on the streets, mother."

"And you think you know a person," said Elizabeth shaking her head in disappointment and looking as though she finally accepted the truth of her ill mannered nephew.

"You think I don't know what you've been trying to do since you've gotten here, you little tart," bit back Veronica, moving around to the other side of sofa closer, perhaps to throttle Red. "But I am wise to you missy and if you ——"

"That'll be enough you two," said James, his head now thundering with pain. "Don't say another word," he added, and for good measure, casted a scathing look at his mother.

"And upon that, I shall take my leave," said Elizabeth. "Jamie, when you are feeling up to it, or if you need anything, just give me a call, and I'll be here as quick as a flash."

She proceeded to the door then turned back around to readdress a woozy James. She cast a look at the two vixens, her gaze lingering much longer on Veronica than Red.

"Jamie," I shall expect you to have this..." she paused, "situation sorted out straightaway. Very well then," she added waspishly. "Goodbye."

And she swept from the house, leaving the three at a lost for words. When the silence was long enough to become awkward, James cleared his throat to speak, but his head was smarting too much for him to declare in a commanding voice. Instead, he lowered his voice to something of a deep whisper.

"Please don't fight. It doesn't help."

He turned his face towards Veronica's, still upset from the phone call she left him the previous night, and he tried to put it out of his mind. But he opened his mouth and defeated the effort.

"I thought you were leaving town. Why are you still here? And why where you at the pier?"

"That night —— before I ever knew what he had been doing all this time —— I asked Uri why did he need my car, and he said I should mind my own business and to never question him again about it. Besides, he paid for the car, which entitled him to take it whenever he wanted. I just didn't understand why he needed my car. So I called the company that locates my car for me. I had a GPS system installed, which does not come with the make and model, unlike Uri's —— you know, if in any event it becomes stolen or if I'm lost or in an accident. I never told him that I had that done. Where was I? Oh, I explained to them that I just wanted to know where my h—" she paused, "I wanted to know where Uri had taken the car."

This near slip of the tongue was not missed by James and Red, but they remained silent during her explanation.

"And the service agent was more than happy to assist me. I took his car, and made my way to the pier, arriving just in time to see Blacky shoot you. It was horrible to see, Jamie, just horrible. I told all this to Capt. Mahony. He was delighted to find out that I had a GPS tracking device placed in my car. But he did not seemed shocked when I told him what I had witnessed. He only wanted to know what is my involvement with you. I told him... I'm in love with you."

The tender moment was short lived when his anger once again got the better of him.

"What a touching story."

And he snapped at Veronica in the manner in which he had done so with Red, which resulted in Veronica immediately quitting the room in indignation. Red, who was touched by Veronica's words, was totally taken aback by James' rude behavior and ill-treatment of the woman he was suppose to be in love with. Veronica had poured her heart out, only to have it stomped on, and Red felt this was most unlike the James she knew. She disregarded any caution she may have felt for his health and angrily reprimanded him.

"She love's you... you ass. And I know you love her too. Why do you have to be so defensive all the time? You'd better straighten up or you're going to lose her. Now, I'm going to do you one and go talk to her. And while I'm back there, you'd better get that thick head of yours on straight, or I will knock it off and put it back on right for you. Okay?" she added softly, leaning in and kissing him tenderly on his forehead, then slapping him hard in the face. "And that was for what you said in the car."

James looked thunderstruck, and Red angrily quitted the room, mumbling harsh words under her breath.

Minutes later she returned dragging a reluctant and teary eyed Veronica behind her.

"Stand here," she said to Veronica. "Tell her Spooner, or I swear I'll give you —"

"I —" hesitated James, his face filled with remorse.

"I love you too, Jamie. If you never say it again, I would know."

Her words rushed through James as if a cleansing wind, and he became calm. He felt ashamed of his actions. She had forgiven him with words he had no defense.

"Is that it?" said Red absolutely befuddled. "I don't believe it. Oh you two deserver each other. That's my cue. Walk me to the door please, Veronica."

Veronica followed. The pair made their way down the corridor and into the foyer, Red speaking in low tones and Veronica nodding in agreement. James was flabbergasted. He thought he would never understand the going-ons of the minds of women. One moment they are arguing with one another vituperatively, the next they have formed an alliance and are plotting to gang-up on you. He therefore sat paranoid, straining his ears to hear and craning his neck best he could to peer down the hall.

"We all love Spooner and can be a little over protective of him at times. He is a real boy scout you know."

"I know," she said. "And thank you, Red.

"It was nothing. I know for a fact that you two belong together. I can see he'll be in good care, in your hands. I trust, when you find the time, you will call to inform us of his progress. Yes?"

"Yes."

"Oh, and doctor's orders, no over exertion of any kind," said Red smiling. "Any kind," she added with raised eye brows.

Veronica smiled.

"You can apologize to me later, Spooner!" Red called across the foyer snappishly. "He was a little grouchy in the car," she added in a carrying whisper to Veronica.

"I heard that!" said James. "I got your grouchy alright."

And the pair of them rolled their eyes in unison and broke out in hearty laughter that went on into the next hour, swapping stories of their irritable yet beloved James.

October follow the latter part of September with great haste, bringing with it a much desired break from the sweltering heat of the summer. The month settled in with its autumn colored leaves splashing themselves against a pale blue sky. Flocks of birds expanded, twisted and contracted across the vast firmament as if enormous sentient cloaks upon the wind. The all too familiar crackling and rustling sounds of busy feet upon leaf strewn sidewalks and streets carried through the wind. It was a day fill with cool enjoyment and a cornucopia of infinite possibilities for children busy at play.

Mr. Berchmier, however, seemed to be one who did not enjoy this time of year. His lawn was an ever plush and deep velvety green which appeared to attract every leaf thrown into the air by children playing merrily and those blown upon the wind, settling there, only to mar his beautifully manicured lawn. He was often seen during the day leaning over as far as he could, without stepping onto the grass, just to remove a few stray leaves. But when a strong gust of wind visited, often tempting leaves to gather upon his lawn, the damage was immense, and Mr. Berchmier found himself, no doubt unwillingly, standing in the middle of his deciduously littered lawn with an electric blower, attacking every leaf that landed in his territory, including a few well aimed others upon the wind.

Inside 427 Redgate Avenue, James found this sight quite amusing. He was resting on the living room sofa comfortably, something he had taken to doing when he felt he had over stretched himself for the day, causing his head to throb with pain. Along with this, he had been pampered over the course of several weeks, healing nicely from Veronica's ministrations and amiable bedside manner. James sat there on the sofa thinking how he and Veronica had not long returned from the hospital visiting William today. They had found him, after many days of traveling back and forth from James' place to the hospital, finally awake and in an agreeable disposition, talking with his mother and Anita Forman about his present condition and how long he would have before he was able to leave. How strange it had seemed to James that William was so adapt to speaking with an American accent. James had forgotten, until he walked in on William conversing with his mother, that his British accent would reemerge out of nowhere whenever he spoke to her or anyone for that matter who had and accent. When William caught sight of James, however, his American accent kicked in over-drive and William sounded as if he was an American born citizen with a heavy African American vernacular that would make even James' cousin Blacky proud. The pair of them had plenty to catch up on, and James made it a point to fill him in on all the details while the ladies huddled near the door conversing. As they spoke, James had the suspicion that Mrs. Barinard, William's mother, did not approve of Williams nimble tongue. She would blink her eyes, casting a slightly disapproving look in Williams direction whenever he would speak.

"Yo, when I'm out, you gotta check out my new whip," he said, referring to his car.

What really seemed to raise her eye brows was the constant use of the word *Yo*.

"Yo... I'm fillin' that."

William seemed to have no problem with his mother's disapprobation, but James remember how uncomfortable he himself began to feel as her eyebrows appeared to travel farther up into her hairline the more William butchered the language.

Presently, a tiny pinch stung James, reminding him of his surroundings and to remain still on the sofa.

"Now don't go ripping what's left of those stitches," she said, pulling off his bandage.

"They still itch, Veronica."

And he scratched very near the mend in his temple.

"They will all be taken out soon. Besides, itching is good," she said, gently removing James' hand from his temple. "That means it's healing, including the ones in the back of your thick skull," she added with a smile. "And quite nicely if I say so myself. Were you always like this as a child?"

"I beg your pardon, madam?"

"Yes, I thought this much. Boys will be boys, and I see you still long for a bit of excitement in you life. I bet you were a real dare-devil. Am I right? Come now, love, do tell."

"Remember the day we visited my parents' home, and you caught sight of me smiling at the ceiling fan? I told you ask me about it later, right?"

Veronica nodded.

"Well... When we were kids, Will and I, there was this fan in my father's study."

And he recounted the entire 'blades of death' event in his father's study to a very attentive Veronica, her facial expressions following in excitement, beaming with shear entertainment and laughter at their dare-devilry.

CHAPTER TWENTY-FIVE

"Oh James," she said brightly. "you've had such a mischievous childhood. You mean to tell me your that parents never found out about the mess you would get yourself into?"

"Never, ever," he said with a grin, remembering the time he saved Blacky's life. "I even had a few mischievous moments with Blacky."

And he regaled the event in vivid detail, with Veronica on the edge of the sofa, looking as if she would topple over any moment with anticipation.

"And then what?"

"Then I pulled him up and we had a laugh," said James nonchalantly.

"I don't know, Jamie," she said with a concerned expression. "If we have a little boy, he might be absolutely rambunctious like his father. Oh, I hope we have a girl," she added as an after thought.

James' eyes lit up, and his excitement could not be contained.

"You mean we are going to —"

"Hold your horses cowboy, let's not get too far ahead of ourselves. We are not, as much as I would love to, having a baby just yet."

James looked defeated but quickly rebounded with a sly grin.

"But we can give it the old college effort."

"No over exertion. Remember?"

"I've been fine for a while now. I'm sure you've heard that there is a such thing as taking a good thing too far or something like that."

"Jamie, my sweet, I'm sure you've heard that good things come to those who are patient. And if we are going to have a wild child like Blacky —"

She broke off. And James took the opportunity to banter.

"My head is not the only thing that's sore and blue."

You know," continued Veronica, ignoring James' last comment, "I think Blacky is working with the police."

"Ah, come off it, Veronica. Blacky, who could win thug of the year award?"

"I know you may be miffed with him, and so was I after that nasty display of thuggery, but I have been re-thinking the incident. He could have killed you that night, but he didn't. It would explain how the police got there so quickly, and why Capt. Mahony has not dropped by to interrogate you yet. I'm sure of it."

"Miffed?" said James half laughing. "Is that what I am?"

"Seriously, James, do you think that one man, who is said to have committed a triple homicide, and evaded the entire police force of a city and the surrounding cities, would not have a manhunt splattered over the newspapers and television for his arrest? There is something extremely fishy about it all."

Indeed. Now that James came to think of it, Blacky was acting strangely. He did appear more so to speak to himself at times rather than to James.

"Yeah, and he kept mumbling things under his breath as if he was talking to someone else," said James aloud, considering Veronica's hypothesis. "On the other hand, Blacky is not all there. So I think we're reaching. If he was an informant, he would have been terminated by Smoke or Rock. Those guys are ruthless."

He indicated with a point of his finger at the back of his head sharply, then for dramatic effect, swung his hand around with the same force to point at a small hematoma on his face.

"Remember how this use to look? And, if he was working for the police, why on earth would Matlock be out to fry him?"

This last point seemed to snatch the wind out of Veronica's sails, but she quickly recovered.

"I know you think me odd to take up for Blacky. I also thought it was odd for Red to do so when she referred to him as family."

"Yeah, she did. Didn't she?" agreed James with a pensive look.

"Figuring out the volatile and intricate complexities of Red's temperament will have to wait for another time," said Veronica. "Granted, Blacky is an exceptionally brilliant individual, as told by you, and could evade the police indefinitely. It just doesn't add up why he stays in town. He must be working with the police. It's the only logical explanation for it all, Jamie. Perhaps there is a woman he's interested in. Men have been known to do crazy things for the company of a lady."

"Don't I know it," he said wryly, then pausing to consider her words. "No, he's my cousin, and I know him very well. He has and always been no good. I just never admitted it. The only person Blacky worries about is himself. And he excels exceedingly at doing so. Remember?" he added pointing to his head again, this time at his temple. "He shot me."

And keen to avoid an argument, Veronica acquiesced in silences with several nods.

26

The Last Letter

Several days later, overlooking the River Thames that reflected London's cityscape beneath a cloud strewn night sky, was a quaint little terrace with chromed and glass railing that sat aloft outside a suite separated by a glass sliding door, which was for the moment ajar. The light that stole through the sliding glass door of the suite, aided by an incandescent light affixed above its frame outside, shown upon parchment and pen guided by a handsome middle-aged man, who sat at a small table enjoying a cup of tea and the night's air, finishing up his letter.

"Live and love with all your heart. Moments in the Sun belong(s) to you." And he signed it, *"Love Dad."*

Alexander placed the letter inside a leather bound journal and closed it, staring pensively at its carvings. His fingers traced the deep curves of the ornate design and lingered a while before tearing himself from painful and longing memories.

"For our son," he whispered in a raspy voice and slid the journal into a very large envelope that was address to Catalina

Marie Barinard, in care of CMB Royal House Publishing, London. "I love you."

"I love you too Alex," came a faint voice across the intervening years, pulling him into the past. "I don't care what people think of us nor do I of my family's disapprobation. I only want to be with you. Now, continue playing."

They were on a wide plinth in the very center of a mall. Alexander was sitting before a grand piano, set aloft, fiddling about with the keys, and his great love was leaning with one hand on the piano, smiling, the pair in the mist of a crowed mall inwrapped in one another.

"Play us another song, my love, before management puts a stop to your wooing," she said.

His fingers touched the keys lightly, and a deep pulsating sound emanated from the instrument. Its heart beat rumbled, ebbing then rising, accompanied by the sweet sound of high notes dancing lightly on air, one following the next in perfect yearning. When he was done, a hush had gone over the great hall of the mall, and she leaned down and kiss him, her fingers in his locks, pulling at them, and his were hands around her waist. A tumult of whistles, whoops, clapping, and cheering rang out. Two enormous smiles parted their kiss. And slightly embarrassed, they gathered up their shopping bags and proceeded from the plinth.

They were now in bed. Alexander was staring down into her eyes, and she, staring up, her hands at his back side pulling, their breath intermixed, labored and united in one exquisite moment in time, breathing in each other, enraptured then falling into utter satisfaction.

And they were now in a wide field of a park on a bright and clear summer's day. The pair were on a blanket beneath a tree, Alexander stretched out, his head in his love's lap, looking up into fingers of light that stole through the canopy of leaves while she read to him.

"I want to do this forever," he said, interrupting her reading. "I want to grow inside of you."

"You are," she said pausing, "growing inside of me."

And there was joy between the two.

There was presently a tap at the door and something incoherent uttered, recalling Alexander to his surroundings. Alexander stood and let out a sigh of great longing then sealed the envelope, proceeded from the terrace through the glass door and into the grand room of the suite.

"Room service," a muffled voice called again from behind the door, this time more intelligible.

Alexander recognized the voice and had been expecting a late supper to arrive.

"Come in Rowan," he said unlocking the door. "Just wheel the cart over to the dining area."

"Yes sir, Mr. Frederick," he said eagerly.

"Take this down to the desk, would you please, and have them send it off straight away."

Alexander handed the package to Rowan and tipped him twenty pounds.

"Straight away, yes, no worries sir. It's as good as done — Is everything okay, sir?" he asked, taking in Alexander's mood and facial expression.

"Moments in the sun. They occur fewer as the years wear on. Just enjoy your life, my boy," he added brightly, slapping Rowan on the back and ushering him out the door.

"Yes sir. Will do," he said presently standing in the corridor, slightly bemused yet all the same gleeful to receive advice from the famous Mr. Alexander Frederick.

After sometime had passed, Alexander found himself sitting at the edge of the bed, staring into a reflection he hardly recognized, his face falling in lines of melancholy. His grey besprinkled hair was much shorter than it was many years ago when he had worn long black dread locks. It was now, however, cut very close to his scalp. His face seemed to him more lined today than it was this time last year. His eyes were puffy underneath but hardly showed, owing to the fact that his low perched spectacles distorted the aged trait. He was a very distinguish looking man with great smile lines carved into his face, possibly remnants of happier times. He raised his hands to touch his face and notice the wrinkles across his knuckles. They looked old now, thin and worn. He thought they looked much like the hands of his deceased father, who often came home late or sometimes not at all. Then he thought of his beloved from long ago, and began to recite.

CHAPTER TWENTY-SIX

"Tender were the fingers
that once touched my line worn face
Dipped in the well of my longing
upon ripples, whence, they left their trace.

Of things once beautiful
'neath laden eyelids of tears
Loving arms vanquished loneliness
with tender kisses releasing fears.

I remember how it was to feel beautiful."

He sighed a large breath and lingered over this thought a while longer then found himself remembering how, as a child, he often missed his father, until one day it all changed. His belief in his father, and all he believed that was true had been destroyed in one night. He thought he must right things with James and not wait a second longer. He picked up the phone and dialed.

"Hi, son. I was thinking about you and wondering how you were getting on," he said, and after pausing for a moment, he continued. "And I want to know if you think I was a terrible father? I did my best not to become like my father, and it seems in some way I have. Give me —–"

Suddenly, there was another tap at the door.

"Room service," came Rowan's voice again.

"Again? Did you forget something, Rowan," said Alexander setting the phone upon the desk instead of hanging it up and striding across the suite then unlocking the door.

It was suddenly rent open with enormous force, knocking Alexander back on his heels. Rowan was thrown into the room, stumbling, then finally falling onto the floor and staring up with immense fear into the door frame from which he toppled.

"No! Please," he cried desperately.

There were two small pops, and he fell back, his expression frozen, a dead stare into nothing.

Alexander, who was looking at Rowan in utter shock and disbelief, turned his gaze towards the door and saw three men push themselves through the entrance. He raised his arms in capitulation, his nerves rattled.

"Who are you? What do you want?" he said, capitalizing on the moment to calm himself.

One of the three men shut the door, and the other kicked Rowan's lifeless body to the side. He removed a metallic cylinder that was fastened to the front of his gun, stowed it in the pocket of his blazer and placed the weapon in Rowan's lifeless hand. The third man spoke.

"I see bravery runs in the family, Mr. O'Neil. I have had the pleasure of meeting your nephew Blacky."

Alexander was confused.

"If you gentlemen are here for an autograph, I'll be signing books on Thursday in the lobby," said Alexander.

"Ha!" laugh one of the cronies in a deep voice.

CHAPTER TWENTY-SIX

"Forgive me, where are my manners. I should introduce myself. I am Uri Sergei, an associate of Blacky, a family member you know as Stephen."

"Really, an associate," said Alexander in sarcastic tones. "I know your kind, with your fancy suits. You're nothing more than common thugs. So, let's dispense with the formalities and tell me why you're here."

"I can appreciate your candor, Mr. Frederick. However, thugs we may be, but common, I think not."

There was a sudden struggle. Alexander had struck one of the men in the face and was tussling with the other who had a gun in his hand. And as sudden as it started, it was over. Alexander was on his knees struggling to stay conscious from a blow to the back of his head.

"Stand him up," said Uri. "Indeed bravery runs in the family, or is it stupidity in the face of futility? No matter."

"What do you want?" said Alexander breathlessly, feebly struggling to free himself from the cronies on either side twisting his arms.

"See, Blacky has something of mine, some information. And your son James has something of mine as well, though I'm sure it's ruin by now. Nevertheless, I am going to teach them both a lesson about taking things that belong to me. And after I am done with them, I am going to start on the rest of your family, just because I'm feeling generous."

"Go to hell," said Alexander, and he spat at Uri.

"Hold him still," said Uri coldly, removing a handkerchief from his vest pocket and wiping the spittle from his face.

And with a murderous expression, he slowly drew closer to Alexander. Alexander thought Uri must strike at any moment, but he drew even nearer to him until they were inches apart, staring at each other.

"You always can tell what type a man you're about to kill, and I can see in your eyes, you know what I mean," said Uri placing the handkerchief in his pocket then withdrawing something thin and shiny.

There was a tiny click. Then he stabbed Alexander in his ribs hard once, twice and a third time. He drew even closer, as if savoring the last bit of life leaving Alexander.

"Yes," Uri whispered into Alexander's ear. "I can see."

Alexander's spoke one last garbled word before dropping to the floor.

"Jamie."

27

Words Unspoken

It was another relaxing Sunday, and the occupants of 427 Redgate Avenue had nestled themselves in what was now their favorite spot on the living room couch. And yet again, James and Veronica had discussed at great lengths whether Blacky was an informant or just another wild hooligan. Veronica pursued her view assiduously, so to the point of nearly convincing James that there must be more to Blacky's behavior than outright thuggery and recklessness. In her opinion, Blacky, being related to James and must have undoubtedly had a good upbringing, was somehow misunderstood. But James found this line of reasoning hard to swallow. He was constantly remembering how Blacky had coldly admitted to killing the three men of Max's old gang, and James could not get past that. The subject was wearing on the pair of them, and they decided it was much too draining to spend their moments together speculating on Blacky's skullduggery.

"I spoke with Capt. Mahony yesterday," said Veronica, attempting to steer as far from the subject as possible, only managing to resuscitate their previous conversation. "He —–" she pause, reconsidering. "You know the ringer on your phone was turned off, so I turned it back on. But I don't know how to work that high-tech contraption of an answering machine of yours."

"Yes, I just want some peace for a change. No interruptions. So go on. What did Mahony say?"

"They found my car ditched in a ditch. Oh well," she added nonchalantly, so much for transportation.

"Did he say anything else?"

"Nothing more. Tell me about your father, Jamie," she said in an effort to lighten the mood, her voice silky and sensual. "Something from your childhood."

"He left a message the other day, I have as of yet to hear it. My answering machine stores the numbers and the messages digitally. And by the looks of it, it's a long one. I'll listen to it," he added reassuringly, for Veronica's expression showed every sign of reprobation. "He was ever present when I was a child. He made it a point to be at all my violin recitals and gymnastic meets. He would read to me and tell me stories, both during the day and before bedtime."

"Oh how sweet, James. Nowadays, it seems there are so many fathers who are too busy doing something other than raising and getting to know their children; their sons suffer a greater lost than the daughters. Mind you, I would never suggest that daughters do not love or are not loved just as much as sons. I do, however, believe the lost a son would incur, is the lost of how to be a man and a father to his son. That is a lost you were spared."

CHAPTER TWENTY-SEVEN

"Yeah, he told me once of how, when he was a child, his father was rarely there. And one night a woman came banging at his parent's door. It was very late in the night, and she was screaming his mother's name, my grandmother Jacqueline, over and over. When he had awaken from his bed and made his way down stairs, his mother was there holding a hammer, just waiting for the woman to breach the large pane of the front door. His younger brother, my uncle Octavius, had also awaken and joined him at the foot of the stair case, standing silently, undoubtedly wondering as my dad did, who was the crazy woman. Interestingly enough, he remembered nothing of their sister Madeline that night. Perhaps she slept through the entire incident. So when their mother grew tired of the woman screaming, she yelled back. *Rufus is not here. I thought he was with you.* Then my father asked his mother, *Do you know her?* And she said to him, *No, but your father does.* I realized later in life how that event, and many others requiring his father's presence, had a profound affect on my father, which caused him to spend as much time home as he possibly could. He made it a point to be present."

He paused for a moment, smiling, Veronica close, looking back at him and taking in his facial expression. She was sitting in his lap and leaned back against his chest comfortably.

"That, I am grateful for," he finished. "You know, one of the stories he told me was about what happens to socks when they go missing," he added brightly. "I had asked the question of why I couldn't find all the matches to my socks. To this very day, I still have that book in the other room on the shelf."

"No way," said Veronica excitedly. "I know the story. That's from *The Adventures of Argil and The Missing Socks,* Oh my goodness, I loved that book as a child. I read that book so many times I nearly memorizing it all. Jamie, our children will be fortunate to have a grandfather such as your father. So many stories he will tell them."

"I never met my grandfather. He died long before I was born. But children, I love the sound of that," said James, grinning broadly.

"Me too."

"How about if we..." said James kissing Veronica on the neck. "And then we can..." he added, sliding his hand under her blouse and feeling her skin against his fingers.

It was supple, smooth. Veronica caught her breath, sliding her hands across his, directing his fingers past her navel, then lower.

"Wait a second," she said. "I don't remember getting the all clear from Anita."

"What Anita don't know ——"

"I have a better idea," she said, gaining her composure and standing up. "Let's watch FEMA. I noticed you have it in your DVD collection and I have always wanted to see a movie based on a book that your father has written."

"Now?" he said incredulously.

She walked over to the entertainment center and added in a seductive voice, glancing over at James readjusting the crotch of his trousers, "There will be plenty of time for that, my love."

"There's no time like time's a wasting," said James shifting uncomfortably on the sofa.

Veronica dashed back to her seat excitedly and plopped rather heavily back into James' lap, causing him to flinch. But James did not care too much for watching the movie, which he had seen several times years ago and heard so much about its internet popularity. Just as long as Veronica was close, her body against his, her scent all around him, he was right with the world. The smell of her hair was sunlight to his senses.

The movie began with credits immediately fading in and out against the main character speaking.

My... they... they're dead, all dead: Sam, Ann, Elle, Marcus, Desmond and the rest of them are dead. I... Calm down Iggy.

A young man of twenty or so was in the middle of a field with a small recorder, documenting some horror that Veronica and James, although he had seen the movie several time, was at present yet to witness. James wrapped his arms around Veronica's torso gently; her arms interlocked with his. He could not concentrate on the desperate man's plight, only the feel of Veronica. He kissed her on the neck and took in the scent of her.

She was intoxication. He kissed her again, and she respond by tilting her head, exposing more of her neck. She seemed to be caught between movie and sensation. The frantic man on the screen continued speaking into the recorder.

Okay, my name is Cornelius Igancious Robertson. I lived in —— well that doesn't matter anymore, does it? If anyone hears this recording, please... please copy it, give it to as many people that you know. Put it on the internet so everyone will know what the government is doing. If they find me, and I am more than sure they will, I'm a dead man. We're all dead. Were should I begin?

It all started here, right here in Madison, Georgia. I was passing this field, off Interstate 20, and saw these overlarge plastic tote containers, large enough to accommodate two adults. They are stacked inside one another like some eerie Tupperware collection, thousands upon thousands of them heaped high, their lids stacked separately. I pulled over to get a closer look. Why did I ever pull over? No one is not even questioning their presence. I looked it up on the internet; they are coffins, FEMA coffins. There are a few other sights like this one. And I found FEMA camps ——

James was now caressing Veronica's left breast; her breath heavy, her right hand in his locks, pulling while he nibbled her neck. Her left hand was across his hand at her breast, and he slid his fingers hungrily inside her blouse. They glided across her skin beneath the silk fabric, and her stomach sunk, quivering from sensations in an effort to catch her breath. The phone rang, but its feeble attempts to gain their attention was lost in the throws of their passion, and the muted answering machine recorded a message never heard. And although audible, the movie playing before them was also not heard.

So I asked myself, 'What the hell is going on with all these coffins in the middle of a field? And why are there so many?' It looks like we are preparing for a holocaust of some sort. Come to find out, I wasn't too far from the mark. I contacted Marcus Gram of——

"Oh, Jamie... yes." she moaned, moving with him then reached behind and beneath her backside. "What's this, baby?"

"It's my flash light, I thought we might need it," he said, trembling with contained excitement.

"J'aime les lampes de poche... I love flashlights," she whispered, reaching inside his pants.

"I love it when you speak French. But, what about Anita?"

"She can get her own flash light."

28

Argile and The Missing Socks

Hours passed serenely with the pair in each other's arms. They lay there naked upon the sofa, inhaling each other's breath, Veronica gazing up, her ear against James' chest, following the sound of his heart beat. He took in her redolence while softly stroking her hair, drinking her in. James was extremely happy and for once found peaceful moments without a thought of Blacky. There was, however, the event of Blacky's skullduggery at the pier. It had so thoroughly eclipsed James' need to know his biological parents that he had forgotten he was adopted and now rekindled his interest, hoping his cousin Paul would call soon with some answers. He thought that he would give it a go later and call his father to find out more information. And now that he had a chance to speak with Veronica about his father, James was feeling closer to him than he had felt in a very long time. James cast his eyes upwards to the ceiling and sighed, feeling extremely well in being.

"Now this is how life should be," he said. "I could do this forever."

"So could I, baby. So could —— What was that?" she started.

"Just the door, Veronica my sweet. Just ignore it."

"Spooner," came a tiny voice from the front and another little knock.

"Is that ——"

"Yes. And oh, how devilishly low she has sunken. I can't believe Red is using Sophie to gain entry."

And the pair scrambled from the sofa, passing each other's clothes back and forth until the both were completely dressed, looking thoroughly disheveled and snickering at their own behavior. Veronica was pleasurably flushed. And after a fashion, the pair made their way to the door and answered it.

"We're not interrupting anything, are we, Spooner? Veronica?" Red asked, once she entered the house.

James and Veronica, who both looked like wide eyed cats that swallowed canaries, began to trip over their words until embarrassment got the better of them and again laughed at one another's behavior. Red, who was ushering Sophie into the living room, seemed too preoccupied to even noticed their odd behavior.

"I have something to tell you, Spooner," she began in a grave tone. "But little rabbits have big ears."

"And big rabbits have bigger ears mommy," said Sophie brightly.

"See what I mean? Sophie, could you ——"

"Would you like to see one of the rooms in the back, Princess Sophie?" said Veronica, understanding that something severe must have happened to have rattled Red to the point of comporting herself in such a stiff manner.

"Does it have a telephone?" Sophie asked. "I just learned how to use one. I talk to my dad on it."

"Yes it does," said Veronica, taking her hand.

And with a distressful look, Red mouthed silent words to Veronica, "Thank you."

As Veronica quitted the room, taking with her a jovial Sophie, she could barely hear Red say something to the effect: "Your mother is very upset. She needs you to come at once." And the rest of what she said was lost in the house's poor acoustics.

"Wow!" exclaimed Sophie entering one of the other rooms. "Look at all the books in here. Just like aunty Bess. And a phone, just like aunty Bess," she added reaching for it.

It was a quaint little room, much smaller than James' parents drawing room, yet a library all the same. There were books lining one of the walls and a computer desk next to the window. Two very comfortable looking sofa chairs sat close, one nearer to the phone at the edge of the desk.

Sophie experimented with the phone for a while and Veronica, not giving much attention to Sophie's delighted comparisons, felt that it would not be enough to keep her interest.

"Sophie, how would you like if I read you a story," she asked while pulling a very familiar children's book from the shelf.

"Yes," she said brightly, hanging the phone up and plopping into the nearby leather chair.

"This was one of my favorite books when I was a child. I'm sure you'll love it."

She sat there quietly and bore an expression of polite interest. And on the whole, Veronica thought she was quite a well behaved child. Veronica began.

"This is one of the tales from The Adventures of Argile and The Missing Socks."

Once there lived, or rather existed, a sock that lay folded with its match in the back of a dresser drawer. Now this sock was just like its match, made of soft wool cotton. It was tan and bore a large dark brown diamond connected to a light brown diamond below it on its right side, and on the left side was the same. A thin brown zig-zag line wrapped around the entire top like gladiator straps, looking very impressive.

One day, when the pair were soiled from much use and thrown into the hamper to await the wash, the socks were for the first time in their entire existence separated. And on this day, one came to life. It was dark and stuffy in the hamper but not as it would have been in a shoe, and somehow the sock new this fine point.

"Where am I? This is not ——"

And before the sock could get its bearings, it was whisked away with the rest of the laundry and shortly thereafter found itself in the wash. After some time of much rubbing against other clothing and being forced down to the bottom of the wash, only to be pushed back up to the top again by the current repeatedly, the sock was placed in the dryer where other clothes had been waiting. A fine dry piece of material was thrown in with the lot and clung to the sock as if glued. Although the sock thought it had a most pleasant aroma, it did not enjoy the clinging piece of fabric. The more it struggled, the less affect the sock had in freeing itself.

"Hang on," a voice called out to an unknown group at large. "We're about to go for a hot ride."

"What? Who said that?" asked the startled sock, and they all began to tumble, each in turn falling over one another, and the thin perfumed fabric released the sock.

"I did," replied a white sports sock with black and green stripes. "Well, it looks like we have a new guy here. Everyone, say hello to —"

"Argile," said the sock, somehow knowing its name.

"Everyone, this is Argile."

"Hi, Argile!" chimed a few other socks, but not all.

"Welcome," said the white sports sock. "Let me introduce you to the gang. That's Pier, Torny, Stacey, Toe-Jam, Splatter, and I'm Rip," he added, expanding his elastic red and black striped top.

"What's wrong with those guys over there?" asked Argile.

"They don't talk," said Rip."

"Why not? What makes them so different than the rest of us?"

"Why not? Why not?" said an incredulous fancy dress sock named Stacey. "Tell him Rip," he added with an air of mischief.

"It's like this, rookie," said Rip. "May I call you rookie?"

"No, Argile will do nicely."

"Very well, suit yourself," said Rip. "They don't talk because they are separated from their matches, and only one of a pair can talk. Their matches are undoubtedly somewhere stuck in a drawer, under the bed, in the hamper, fell on the floor on the way here or more than likely clinging to some garment hanging in a closet. Much like what has happen to us all, but we are in here instead of out there."

"Believe him," said Toe-Jam, whose threads at the end were wore to the point of nearly forming a hole. "It happened to me. I spent all summer holding onto a sweater once. Sometimes it takes months before you are found, or you could end up in the wash several times, if you are so lucky to be mistaken for a match to another sock.

CHAPTER TWENTY-EIGHT

"Like I was saying," continued Rip. "It also happens when ——"

Just then the door to the dryer opened and an identical match to Rip was thrown in, and the door was once again close.

"Then what Rip?" asked Argile, who had listened to every word attentively and with much anticipation.

But Rip did not respond. And after several attempts at getting Rip's attention, a very colorful tie-dyed sock by the name of Splatter spoke.

"Give it up Argile. It's no use. He can't hear you. That's what he was trying to tell you. Only one sock of a pair can speak and only when we are apart from one another. That's his match that just got thrown in here."

"Oh," said Argile understandingly. "I see. What about that sock over there, it looks like you?"

"I beg your pardon," said Splatter. "That sock looks nothing like me. The colors are all wrong. I am red, gold, and green with brown swirls, and that sock has brown swirls with red, gold, and green. Thank you very much," Splatter finished, as if defeating Argile in perfect reason.

"If you say so," said Argile, thoroughly confused.

"Tell him about the socks that never come back," said Toe-Jam with contained excitement.

"Oh not again," said Pier in a hardy tone. "Will you give it a rest. There is no such thing as The Golden Loom; so let's not even bring that up again. It's just a dresser drawer myth to explain what happens to the socks who decide to set off on their own and to never return."

"Is that possible?" asked Argile, thrilled.

"Where there is static, there is hope," said Toe-Jam.

"Don't go filling his fibers with such rubbish," said Pier. "Know your place and don't go running off half stretched somewhere and end up in the street all tattered and torn. Keep your head down and you may have the opportunity to make a lovely hand puppet for some lucky child."

"Yeah right. Or an old scrub rag," joked Stacy.

And the laughter mounted.

"Seriously," said Pier, a little irritated at their jubilance. "The only way you are going to get out there, is if you are paired with another sock that looks like you. That means one other than your match. You will then be taken around all day, awaken and alert. If you are not covered with a long pant leg, you will be able to see the world around you."

"Ah yes," said Splatter. "That happened to me once, and it was a wonderful feeling to be able to experience the outside. The person who wore me was a little girl, with high top tennis, a pretty cute little skirt and ——"

"Okay there isn't much time left in this dry cycle," cut in Toe-Jam. "Let's save the fashion foray for later. What you really need to do, Argile, is to stay away from the fabric softener sheet. It is that sheet over there that was thrown directly on you. It keeps you from clinging to anything, making you slick as new, but you smell real pretty. Next time, do your best to stay in the back of the dryer so that it does not touch you, then you will have the opportunity to escape with the help of static. Remember," he added, "when escaping, static is your friend."

The door to the dryer was opened and they were all heaped out into a basket with other clothes. Argile thought he glimpse a sock that looked very much like himself as he fell towards the basket, and darkness overcame him, then there was nothing.

The next time Argile was placed into the dryer, he had the most incredible story to tell. Everyone from before was there, and the last of the other clothing were placed in the dryer. The door was shut, and the cycle began. Rip, Pier, Torny, Stacey, Toe-Jam and Splatter were all curious.

"Why do you have those strange marks all over you?" asked Rip.

"I'll tell you, and you will not believe where I've been," said Argile. And upon their curious looks, he quickly added, "I have been on the outside."

"You're pulling my leg," said Stacey in disbelief.

"What leg?" joked Toe-Jam and Splatter. "More like elastic."

And the two laugh heartily.

"Get out of here," said Torny, "How did you accomplish that feet?"

The laughter was even more contagious, and Torny began to laugh at himself.

"Good one, feet, you're killing me, stop," they said, congratulating Torny on his well executed line, and the laughter became a ruckus.

Rip and Pier, the oldest of the socks, were silently waiting for the commotion to settle so that they could hear the entire story. When the hilarity did not cease, Rip and Pier raised their voices for order. The rest snickered themselves into silence.

"Okay, rookie," said Rip. "You have the floor."

"As if," said Stacy, and their giggles were immediately dashed by sharp looks from Rip and Pier.

"It all happened to us when we were in the car," said Argile, "me and my match."

"Impossible," said Pier indignantly.

"Give him a chance," replied Rip. "Please continue."

Pier looked scandalized, but held his silence.

"I woke up, and there I saw in the front passenger seat of the car, a woman pulling my match from the dash board and placing it into her purse. Then she was hit in the back of the head with the sandal thrown by the child that wore me He was throwing an awful fit. The window was down, and I knew I was the next to be thrown. He tugged on me and stretched me until I could stretch no more. I held on as long as I could, but it was pointless. I snapped from his foot like a sling shot, and that disagreeable little boy tried to throw me out the window. So I wrapped my elastic top around his fingers and held on until he stopped flinging me around. When he was tired, he place me in his mouth and began to suck and chew. Yuck!"

"So that's were those marks you have all over come from," said Rip.

"Yes, and get this," he continued. "He loved chewing on me so much that they just let him gnaw on me the entire time we were out driving. It kept him quiet. I nonetheless," he added happily, "saw tall trees, building, a bright blue sky, and birds flying by. There was so much to see. We went to the park, and I saw socks of all kinds on many different legs of all shapes and sizes ——"

"Did you see it..." cut in Toe-Jam. "The Golden Loom, you must have?"

"There he goes again with The Golden Loom," said Pier.

"Sorry," said Argile. "I didn't see it this time. But I will look for it the next time I'm out."

"That's the spirit," said Rip. "Always believe in yourself and your ability to make things happen. Never give up. And Toe-Jam," he added, "hold on to your dreams."

And Argile thought he might, if the opportunity presented itself, attempt a planned trip to the outside. And maybe if he liked it enough, would stay a while and search for this Golden Loom.

Veronica closed the book, peered over her shoulder and caught a smile from Red, who was absolutely beaming with appreciation.

"Yea!" cheered Sophie, clapping her little hands for all she was worth.

"Bravo. Veronica. That was sweet of you to read to Sophie. You're very good."

"Thank you."

"Sophie darling, it's time to go. Say goodbye to Veronica."

"Goodbye," she said brightly, bestowing a great hug upon her as Veronica gathered her into her arms.

CHAPTER TWENTY-EIGHT

James was waiting in the living room with a rather disturbed look on his face. After James exchanged goodbyes with a solemn Red and a beaming Sophie at the front door, Veronica asked James what had happen to have brought Red so far out of her way.

"I need to go see my mother. Will you come with me?"

"Of course, my love. What has happened?"

"It's my father. He's... he's dead."

29

A Poet's Rite

It was a call from Cornelius Robertson — Alexander's closest and dearest friend, as well as his lawyer of many years — who informed Elizabeth the traumatic news of Alexander's death. And as disturbing as the news was, Elizabeth was not prepared for the manner in which he had died.

"He was murdered, Bess," Cornelius had conveyed to Elizabeth. "Killed like an animal."

His tone was harsh, angrily bitter and unapologetic, but the unwelcome words were from a familiar voice nonetheless. Inspector Jonathan Garrison, of the London Police force, had indeed contacted Elizabeth moments after Cornelius' call and left a contact number, if Elizabeth did so choose to return to London in order to properly identify the body. But Cornelius had commissioned himself the quicker and felt that it was perhaps for the best that he should contacted Alexander's family first, instead of them learning the tragic news from London officials.

CHAPTER TWENTY-NINE

She sat presently in the study, still in shock and disbelief, yet she gather what little resolve she had to explain the details of Alexander's utterly horrid demise to her son. James and Veronica sat there before her, absolutely staggered by Elizabeth's recount of how a bellhop by the name of Rowan Perkins —— who must had been a crazed fan, as reported by Inspector Garrison —— forced his way into Alexander's suite, and after a struggle, was disarmed and shot with his own gun by a gored Alexander Frederick. None of which was told to them made any sense whatsoever. James could not rightly understand why would a fan do such a thing. Perhaps they have the wrong Alexander Frederick, he hoped. His father's work never inspired anything other than an admiration for poetry and a love for philosophy or on several occasions, as he remembered, totally enamored followers. That's if one did not count the FEMA internet scare, and no one in England, or for that matter the whole of Europe, would ever count that as a divisive piece of work, but rather entertaining. He mulled over these things in his head with no consolation.

And just as James' feeling of disbelief turned into rising anger, the desperate plea in Elizabeth's voice caused him to disconnect from any sort of bereavement process he would have undergone, and he became emotionally numb. He was the man of the family now and needed to immediately assume the role of managing his father's affairs without falling apart, which included at present the urgent necessity to return Alexander's remains home to his loved ones. So it was with deliberate haste that James called Graves Funeral Halls to requisition the remains of his father to be flown home. He booked a round trip flight for himself to London so that he may identify his father's body before transport, as well as having the honor of being Alexander's escort.

❦

"TWA's flight 447 to London now boarding," issued a pleasant voice four hours later over the airport's intercom system.

"I wish I was coming with you, Jamie," said Veronica. "Yes, I understand. We have already discussed it. I need to stay here to keep Mahony from... How was it you said?"

Passengers were now cueing to the right of the final check boarding pass counter attended by a service agent standing behind it. And behind him was a digital sign blaring both TWA's arriving and departing flights.

"Do his nut. You know, losing his mind... flipping out," said James taking his place in line behind an older woman with a long umbrella and whose hair was extremely stiff looking and dark against her pale skin.

He over heard her talking to someone in line, saying something to the effect that she heard it rains all the time in London. And at great lengths, the woman carried on in a worried state.

"Is this an Airbus? Because I heard that they are falling apart in mid flight these days, held together only by duct tape."

"No ma'am," said the service agent politely. "It's a Boeing 747."

And the woman looked thoroughly satisfied.

"I just wanted to hear you turn that colorful phase again," said Veronica, giving him a buss on the cheek before stepping back.

He handed his boarding pass to the flight attendant, who manned the door to the boarding bridge and promptly scanned his pass with a high-tech handheld electronic gadget. James then turned and casted Veronica a knowing look with a winked. She blushed slightly with a wide smile.

"Don't let Red and my mother get you off your stride," he said, taking his boarding pass back from the attendant and waving goodbye.

"You have a safe trip, Jamie. And not to worry," she called out to him as he disappeared into the boarding bridge leading to the door of the plane. "We will be like old girlfriends."

"That's exactly what I am worried about," he mumbled to himself and thought the grinning flight attendant, presently greeting the passengers at the opening of the plane, must have heard him.

After a fashion, everyone was settling into their assigned seats and stowing their possessions in the overhead compartments, everyone except the woman with the long umbrella and dark stiff hair. She inconvenienced the passengers in her row by fumbling about with her umbrella, waving then finally smacking one passenger with its handle. This she did with an unabashed and determined attempt to situate it between the cramped leg-room space of the row. James wondered why on earth did she bring an umbrella on board. Surely it would be difficult to stow. Had not she realized that she could very well buy an umbrella once she reached her final destination? Finally the flight attendant, who had watched the woman's dumbfounding behavior from a safe distant and felt now it would be prudent to intercede, approached from behind and tapped the woman on the shoulder.

"Madam, allow me to stow that for you," she said, reaching for the umbrella.

The other passengers in the row looked quite relieved.

"No thank you," said the woman holding the umbrella tightly in her grip.

And they struggled for a brief moment before the flight attendant realized there was no use in trying to secure the cursed item. The flight attendant walked away to consult with what James thought was more than likely her supervisor. The woman stood and try to stow her umbrella, this time in the overhead compartment. And at James' (and everyone who was attentive) astonishment, she managed to force the nuisance of an item into the small space, then closed the overhead compartment. She did this in a bit of a rush while simultaneously ducking under and taking her seat. The resulting outcome was something no one was quite prepared to witness.

While the pilot gave the announcement for the crew to prepare for take off, the returning flight attendant, who was now giving the safety demonstration, could not understand the stifled laughter that was going on, until she cast down the aisle and saw a wig swinging animatedly from the overhead compartment above the woman with whom she struggled with minutes earlier. It seemed the snickering was literally completely over the woman's head. Her head was dressed with what looked like a stocking cap, and small pieces of her hair stuck out from beneath it around the edges.

James wondered with astonishment, how in the world did that happened. He closed his eyes, trying not to laugh, but his stifled laughter caused his chest to jump as though he were coughing silently. He thought it was an odd yet perfect beginning to a what would be a very long flight. He closed his eyes with a growing smile and tried to imagine what it would be like if his locks, although permanently attached, were to slide off his head, and he felt a small amount of pity for the woman.

James found himself in the lobby of The Swissotel Howard, which had not change much in the many years of when he had visited London. Its tall ivory thresholds, remnant of traditional archways, were trimmed brilliantly with gold. Fluted columns also with like trim, set atop marble plinths, effecting something of a French and Greco-Roman grandeur that contrasted impressively with the marble tiled floor. The designs that framed the white archways, drew themselves in sharp relief magnificently upon the recessed ceiling, from the corners to finally the center, encircling the base of an elegant chandelier that hung with sparkling crystal candles. James crossed the length of the lobby, passing a beautiful red top table with phalaenopsis orchids placed in a glass vase as a centerpiece. He reached the elevator, which was framed by a shiny black marled wall, and pressed the gold button. The door to the lift opened, and he stepped in. It closed after him, and he was for no particular reason he could figure, suddenly filled with dread after pressing the number four button. Then the elevator, instead of ascending, stuttered and dropped, and James' heart fell into his stomach like a brick. The lift's speed increased with its descent, and James felt as though his feet were about to leave the floor. He crouched down to brace himself for the impact, but the speed increased even more. And to his great horror, his feet left the floor. He could not calm himself, and fear overtook him. Any moment now, he would slam into what he thought was by this time the center of the earth.

James was jarred out of his sleep panting. The airplane's landing gear greeted pavement. It touched down rather hard on the tarmac for his taste. He was thankful, however, to be awaken from his horrific dream. The breaking system engaged immediately, and everyone lunged forward in their seats, some looking rather unnerved. But in comparison to the dream he just had, James felt it was nonetheless a fairly altogether excellent landing. The pilot's calm and commanding voice over the airplane's intercom reminded everyone to stay seated while they taxied to the assigned gait. And he thanked everyone once again for flying TWA Airlines.

The woman with the malfunctioning wig was now groggily stirring. She had apparently retrieved her headdress that was stuck in the overhead compartment door. And after falling asleep on the long flight, she presently found herself awakened with her wig atop her head all askew.

Shortly thereafter, the aircraft came to a complete stop, and many hands were immediately busy with the post landing ritual of pushing tiny buttons on their mobiles. James took out his well preserved and now fully charged cell phone, which still had the thin manufactured plastic stuck to it, and began the ritual also. He dialed Cornelius Robertson's number.

"No worries mate," said Cornelius a few moments later on the other end of the phone. "I'm inside the terminal as we speak. I saw your plane pull in."

When James hung his phone up, he immediately received a sharp blow to his forehead, and swore loudly. He had not been paying attention and neither were several other passengers, who were now nursing growing knots, painfully sore eye sockets, and bruised body parts of their own. The woman with the malfunctioning wig had a problem retrieving her umbrella, and after freeing it from the overhead compartment, she swung it carelessly in the air and struck anyone who was unaware, then offered her sincerest apologies over and again for the damage done. Not long after this rather painful encounter, James exited the boarding bridge from the plane to the terminal, nursing the smarting bruise on his forehead. He thought it serves him right to laugh at someone's pain. The universe must be laughing back right about now.

"Rough ride there, James?" inquired Cornelius, casting a concern look at James' forehead and noticing a few others entering the terminal and nursing bruises of their own.

"I'll be fine. Just had a run-in with an umbrella."

Cornelius considered him for a moment.

"Welcome back James. Permit me. There are a few things we need to cover, such as your father's will; however, at present I am sure you'll be wanting to see your f-father's..." he faltered, then recovered, finding the strength in his voice, "your father's body."

James took this as a sign that Cornelius was in much more emotional pain than his face would betray. Cornelius Robertson was a rugged looking man with a deep scar across his left cheek, yet James thought he must have retained some handsome attribute from his youth which detract from the marred feature. He conveyed to Cornelius that he wanted to see his father as soon as possible, in order to carry out the business of getting him home and laying him to rest. He secretly hoped the entire ordeal would soon come to a close. But forty-two minutes later, nothing was to prepare him for the shock of seeing his father in the morgue.

"That's him," said James, as Inspector Garrison pulled an enormous drawer from out of a stainless steel wall of many.

It was real now. It had been finalized once he set eyes on him. James' father was dead. His life pointlessly taken away from the ones he loved. Gone. Never to be spoken to or heard and understood. Never to feel the sun on his face or sit in the glow of a full moon. Never to enjoy life's many treasures he had so often written of. Never to write another letter. Never to breath another breath. Never to wake. Never to be.

James was in a most morose mood and did not care to listen to the retelling of how his father was killed. It was the indignity of Alexander's state that fueled James' need to get on with the business of laying him to rest.

"There are a few papers the department will need you to sign, sir," said Inspector Garrison. "At your leisure, of course. I'll take my leave now," he added, then quietly swept from the room.

Alexander lay there rigid, his face filled with more lines than James remembered, his hair brushed with much more grey. James thought Alexander's naked form looked cold, and wondered why wasn't he covered with more than just a small white sheet. It was insufficient for a man who had given so much and asked for very little. What a meaningless end to someone so admired. And James wondered why was he able to look upon his father's aged and lifeless form and not feel compelled to cry. He figured maybe there would be time for tears later. Right now he had to get his father home to the rest of his family.

"I'll be there, James," said Cornelius. "At the memorial, I mean. What every you need, you only need to ask."

"You think you could officiate the ceremony. I think he would have like that."

"Yes, it would be an honor. And have you made plans for transport?"

"I have, it's been taken care of. Tomorrow we leave together for home."

"You are aware that your father's will specifies his remains be cremated, and there should only be a memorial service?"

"No, I didn't."

"Then you must come to my office and I will read it to you. I am surprised that he has never mentioned the will to you or your mother."

And sure enough, twenty minutes later, after making arrangements with Inspector Garrison for the removal and transportation of Alexander remains, James found himself in the office of Cornelius Robertson, reading his father's last will in testament.

I, Alexander Frederick O'Neil, a resident and domicile in London, England, do hereby make, publish and declare this to be my last will in testament: Hereby revoking all wills and codicils at anytime by me, here before me, by me. I direct there be only a memorial services. It is my wish that my body be cremated and my ashes scattered over the earth. I give and bequeath all of my right title and interest to the following: My will property know as O'Neil Manor, located in Virginia Beach, Virginia on O'Neil Lane, to my wife Elizabeth Vittoria O'Neil. I give and bequeath the following sums: One million dollars to The American

Alzheimer's Research Foundation; One million dollars to The American Cancer Research Foundation; And appoint, my son, James Benjamin O'Neil, as my individual executor, hereunder, with the sum of One Hundred and Fifty million dollars for the performance of his duties as executor. I appoint James Benjamin O'Neil as trustee of each trust created hereunder. James Benjamin O'Neil will appoint as a coexecutor for such bank or trust company, that he, in his absolute discretion, shall deem appropriate.

The reading of the will went on longer than James cared to listen. And when it seemed it would stretch on even further, Cornelius found the end.

I appoint James Benjamin O'Neil the director of the foundation along with four additional persons as James Benjamin O'Neil shall designate. I have here unto set my hand and affixed my seal to this my last will in testament on this Twenty-Fourth day of July, 2004.

Alexander Frederick O'Neil.

"Well, that says it all. Doesn't it?" said James, rather fatigued from the legal jargon coupled with his jet-lag. "I'll make sure his wishes are carried out. As far as scattering his ashes on the earth, I have no idea where he would want me to do that."

"When the time is right, I'm more than confident that you will know," he said, handing the will to James then pausing a moment before continuing. "I'm reminded of one of your father's quotes. *When I have passed and rid myself this mortal coil, and all the lilies and alstroemerias are in bloom...*" he went on, quoting until he reached the passage's end, dawning a distant stare and a knowing look upon his face.

"I like the sound of that," said James, tossing the will aside and reaching for a note pad to the left of Cornelius.

He tore off a sheet then grabbed a pen from a cup that sat to the right of the note pad, and he began to scribble.

"Well, if you don't mind, I'm wiped out," he said after copying the words and placing the pen back into the cup, then folding the paper into his pocket. "I really would love to get some food and rest. Could I trouble you for a bite to eat before we head to the hotel, Cornelius?"

"Say no more, my good man. I'm at your disposal. By the way, I'm having your father's things sent to your hotel room. It's not much, but they are his things. And in being that, they are important."

"Thank you."

CHAPTER TWENTY-NINE

"You know, your father uses to scribble on pieces of paper many years ago, just like you. But, he got more organized as the years past. My advice to you, James, is to get a PALM."

"Why would I want to do that? I have two perfectly good ones with fingers attached to them."

"Hahaha! Your father wasn't keen on technology either. What a pair. What a pair."

The next day came without hesitation, bringing with it a blood-shot and wide-eyed James. He had not gotten the desired sleep he so desperately needed. He was up most of the night on the phone convincing Elizabeth that his father's wishes, of being cremated and having a memorial service only, were to be respected. She did not like much being told what to do by her deceased and once estranged husband, but there was the house he had left her, and James felt it was incentive enough. So she grudgingly acquiesced to Alexander's wishes.

Veronica, on the other hand, was chiefly supportive and gave no indication to the contrary, nor implied that she was being denied equal phone status with his mother. James felt as though she was perfect in all respects and looked forward to reuniting with her. After speaking with Veronica, he called the airline to insure that his father's body was received at the airport, and an airline official confirmed that Alexander's body will be placed on the departing flight as soon as the plane arrived. James' bags were packed. His father's personal effects, which were sent over to him, were carefully boxed and addressed to his mother's home. He gathered his things, took one last look at the room to insure he had not forgotten anything, then left.

30

Memorial

No cameras were allowed entry. No reporters allowed interviews. Many came from far and wide on this solemn yet beautiful autumn day to pay their respects to the memory of Alexander Frederick O'Neil and to his loving family. James and Elizabeth stood inside the entrance of one of the large halls of Grave's Funeral Halls, which was an enormous and luxuriously structure that housed several other memorial halls and many smaller pollers. As they welcomed those who came to pay their respects, James could not help but think of the time he and his father missed spending together as a result of James own stubbornness. It was time he could never recover. And all he could do now was stand there welcoming and receiving commiseration and thinking how selfish he had been.

Veronica, on the other hand, had earlier reserved a spot for her and James on one of the uncomfortable pews to the right of the hall. She kept peering back at James over her left shoulder in an effort to ascertain his state of mind.

Elizabeth, was totally the opposite of James. She was constantly sobbing into a handkerchief, barely stringing several words together to effect a thank you for the condolences afforded by solemn attendees. James had shown no emotions to the matter whatsoever, and Veronica wondered if he was in shock or suppressing painful emotions. She had asked him many times, very near to the point of becoming an irritant, how he was doing or if he needed anything. She felt useless because he seemed to need no support from anyone. Veronica felt, if there was a time in life to be emotional, this was certainly it. She kept a worried and close eye on James, wondering how long could he remain stoic. And James realizing this, would from time to time shoot a counterfeit smile in her direction to assure her that he was okay.

The procession of solemn faces sauntered in and took their seats in uncomfortable wooden pews on both the left and right sides of the hall. After some time, many began to stand along the walls for want of a place to sit, while the sunlight casted its diffused glow through the skylight upon populated pews. A red carpet ran center length of the enormous room. At the front, where the red carpet ended, was a large picture of a younger Alexander supported by a great easel. A white and marble top roman-style pillar, flanked by beautiful floral arrangements of asiatic lilies and alstroemerias, stood before Alexander's image. Upon the pillar rested his remains in a brilliant golden urn with hieroglyphic markings all over it and a black onyx plinth beneath it that read in large gold lettering: **Here rests the remains of Alexander Frederick O'Neil. The rest lies within our hearts**.

CHAPTER THIRTY

The hall was filled with subdued sounds of sobs and whispers from family, friends, and many fans, who undoubtedly had followed his work religiously over many years. Among the attendees James found himself familiar with were: Elizabeth of course, who had taken her seat in the front most pew next to Red and Sophie, was still weeping into a tear soaked handkerchief; Aunt Olivia, who sat alone and wore a large black hat with a single matching feather; Aunt Maddy, whose vastness caused the entire pew on which she sat to shake as she sobbed into a red handkerchief matching her hat, while several fans of Alexander kept cutting their eyes at one another whenever Aunt Maddy caused the pew to tremble; Mrs. Barinard, who sat quietly behind Aunt Maddy, bearing a solemn look; James' best friend William, who sat next to his mother, both accompanied by the lovely Anita Forman, who sat to the right of William, periodically glancing at her pager; Capt. Mahony of the 23rd precinct; Laura Sanchez, a reporter for Channel 3 News, who promised no cameras or attempted interviews of any kind, sat scribbling on a small pad; and Alexander's old and dearest friend Cornelius Robertson, whose tough and ridged exterior commanded attention when he stood. He had gotten to his feet and turned to insure that the door to the hall was closed before approaching the podium to speak. James took his seat near the front with Veronica. An even quieter hush fell over the wall to wall room of attendees. Not even the smallest sniffle could be heard. And with great solemnity, the ceremony was now underway.

"My names is Cornelius Robertson. Alex was my best mate," he began in tremulous tones, then cleared his voice and found its strength. "There is so much that I can tell you about Alex, but my fondest memories of him are during our days of journalism at the London Times. In all my life, I had never —— and to this very day —— met a more talented writer. He was referred to me by a very close and mutual friend of ours."

James thought he saw out of the corner of his eye Mrs. Barinard shift uncomfortably in her seat. He, however, figured that she too felt the chairs were a bit hard for her taste.

"I was a junior editor," continued Robertson without interruption, "and was working on an expose´ entitled Internet Addiction and was asked to interview Alex. I immediately took to this cheeky and exuberant young fellow, who was so full of life that it was contagious. After speaking for two hours or so, he revealed that he was working on an internet project of his own that was very akin to what I had been working on; however, his was something far more intriguing. For those of you who do not know, Alex was the creator of the FEMA internet panic, which catapulted him into instant stardom and got him into a spot-of-bother with the American government. It was very much like an old wireless production —— you know, radio, before television. He had asked me, the day of the interview, if I would have a look, or rather, have a listen to what he was working on. It was an audio recording of a frighten America bloke's voice, who was desperately trying to describe what happened to him and his friends. We sat in the office listening to the voice spin a tell of internet intrigue, governmental corruption, and interviews that led to the deaths of the character's mates, who had aided him in his search for the truth. It was such a thrilling tell that I pulled strings to get him a job at the London Times. He and I spent most of our days off working on the script for the recordings and making them sound as authentic as possible. He was brilliant with the voices of the interviewed friends and did a brilliant job with the frighten American's voice Iggy. Each weak we would post a recording to a message board. First we posted the same one at different sites that demonstrated a lack of trust or an acute paranoia of any form of government. And after that, we found that one recording was being e-mailed to many people on the net. Shortly thereafter, we began to post them periodically at different message boards. And before we knew it, there was an internet scare the likes of Orson Wells' War of The Worlds. It was the perfect urban legend.

He paused a moment, and surveyed the hall. James thought he appeared rather pleased with himself at telling the story, and perhaps this was not the first time Robertson told it.

"Some of you may have known him best for his beautiful poetry and his ability to weave his philosophy between the lines. He was many things to many people, but to me he was my friend, my best and only friend. And he forever changed my life. He will always be —— in our ——"

Cornelius Robertson eyes welled, and his tough exterior broke. He was now weeping and could not go on any further. He stepped away from the podium. James watched him walked to his seat and wondered if Cornelius and Alex were as close as he described. Could he possibly have been privy to any of his father's secrets. James felt perhaps it would be possible to tap him for information. But when he realized the silence laps much longer than customary, James quickly stood and walked over to the podium.

"Yes," amended James. "He will forever be in out hearts."

He smiled consolingly at Cornelius Robertson, and nodded. And for a brief absurd moment, James wondered were did Cornelius ever get that large scar across his cheek. Was it from a dangerous adventure, an accident, a self inflicted wound, or an attack of some sort. A loud cry from Elizabeth followed by one from Aunt Maddy reminded him of his surroundings.

"I am James Benjamin O'Neil. As Cornelius has already stated, most people think of Alexander Frederick O'Neil as a brilliant philosopher."

He smiled at Veronica.

"A brother."

He cast a smile in his Aunt Maddy's direction, who stifled her sobs.

"A husband."

He looked at Elizabeth, but she only cried louder into her handkerchief.

"Yes, many things to different people, but I knew him as my dad. He was always there, always teaching. He felt that the job of a child was to learn as much as he or she could, and on occasion —— as he so colorfully put it —— *rip and run the streets*. And the job of the parent was not to *rip and run the streets,* trying to recapture their youth, but to aid in the development of the child. Children were not to, under any circumstance, raise themselves. Nor were they to be put in a position to cover for the ineptitudes of absentee parents. He believe that it was important to get education early in life so that later you would have the time and resources to devote to the children. Always be accessible. Always be approachable."

James believed every word that came from his own mouth, but could not feel them. He knew they were true, yet found no solace in them. He did not understand why he was feeling this way. What was this feeling of detachment? With so many people around him suffering the lost of his father, why wasn't he? He wished that he felt something other than this numbing sense. It was most disconcerting. He looked up, and to his enormous surprise saw Blacky standing in the back. And for the first time in days, he felt something. It was not sadness, or guilt, but rage that began to rise in his chest. James calmed himself in order to recite the passage from one of his father's works. He pulled out the piece of paper on which he scribbled in Cornelius Robertson's office.

"When I have passed and rid myself this mortal coil, and all the lilies and alstroemerias are in bloom, scatter my ashes not in the wind or upon the sea. Lay me upon my love and let me sink beneath the earth and become one with her. — Alexander Frederick O'Neil."

He paused for a moment of silence.

"Thank you again for coming. Please feel free to come up here and share your thoughts," he said rather abruptly, then stepped down from the podium with anger shadowing his face.

Veronica cast a look towards the back of the hall and saw what it was that disturbed James and attempted to grab him as he passed her. She caught hold of his arm, but he shrugged off her grip and made a beeline for Blacky.

"Jamie... Jamie...," she called out to him in a room now stirring with more people standing and cueing to view the remains and say their last farewells.

"May I have a word, Mr. O'Neil."

"Oh, Capt. Mahony," James said trying to skirt pass him, but his attempts were thwarted by the growing congestion. "I have to take care of something very important. I promise to return in two seconds."

"I just want to offer my condolences."

"Thank you Capt. Mahony. That means a lot. Now with your permission."

Mahony stepped aside, and James made his way through the throng, wondering what on earth possessed Blacky to be so bold as to show his face today, here of all places. Rage was swelling inside James' chest, and he thought once he got his hands on Blacky, he would teach him a thing or two about pain.

Several minutes later, outside the building, next to the well mulched white and yellow pansies and chrysanthemums, James found Blacky conversing with someone on the phone. He could not help but overhear the plea in Blacky's voice as he whispered.

CHAPTER THIRTY

"Didn't you hear me. We can't do this anymore. It's getting way too dangerous. I don't want another family member of mine to end up dead."

"Blacky!" bellowed James. "What the hell are you doing here?"

"Do you mind. I'm on the phone, Spooner."

"Damn-it, Blacky!"

James' face was contorted with anger.

"Call you back," Blacky said without heat, snapping his phone to a close then taking a step forward in James' direction. "He was my uncle, Spooner, in case you have forgotten. I know he was your dad, but you're not the only one who loved him."

"You don't love nobody but yourself. You think I've forgotten you shot me!"

"You seem fine to me, Spooner. And that's a little unkind of you to say I care only about myself. Now keep your voice down, cuz. Try not to take things so personal."

But, it was too late. Several of the people who came to pay their respects had come trooping outside to investigate the commotion.

"You shot me, you ass! It doesn't get any more personal than that!"

James was seized by a sudden and intense desire to strangle him. He lunged for Blacky but was halted, however, by someone with incredibly strong hands. James did not think to look to see who had accosted him. His only thought was to get his hands around Blacky's neck. Blacky rent James' hands away from his lapel and threw him off.

"You broke my heart, Blacky," James said, his quivering voice cracking with anger. "I believed in you. Go. Just get the fuck out before I sick Mahony on your dumb ass."

"Spooner —" said Blacky, utterly shock by his vituperation.

"I said step, Blacky!"

Veronica, Red and Sophie had made their way though the now swollen group of spectators to see what exactly was occurring. Veronica stood there with a look of incredulity on her face. Red stood there with tear filled eyes and a clapped hand over Sophie's mouth, muffling something inaudible she was saying while pointing her finger at Blacky. He was now making a speedy get-away before James decided to make good on his promise. James turned expectantly to see William, whose grip must have been that of the person holding him back. And to his surprise, it was a very handsome and clean shaven Alfred Clark.

"Al?" he said, pulling himself together.

"In the flesh, Spooner."

"You don't look the same, said James, still stunned by Alfred's stateliness. "Veronica, this is Alfred Clark."

"Please to meet you. You look nothing like how James had described you."

"Please to meet you as well. I know. Sometimes I don't recognize myself when I look in the mirror these days. And James, I see you've found the infamous —"

"Yes," said James.

"Or should I say he found you? You know, I understand about dangerous family members," said Al. "Robert Lee aka Smoke. Remember?"

"I didn't even recognize him," said James surprised. "But let's not talk about them right now," he added, attempting to lighten the mood.

"Very well," said Al. "And how are you, Red? Long time no see."

"Yes, it has been a while," she said rather snappish.

"And is this your —"

But before he could ask, Red pulled Sophie away quickly, and the pair disappeared in the somber crowd.

"My father's death is hard on us all," said James rather apologetically yet confused.

James could not rightly understand Red's abruptness with Al, and wondered if it was the sad occasion that had her upset or was it Al with whom she had taken issue.

"You know how Red can be, Al," I'm sure she meant nothing by it."

James had cast a furtive glance in Veronica direction and knew that she was thinking, *yeah right, sure she meant nothing by that. You must have done something wrong to piss her off, perhaps a forgotten disagreement from long ago or just because you were born.* The corners of her lips began to curl as she looked away, and James suppressed a grin.

"I'm sorry for your loss, Spooner."

"Thanks, Al. And you look fantastic, man. How did you manage this incredible transformation?"

"It was the fifty dollars you gave me."

"You seem to have done a lot with a little."

"Jamie," interrupted Veronica, trying not to sound too disinterested, "I see Cornelius Robertson and I'm going over to pick his brain."

"Okay, love."

She kissed him on the cheek gently and departed.

"You've done alright for yourself, Spooner," said Al, watching Veronica disappear into the room full of family and friends. "She is beautiful. I wish you two all the luck."

"Now about —"

"Yes, the fifty dollars. I rented a room at Motel 6, a cheap one I might add. It was better than staying on the streets. I never had such a good night sleep in such a long time. I had parked my shopping cart full of — well you know my stuff, outside under the stairwell to the second floor. When I woke the next morning, I found that it was missing. Imagine everything that you own, gone in one night. I was first upset. Then I realized I had spent a night in a reasonably comfortable bed. I had a hot shower. I washed my clothes, and they dried on the heater, all in the span of a night. It was a beautiful morning and I felt different about myself."

"Fantastic, but —"

"I'm getting to it. I'm getting to it," Al said, the palms of his hands turned toward James halting him. "I took the remaining twenty dollars to get something to eat at the mom-and-pop store a few blocks down and used five of it to buy one of those lottery tickets ——"

"And you won," interjected James exuberantly.

"Yes, I won two hundred thousand dollars," he said, reaching into his pocket. "And here's your fifty back," he add, separating it from a large roll of bills and stuffing it into the lapel pocket of James' jacket.

"Uh, thanks," said James, still amazed at Al's good fortune.

"No, thank you, Spooner."

"So what will you do know?"

"Live, Spooner. I am going to live," he said patting James on his left shoulder. "Oh, time to go," he added, looking at his watch. "Don't want to miss my flight to Jamaica. Good luck to you and Veronica."

James was once again inside and suddenly felt as though the walls were closing in on him. He took in several deep breaths to master himself and. And as he did, a heavy and gruff woman's voice spoke to him.

"Feeling a little overwhelmed are you?"

"Aunt Maddy," said James, a little taken of guard. "Yeah, It's a lot to take in. So many people from different backgrounds are here."

James thought he smelt distilled spirits on her breath and figured perhaps there may be a flask in that small purse of hers dangling on her arm. He felt she had not changed at all since he was a child, and perhaps this occasion would call for a stiff drink.

"My dear brother Alex was a friend and comfort to many a diverse individuals. Me, I prefer to stick to my own kind. He particularly loved him some white women," she said with an air of disapprobation. "I never understood that part of his personality."

And as if from nowhere, James reached out into the crowd of people and pulled Veronica into his arms.

"Aunt Maddy, may I introduce you to my girlfriend, Veronica."

Veronica was taken totally by surprised but was pleasurably flushed nonetheless from his reference to her. She shook hands with Aunt Maddy.

"Well. So it's true," she said rather brazenly. "You O'Neil men do love you some white women. You are more like you father than you could ever imagine."

"Okay then, Aunt Maddy," said James slightly flummoxed. "Good seeing you again."

"Pay her no attention," said Cornelius, who had followed the entire exchange nearby with absorbing interest. "She's just still upset with me for standing her up years ago. And now has an issue with mixed couples."

"I went halfway around the world, only to be left sitting in a pub, or whatever you Brits call it, all night long with no word from you, Cornelius," she said, his name forced from her mouth with contempt. "And how dare you presume what makes me tick."

"Madeline, come now," said Cornelius most gentleman like. "That was many years ago. Surely you have forgiven me by now."

CHAPTER THIRTY

"Don't act like you cared, Cornelius. And don't talk to me in that skilled lawyer's tone of yours. I am not bamboozled anymore by your smooth words and that hypnotic accent of yours. You and that brother of mine were always up to something. You loved him more than you loved me. Remember, I know how you got that scar across your cheek. Still carrying his secrets, aren't you? I thought so," she added after no retort from Cornelius.

She stormed away into the throng, her large girth easily clearing her path..

"What the hell was that all about," said James half bemused, half laughing.

"You were right about her, Jamie," said Veronica with a stunned look on her face.

"She is a piece of work," said Cornelius, shaking his head as if clearing it.

But, Aunt Maddy knew more than what most people in the family did. James had not realized the validity of this general consensus until now. And it would seem that Cornelius was also privy to certain information that his Aunt Maddy had. Now was the time to ask.

"You know," began James, "he told me in a letter before he died that I was adopted. Did you know anything about it?"

"I know were this is going, my dear boy. So I will pose you this. He was a good father, was he not?"

"Yes, he was."

"The only father you had ever known, correct?"

"Yes, but —"

"Then leave it at that. Why besmirch the memory of him?"

And he looked into James' eyes, and James understood that Cornelius' must be filled with more pain than James himself realized.

"Your father was your father, and that's all you need to know."

"And a good man he was, just like his brother Octavius," said Aunt Olivia, approaching from behind James and Veronica. "I do so miss Otty."

"By your leave," said Cornelius bowing his head slightly, "Veronica, pleasure to have met you."

And he left the three of them there commenting delightfully on his good manners and diction.

"I miss uncle Otty too," said James.

"Jamie," Aunt Olivia said a little hesitantly, "I'm sorry about what happened with Stephen. You know since his father died, it has been one thing after the next with him. And then his brother Max was killed, and then Paul left to get away from... Well I don't know why he prefers Europe to the United States. I'm doing it again, making excuses for Stephen."

"It's okay Aunt Olivia. I have also made excuses for Bl—— Stephen myself. It's out of love and our image of what we expect him to be. Don't beat yourself up too much. You are a mother who loves her child. It's harder for you than it is for the rest of us."

"Thank you for saying that, Jamie. He always looked up to you. You were his best friend. The only one he could count on to be there for him."

CHAPTER THIRTY

And James felt a stab of guilt. On the contrary, he had not been so understanding outside the building. He was angry and wanted to hurt Blacky and did not care how he did it.

"Excuse me, Jamie," she said in a whisper, "I have to go. I see that annoying cop coming this way to harass me again."

"She such a sad woman, Jamie," said Veronica, following with her eyes Aunt Olivia's progress to the other side of the room.

"Yeah," said James, "bad news."

"Excuse me?"

"Here comes bad news. It's that cop Matlock. Why is he here?"

"Ah, Mr. O'Neil, my condolences. And Mrs. Sergei."

"That's Thealcey, Detective Matlock," said Veronica rather harshly.

"Forgive my impertinence. I meant nothing by ——"

"Why the hell are you here, Matlock?" snapped James loudly.

And the entire room became silent. All eyes were on them, Veronica a little embarrassed, but James was livid and had no patients for Matlock. James was beginning to look as though he was out of control. And realizing his anger was more than likely a prelude to another scene, he lowered his voice.

"Get out."

"Detective Matlock," Capt. Mahony said, appearing out of a curious bunch of by-standers. "A word with you outside, if you please."

The pair of them left the hall, and the room soon returned to its previous solemn state of murmurs, as if James' outburst had never occurred.

The evening wore on, and many family members had adjourned to O'Neil Manor. The beautifully ornate urn that contained the remains of Alexander rested in the large circular foyer upon the white marble pillar. Elizabeth seemed more herself and far less doleful than she was at the memorial service. James figured this was owed to the fact that she now had his father back home, even though it mattered not that he was deceased. The gathering was wearing on him, and he suspected that Veronica may have long tired from discussing the many works of Alexander Frederick with his readers and family. James had observed that she and Cornelius had much to say to each other on the subject of Alexander's work. They appeared as if they could go on for days. He, however, stood there alone peering into his drink and watching the ice melt into what was now a pale and watery cranberry. And when he had his fill of the evening and felt as though he could go no longer without getting a breath of air, a soft voice spoke into his ear.

"Cornelius is a fascinating man, but if you don't mind, Jamie, I'd like to go home now."

Home, what a wonderful thing to hear Veronica say. They were really together now, and his parent's place never felt less like home than at this very moment. Home, where the pair of them were starting a new life.

"I like the sound of that, love. Get your coat, and I'll inform my mother that we're leaving."

"Jamie, have I told you ——"

"Told me lately that you love me? Your eye say it every time you look at me. Now let's get out of here."

After brief salutations with many of the invited party —— and a lengthy one explaining to his mother why he and Veronica would rather stay at his home and how very much he appreciate her invitation to stay overnight —— James and Veronica were off.

Hours later, after James and Veronica were settled at home, James found himself tense for no apparent reason other than the fact he found it hard to mourn as others did. And after a bit of soul searching, he realized that he was kicking himself for not contacting his father when he should have. It was guilt, and he knew it. Veronica noticed that James was a bit agitated at something and assured James.

"Your father never stopped loving you, Jamie, and I am sure that he knew the same of you."

"I should have ——"

"Yes, my love. But you did not know how short his time was."

"*Always appreciate what you have. It could be taken from you in the blink of an eye.* That's what he used to say. I just never thought ——"

"No one ever knows, love. As sure as death is, it's often hard to predict. But they live on in us. We keep them alive as long as we think of them."

"You're right. I think now I will give that message of his a listen to."

He walked over to the answering machine and started pushing buttons on it, scrolling through a list of names and numbers that appeared on a small LCD screen.

"I'm not a high-tech person, but I really like this machine because it holds a lot of info, and it's digital."

James located his father's message and pressed play.

"Hi son," came the crystal clear voice of Alexander from the answering machine.

"Hi dad," said James as if the both were actually conversing.

And Veronica's eye welled with tears.

"I was thinking about you and wondering how you were getting along."

"I'm doing good, dad, I found a beautiful woman, you'd love her. Her name is Veronica," he said as Veronica took his hand. "She's here with me."

"Hello Mr. O'Neil."

"And I wanted to know if you think I was a terrible father."

"No, dad. You were the best."

CHAPTER THIRTY

"I did my best not to become like my father, and it seems in some way I have. Give me ——"

"You were more than what a son could ask for —— Dad? You there? Dad?"

"Jamie, sweetie," said Veronica delicately, "Remember, this is a recording. It sounds as if he sat the phone down."

They could here Alexander in the back ground calling out Rowan's name and were horrified.

"That's the guy who killed my father."

"Oh my goodness, Jamie. It's recorded. Turn it off."

"No," he said resolutely. "I want to hear it."

There was the loud sound of a door being forced opened and a scuffling sound followed by a man pleading. But, it was not his father's voice. Then there was the sound of muffled gun shots. They listened closely and could hear Alexander ask the intruder his name and what was it he wanted. Veronica gasped when she heard the voice speaking to Alexander.

"Rowan must be the one that was shot. Who's voice is that," said James thinking out loud. "Did he say Blacky?"

"It's Uri's, Jamie. Oh my goodness. That's his voice. I'd know it anywhere."

There was another scuffle then something about Blacky and James having some property of Uri. James did not know if that something spoke of was one in the same. Then there was the sound of what James realized was Alexander being stabbed repeatedly then falling to the floor. His heart leapt with terror, pounding into his throat, and he could not speak.

"Remember to get his prints on the gun as well," said a faint voice."

James could here the men vacate the room, and envisioned his father dying alone, while he stood there helpless to do anything but listen.

"Jamie, sweetie, turn it off. Please... turn it off'

He reached a shaky finger for the button. And there was a fumbling sound as if the phone was dropped.

"Wait," he said.

"I love you, son," came the raspy voice of Alexander.

And James' world was rent in two. He felt as though something reached inside and snatched all that he believed was good in the world from him. It felt as though he had received that murderous blow from the knife, and the pain stabbed him in the chest. He fell to his knees and bellow in a loud agonizing roar. Veronica had never heard a man make such a sound. It was filled with immense sorrow, so much despair. She knelt down and threw her arms around him and held him as if holding a man together who was about to brake into a million pieces. She knew everyone had their limit, and James had finally reached his.

"Let it out, Jamie. I got you, baby. Just let it out."

And he collapsed uncontrollably into her embrace, weeping until he could weep no more.

31

Moments In The Sun

It was the following day of James' agonizing meltdown, and the disturbing news surrounding Alexander's death loomed over 427 Redgate Avenue. However, a good long cry and night's rest had made him much more amiable than he had been in days. It was liberating to have finally let go all the pent-up emotion and grieve properly. He also finally came to grips with what he had heard on the answering machine and called Capt. Mahony with the new found evidence, only to find himself leaving a very lengthy message on Mahony's answering service. James thought he would, later, make his way downtown and present the evidence in person. It was, however, presently around the time the postal carrier would deliver the mail. So he remained home in hopeful spirits.

Veronica had taken in the morning's newspaper, which finalized the departure of Alexander Frederick to the rest of the world who had not heard it on the local news for the past several days. She sat quietly reading in the room James used as a study. And as she did, she held the silver ornate necklace belonging to

James in one hand, her thumb tracing its carvings as though it was some meditative amulet. She paused for a moment, then thought perhaps she would give it a good cleaning, for its general appearance of neglect had shown in its tarnished features. Afterwards, she returned to her previous perusal of the newspaper. When she was done skimming through a small section on the front page, she threw the paper onto the desk, exposing a small section of the article of which she had been reading.

Mourners from near and far bid author farewell

With final praises from his family, friends, and a host of fans, Alexander Frederick O'Neil, the noted author and screenplay write, was mourned and life celebrated Monday at Graves Funeral Halls. His remains were transported from England and...

The paper was folded in half, and the rest of the article was cut off. The press' continuous coverage of Alexander's passing was beginning to wear on Veronica's patience and increase her desire for material that was far more sanguine. She therefore selected one of many books from James' shelf to entertained herself while James busied himself awaiting a visitor.

CHAPTER THIRTY-ONE

They were waiting for Mrs. Barinard to come straight away after caring for William, whose condition had miraculously progressed all for the better since being back in his home. It did James' heart good to think how very strong William appeared at the memorial service, and to have his mother fuss over him, was much to her credit his good health. Mrs. Barinard had given James a call earlier and told him that she possessed something very important his father wanted him to have. That was odd in itself. James was not aware that the pair of them ever kept in contact. It was that time in the hospital, however, that she avoided a direct question about her relationship with his father. But it was not the only reason James was hovering about the front door and stealing glances for a particular visitor through the peep hole. It was because of the postal carrier.

Waiting for the mail was a constant and reoccurring act that James had as of late added to his daily rituals. He had been eagerly anticipating some word from Paul, and he was sure it would come by mail post, if not by phone. The mailbox outside the door made a groaning metal sound and was immediately followed by a clanking that James recognized as the sound of the mailbox lid closing. He opened the front door and reached his hand outside, drawing from the box —— which was attached to the siding of the house beneath the porch light —— a single letter with many rather large postal stamps crowed in one corner of the envelope. And to his very happy surprise, it was from his cousin.

"Veronica!" he called out. "I have word from Paul."

She came walking out of the back, with a cleaning cloth rubbing James' ornate necklace, just in time to see James ripping open the letter, and the pair adjured to the bright lights of the kitchen excited with hungry eyes.

"Wonderful. Let's have a look," she said.

And he began to read.

My Dear Cousin;

Do accept my sincerest apologies for taking so long in responding to your query. And may I offer my condolences for the lost of Uncle Alex. He will always be remembered by not just family, but millions. Even some here in this part of the country have read his works. Presently, I'm in the rural part of the country where there are less cellular bars in more places, and I'm finding it difficult to locate a pay-phone or at least a phone that I might exercise a great deal of liberty. So writing you would be far more advantageous than trying to call you with what we have found. Please refer to the enclosed documentation. I'm sure that high-tech answering machine of yours wouldn't be able to hold what I have to tell you. Although much time has transpired, we were quite successful in our find. Mind you, we unearthed information only on your mother, nothing at all on your father. By the way, I was quite shocked to find that you were adopted into the family. I was therefore equally intrigued to discover the name of the woman, Marie Bar, that you had provided in your last message, led my sources to a woman who lived in London and was very much in contact with uncle Alex. What is even more interesting is that Marie Bar was the mother of two children, one British and the other African British. The latter would be you. Now here is where I believe societal prejudice rears its ugly head. The first story that we uncover was told to us by a Mrs. Thompson. She spoke of a woman who could not take care of her two children because she hadn't enough to cloth and feed them. So she decided to put one up for adoption, hoping that the child would be given to a good family. But we uncovered another story, that after careful consideration and authentication, we found it to be accurate. Marie Bar's very wealthy family did not approve of her having children out of wedlock, and to have two distinctive looking children was too much for her aristocratic family to handle. They therefore coerced Marie Bar into giving up one of her children, under the pretext that neither would ever inherit the family's fortune if she did not acquiesce. So to save face with the family, and to save one child's inheritance, gave in. This second story was conveyed to me by the now retired Helena Carter of Kent, London, who was at the time the assistant to the director of the BAAF, British Association for Adoption and Fostering.

Now here's the kicker. Marie Bar disappeared almost immediately after giving you up for adoption. It was as if she vanished into nothingness. That's where the trail got cold. Then recently a source working in the DVLA, Driver and Vehicle Licensing Agency, located Marie Bar's cold trail and found that she had been using a bogus name in an effort to protect her family from a scandal. The more we dug, the more tight-lipped people were. Mind you, now that she had given you up for adoption, she was free to use her family's name again. James, her name is Catalina Marie Barinard. She owns C.M.B. Royal House Publishing, the very same company that has been publishing your fathers books for years. And if that is not enough to choke on, she is the daughter of Lord William Barinard, and she has a son named William Barinard who presently resides in the U.S., remarkably in your hometown. If you can find him, your brother, you would undoubtedly have found your biological parents. How odd it is, cousin, that you have a brother that you've never met and in the same town in which you reside. Good luck finding him. And please inform me if and when you find him. Take care.

Sincerely,
Paul

"It's all documented here," said James. "And she's coming over today. Now how's that for timing?"

"Jamie, this letter says that William is your brother and Mrs. Barinard is your mother," she said with much excitement.

"Yeah I know. That's what I meant to say," he responded with equal enthusiasm. "All this time William and I have been best friends for —— well since we were kids. This is getting way too bizarre for me. I've known her all these years, and even till this day, she has kept it from me. And my father said in one of his letter, that I had no brother or sister. More lies. Damn-it."

He swore loudly, causing Veronica to drop the silver necklace.

"Sorry, sweetie."

The necklace had hit the wooden floor of the kitchen then bounced hard and lay there as if broken. Veronica's face colored up with embarrassment.

"Jamie, I am so sorry. I ——"

"What's this," he said, picking up the necklace. "It looks like a locket."

And sure enough, the top of the ornate locket had twisted on its hidden pin, exposing the inside edges of the bottom half.

"I take it you did not know it opened up like that?"

"I never suspected it could," said James holding it in his hand as if for the first time ever.

"Well then, open it, love."

His heart began to race as he rotated the top half of the locket with slightly trembling finger, fully exposing the bottom half, where a small photo of a beautiful young woman rest.

"Oh my goodness, Jamie. I think that's ——"

"Mrs. Barinard," he finished her sentence. "And here is the proof. Why would my father give me a picture of her encased in a locket, if he didn't want me to know someday that this was my mother? For that matter, why did he keep it all these years?"

CHAPTER THIRTY-ONE

"Perhaps," she began pensively, "it's the only thing she could have left you, Jamie. You know, some part of her, without drawing suspicion," she added weakly. "I don't know. It really doesn't explain why your father had it."

"We'll ask her when she gets here. Wait a second. Why hadn't I noticed this before, there is a C and a B that's crafted into the design so beautifully. Can you see it?"

"Yes," she said, taking it into her hand and giving it a thorough examination. "I never would have guessed it was a locket, Jamie. It's so thin and —"

"Fancy," finished James. "I'm sure it's hand crafted and one of a kind. No, that's not true," he added, the memory of another locket springing to the forefront of his mind. "She has one just like it hanging around her neck. I wonder what initial she has engraved in that one?"

There was a knock at the door, and the pair froze where they stood, just looking at one another absurdly. Another knock came from the front and Veronica raised one eye brow at James.

"Okay. I'll get that."

After a fashion, he made his way to the door, tidying up as he went.

"Hello, come in, Mrs. Barinard. You know Veronica, the love of my life."

"Good evening," said Veronica.

"Good evening to the both of you. How have you been?" said Mrs. Barinard, carrying a rather large manila envelope package in her hand.

"We're good," said the both of them.

"Something to drink?"

"No thank you, Veronica my dear. I am come only for a mo——"

"Mrs. Barinard," James interrupted as delicately as he could. "I know that you and my father are more than an acquaintance, more than just his publisher."

"That's what I want to talk with you about," she said. "This is your father's journal. He sent it to me before he died and wanted me to give it to you."

She handed him the package.

"Is that all?" said James, expecting for a brief moment some great confession on her part.

"Yes, that's all he wanted me to give you."

"Then I need to show you something. You see this locket?" he said, taking it from Veronica and holding it at Mrs. Barinard's eye level.

Her eyes widen in disbelief. But James continued before she asked from where he had acquired the locket.

"It looks like just another pointless fancy emblem on it, but if you take a closer look at it, there are two ornate markings I've until now realized. There is a C and a B, but we will get to that a little later. You see, Veronica dropped this today and it slid open, but not like any other locket. It rotates like this at the top. And guess what I found? A picture of you."

CHAPTER THIRTY-ONE

Her eyes widen even more in disbelief, and James thought he saw her searching for an answer to why there was a picture of her in his locket. So to explain his point further, he continued.

"I got this locket from my father many years ago. Now why would my father have a picture of you in this locket, Mrs. Barinard? Or should I call you Marie Bar? Yes, I know your alias because my cousin Paul did some research and found that you are from a very prominent English family. It took him a while to make the connection, but he found that you had two babies, one black the other white. And according to my mother, Marie Bar is the woman who I was adopted from. In addition, he also states in this letter why you put me up for adoption."

He held the letter up eye level with a snapping force.

"You were embarrassed enough with one child out of wedlock but to have two and the other being black, was too much for you. What would people say? It ruin what ever chances that you could of had in getting back in the good graces of your rich family."

"Your cousin has got it all wrong, James," she said politely.

"Does he?" James said, and his voice was not as polite as Mrs. Barinard. "Sound pretty straightforward to me. And what of William, were you going to ever tell him we are brothers? This CB stands for Catalina Barinard. Doesn't it? You were that mutual friend, that Cornelius Robertson was talking about at my father's funeral. I saw the look on your face when he mentioned it. You are my real mother, aren't you?"

"No, my dear. The letters stand for Catherine Barinard. And no, I'm not your mother. That's a picture of my sister Catherine. She died giving birth to you. My sister's husband, Arthur Frey, would not claim you after you were born because you were clearly not his child. So my family, with their money and influential connections, covered up the circumstances surrounding your birth and my sister's death to avoid a scandal. They wanted me to leave you there at St. Agnes, but you were so beautiful that I could not help but take you in my care."

James did not expect this explanation, but he quickly absorbed what was said and fired back.

"If Arthur Frey is not my father, then who is?"

Her voice was quivering now while she tried to speak. She seemed to be holding back years of suppressed emotions.

"Please Mrs. —— Aunt Catalina," he said, placing a steady hand on her trembling folded arms. "Take your time."

"Let me try to make some sense of it all. Earlier that horrid night —— the night that your mother died —— she had been arguing with Arthur, telling him their marriage was over, and she was going to leave him because he was rarely present as a husband and would make an awful father. She omitted the fact that the baby she was carrying wasn't his; so he refused to let her go. He told her that she was going nowhere, and it was till death they would part. She conveyed all of this to me over the phone after he had left to take care of some unfinished business at the office. Catherine was so upset that she went into labor. She was all in a tiff, screaming about blood, and I had to do something. So

I called your father to go there and wait with her for the ambulance. He arrived there within minutes, and when I was satisfied that she was in good hands, I headed to St. Agnes where I was sure she would be taken."

"But my father, what of him?"

"I'm getting to it. Now, as I already said, you were born that night. I met your father there in the waiting room, worried, only to inform him the terrible news of my sister's death. Because he could not at the moment, I took you in my care, along with my son William, whom I gave birth to earlier that year. Then one night, shortly after you were born, Arthur came by my flat in a towering temper and with murder in his eyes. He found out the man who Catherine had a baby by was there, your father. But when he arrived, your father and his best mate Cornelius Robertson were there. Cornelius tried his best to keep the two apart and tried to defuse an already tense situation. But Arthur was determine to get his hands on your father. One thing led to another, and Cornelius was slashed across the face with a knife. Your father, fearing for our safety I'm sure, managed to put Arthur in a choke hold. Arthur was struggling, but your father was powerfully built and very angry. He snapped his neck as if it were a small branch, killing Arthur."

"And Arthur Frey?" said Veronica, now positively absorbed in the narrative. "I remember hearing on the news a while back that he disappeared."

"Yes. We covered it up."

"You what," said James astounded.

Veronica's hands flew to her mouth, cupping it; her eyes enlarged. She seemed to know what Mrs. Barinard was going to say.

"They, your father and Cornelius disposed of the body. No one ever found it."

"Then who is my real father?"

"Your father is your father. Don't you get it?" said Mrs. Barinard.

Veronica's jaw dropped behind her hands. It was obvious that she undoubtedly comprehend more than what James had considered. James stood there bemused and slightly irritated that Veronica was quick on the uptake.

"James," began Mrs. Barinard, "your father, Alexander, was very much in love with my sister, and she was going to leave Arthur and run away with him. It drove the pair of them mad to be apart. He was so tender with her, and she glowed every minute they were together. But my dear sister, your mother, is gone now. Forever."

Mrs. Barinard was sobbing now. She reached into a small purse that was dangling on her wrist and removed a handkerchief, then dabbed her tears. She pause to collect herself, then continued.

"That's when we, Alexander and I, came up with the story and idea for him to adopt you. But he told me to keep my identity a secret so the kids can grow up together knowing one another. Shortly after your adoption, I changed my name back to make sure that no one made the connection and to protect the Barinard family name."

"My dad really was my dad," said James a bit teary eyed. "And you're my aunt."

"Yes, and you look very like your father, is what they all say. And true. I am surprised that Elizabeth has not suspect this."

"I am sure she has," said James. "She seemed to have no problem with my dad calling her to give me the message that something had happen to William and without even questioning how he came about the information. And I am sure you gave that information to him. If I figured that much out, I'm sure she must have and also about my dad being my biological father."

"Yes, I told him of William's circumstance. I'm sure your mother suspects more than she has led us to believe."

"William told me long ago that his father had died, but you use the name surname Barinard. Why is that?"

"We never married, his father and I. My family disapprobation of my having a child by a, forgive me, commoner, wore on William's father. He could not stand the ill treatment from my family and was off, never to be heard of again until years later. I was told that he had died somewhere in the country side of poor health. But that's not important. I took the title *Mrs.*, so that William would always appear to have had a father. You see, at my age now, a single woman like myself would be called a spinster. And to have a child at the young age that I did, with no husband, well... It just looks better with the title *Mrs*. Now that you have the journal, do cherish it. It's comprised of words left by two people who loved you and loved each other very much. I must go now. William will be expecting me soon. We have an appointment with the lawyer and hope to have this shooting incident behind us once and for all. I will inform him of the nature of this visit. Everything. And I am sure he will be thrilled to know the pair of you are related, first cousins."

They walked her to the door, and she kissed Veronica on the cheek, then James.

"You two remind me so much of them. Love each other every moment life allows."

Her words lingered long after she had gone, and the pair witnessed the effects of her words reflected in each other's smiles.

"Open it," said Veronica.

He did, and there was a letter with the journal. He unfurled it and began to read.

Dear Son;

With ernest sincerity, I pray this letter finds you thriving in the best of health. Your happiness has always remained paramount in my life. I have lived to experience the disillusionment of my hopes and aspirations, and when all had become bleak, fortune allowed me to see my aspirations resurrected, blossomed from winter's bed in the brilliant form of you. The opinions of busybodies would refer to you as an illegitimate expression of fracture fidelity. This mattered not. I would do all in my power to protect you from vicious and nefarious tongues. Any slight on our ray of sunshine, however, caused our joy to diminish not, nor did it begin to besmirch the incomprehensible love we felt for you, my son, our last and most blissful moment in the sun. Find yours. Love and live with all your heart. Moments in the Sun belong(s) to you.

Love,
Dad

"Are you okay, Jamie," asked Veronica, the both of them finishing the letter at the same time. "He had quite a way with words."

"Yes, I'm fine. And he did have a way with words."

The journal had the same ornate art of the locket. Veronica ran her hand across its grooves with trembling fingers.

"This is the book," she said with nervous excitement. "The one that no one has ever seen. "Moments In The Sun," she read the engraved title then opened it and began examining its contents.

"See how the hand writing changes here. Your father didn't write in two different styles. He wrote in one, and the other was from your mother. These are love letters or poems, if you will, which they wrote to each other. That is what Mrs. —— your aunt was saying," she added and began to read aloud what she guessed to be Alexander's hand writing.

Moments In The Sun

How now do I impart moments of joy, moments of pain? Endless moments I count between your kisses; and forget them I ofttimes pray, in forgetting them, forget you. I am not myself today; the clever whip that quips, masked behind winks and smiles, tires from pretense. I do feign to not love you as much as I do, reluctant that I may disquiet you. I fear my heart's true nature rests upon the tip of my tongue. Dare I speak it? And if I comport myself in all ernest, I fear also you'll never know the depth of my love that words fail.

I see in your eyes, the longing to throw yourself into my arms. I hear bridled words unspoken behind the gentle gestures and sweet accord of your silent lips. You are most beautiful when conflicted so, and I can't help but desire to take you in my arms and promise

that we can make a future of this. Yet still you hold back, and I dare not reach.
I die a little.

I am now tired, deflated and defeated, vision blurred and falling into a million pieces (that need you). It pains to do this. There are not enough tears to cleans, not even for a moment. Perhaps I am not yet skilled enough to let you go. Perhaps it is more fear than skill. I am a winged creature afraid of falling, afraid of flying. I fear it is you who have given me wings.

Although I long for it, today I cannot listen to your voice. It is too sweet a thing and fills the canyon of my longing. It is my opiate, and suffer I do from incomprehensible withdraws of you. If your need is as great as mine for you this moment, forgive me, my love. I do not mean to torture you. I thought I could love you in small portions.

Lock this in a box from me; take it away. Never tell me where you have hidden it, even if your heart inclines you so.
I die a little

You have written yourself into my heart, and now I must write you out.
Today I write in blood.

There is no light inside (me) when you are gone
'cause I am filled with emptiness
and ache from the loneliness
that echoes memories of you
have mercy and free me from this addiction
you
let me go my love
end this torment
end my pain.

I find moments in the sun
you
heavy in my hand
fingers curling rays
spilling over me.
I want to grow inside of you.

They looked into each other's eyes and together understood that there will be plenty of time later to read. James took it from her hands then placed it onto the kitchen's pass-through. And they headed towards the bedroom. Their ips locked together ardently, only to be interrupted by another knock at the door.

CHAPTER THIRTY-ONE

"Who is it now," Veronica said with disappointment in her voice, her kissing lips barely forming the muffled words. "Go see who it is and send them away so we can... you know," she added with a flirtatious raise of the eyebrow.

James waste no time in answering the knock. This time when he opened the door, it was Red and Sophie standing there, beaming.

"Spooner!" yelled Sophie with excitement, and she launched herself into him, bestowing the tightest hug her little arms could give.

"I hope we are not interrupting," said Red. "We were just passing by, and Sophie wanted to say hello."

"Well," began James, wishing he had checked the peep hole before answering the door. "Now that you mentioned it —"

"No, not at all," said Veronica, cutting across James when he failed to affect a warm welcome. "Do come in."

"Well..." amended James, "You know how I love it when people pop in. Wonderful," he added, shooting a furtive glance at Veronica and rolling his eyes in exasperation.

His facial expression was missed by Red and Sophie. All James could think of were ways to rid himself of the intruders. They all chatted while adjourning to the living room, James mind still at work on how to delicately eject Red and Sophie. Then there was a third knock at the door.

"Good gracious," said James a little too irritably. "Who is it now?"

He dashed to the door, and without checking through the peep hole again, swung the door open. And to his enormous trepidation, he swore.

32

Out of Favor

Far away in a dark warehouse, located somewhere in the forgotten part of the city, Blacky stepped into the dimly lit space of a great room and stood there silently. He was impatient and did not like to be kept waiting, particularly when his quorum was aware of him being a stickler for punctuality. Blacky thought wryly, what is it about warehouses and criminals? It seems they go together like a B movie and zombies. Blacky began to feel disconcerted. Something was not quite right. He had never met with Uri Sergei in such a secluded place that was closed off to the outside. There had always been a large enough area, such as the pier, to give early warning if police were about to intervene. He inwardly cursed himself for not realizing it sooner. It was a set-up.

"Careful now," came a voice from behind him. "You wouldn't want to go whipping that gun out, would you? So put your hands where... Yes, you know the routine."

"Where is Sergei?" asked Blacky calmly, his hands held in capitulation.

Another man stepped into the light with a pistol in hand, and removed the one from Blacky's holster beneath his arm pit.

"I'll be needing that back when I'm done here," said Blacky

The two men laughed.

"It's true, you got a pair of big ones on you, boy," said the first man poking Blacky in the back with a gun. "We're going to take you to him after we are done here. I take it you don't have the list on you. Right?"

Blacky said nothing to this

"Sergei thought so," said the other man standing before him. "So he has taken out some insurance."

Blacky realized the only place Uri Sergei could be was James' home. The night at the pier had sealed James' and Veronica's fate. Revenge was not the only thing Uri wanted, but the list just might make it a two for one. Sure Uri did not know that the list was hidden in James' car, but he did not need to know that. He would undoubtedly use his family as leverage. There was no time for small talk. He had to act now.

"Didn't your mother ever tell you not to..." began Blacky.

And he spun around back, slipping past the arm of the goon and grabbed him around the neck in a choke-hold. Blacky forcibly secured the man's weaponed hand but was unable to remove the gun. The man in front fired into the chest of his comrade, with whom Blacky used as a shield, and they both were thrown backward.

"...play with guns," finished Blacky, squeezing the fingers of his struggler and firing two shots into the head of the second man.

CHAPTER THIRTY-TWO

The man whom Blacky had seized by the neck was strong. Although shot by his comrade, he was still putting up an enormous fight. Blacky tightened his grip around his neck and hand, and another shot rang out. The man struggle less until he slumped forward, releasing the gun into Blacky's hand and falling to the concrete floor with a thud.

"Thank you," said Blacky, now bending down and prying his own gun from the other man's lifeless grip.

He took off in a mad dash, afraid for the first time in years. He thought, what would he do if he lost his family? He mustn't. He must get there at all cost and handle the situation himself. To call the police would be a sure way of killing them. He could not have them bungle a hostage crisis. There is only one person he could ask for help.

"There is something strange about you, Blacky," said Smoke, ten minutes later in another nearby warehouse. "Something that I can't rightly put my finger on. You come back here asking for help. Well, not exactly. Let me get this right. You want me to help you tool-up so you can go commando on someone that has offended you. And you come to me because you feel I own you, right?"

"That about says it all," said Blacky nonchalantly.

"Ah," began Smoke pensively. "There he is again. That cool calculative Blacky I know from prison. "Tell me Blacky, how was it that you were able to endure solitary confinement twice the amount of times other inmates and came out remarkably rejuvenated? Don't answer the question," he add, pausing. "Better yet, are you five-o, Blacky?"

"What the fuck, Smoke! We are wasting time here," bellowed Blacky, then immediately mastered himself. "No, I'm not the police. What I am is a man who had your back in prison, you and Rock there," he indicated with a head gesture, "you remember how I stop that inmate from shanking you in the yard. Come on man, this is the last thing I'll ask of you and Rock. I got to protect my family."

"I say friendship in this case is not enough, even if you did save my life. I need to know what's going on."

"Uri Sergei reneged on our deal," said Blacky. "He wants it all for himself. And I'm sure he means to do harm to my family."

"See now," said Smoke. "Don't you feel better getting all that out in the open. Still, I can't help but feel like you are holding something back, Blacky. But I'm going to help you anyway. After this, Blacky, stay away. You're too hot."

"Indeed."

Smoke turned to Rock and said, "Take him out back and let him tool-up. Make sure he takes a vest with him. You're fast," he added, addressing Blacky. "But you can't dodge bullets. Make sure he leaves out the back. Damn place getting to be a regular Grand Central."

And when Blacky had left the room, Smoke looked at the rest of his men, shifting his eyes back and forth in deep thought.

"Pack it all up. Our boy's five-o."

33

Paid in Full

Hello Mr. O'Neil," said Uri politely, his ill-disguised malevolence dripping with every syllable spoken. "I'm looking for my wife. You know, very beautiful, dark hair, shapely, about so high," he indicated Veronica's hight with a leveled hand. "You wouldn't happen to know where she is, would you?"

James knew the question was rhetorical and simply gave him and his four goons a once over, assessing his ability to overcome them if needed. And coming to the conclusion that he was out muscled and out numbered, he proceeded to slam the door but was thwarted by the strong arm of one of Uri's cronies blocking his attempt.

"Aren't you going to let me in?" said Uri with a sinister grin. "You wouldn't want to give the wrong impression of being inhospitable."

James attempted to slam the door once more with the force of his entire body; however, a big boot of Uri's crony was wedge between the door and frame now, and he was exposing his gun from beneath his blazer, silently threatening him. But when James did not acquiesce to his silent demand. Uri coldly pull out a pistol and pointed it at James' groin.

"Don't even think about warning them."

"Come in," said James nervously staring at the gun, and his anger began to rise in his chest.

James remembered his father's phone message, how he listened helplessly to how Uri invaded his father serene world and now it was happening all over again. He remembered his father's last words, and the monster within his chest became furious. He caught sight of his Louisville Slugger and thought now is the time. He would take as many ——

"Don't," warned Uri with a prod of his pistol against James' spine.

Uri shoved James a few steps then stowed his weapon, and his cronies bulldozed their way into the foyer with their weapons presently drawn, fanning out into the rest of the house. One now held a gun to James' head at arm distance, prodding him with it, marshaling him into the living room. And at the site of this, Veronica and Red's jovial expressions tuned to that of sheer horror.

"Uri," cried Veronica stunned, her voice trembling with fear. "What are ——?"

"Silence them," he said impassively.

And two of his four cronies grabbed the struggling women each in turn, forcing them to the floor and taping their hands together and mouths shut.

CHAPTER THIRTY-THREE

James saw that Red was absolutely terrified for Sophie, who was off in the rear of the house exploring. What if she came into the room unexpectedly and was killed? Her absence went unnoticed by the intruders. James stood there praying that Sophie was far too occupied with some book or at play to be interested in the going-ons of adult affairs. Or maybe she was somewhere in the house hiding. And though the thought of Sophie's safety was not troubling enough, she came skipping into the room nonchalantly, as though all was right with the world, and she cast around.

"Five men, four guns." she said sing-song like and turned, skipping away back into the part of the house from which she emerged.

The gunmen stood there utterly bemuse by her lack of fear and were slightly amused by her audacity.

"What the hell you're waiting for," said Uri in disbelief, gesturing animatedly with both hands in the direction of her exit. "Go get her."

One of his men galumphed out the room after Sophie, which then prompted Red to began hysterically screaming muffled and inaudible words into the gag around her bound mouth. James, who remained still with another warning prod of the gunman's weapon to the back of his head, thought she was trying to say something that may had been, *"Run Sophie... Run baby, run!"*

But she was savagely smacked across the face by a nearby goon and fell silent. She whimpered slightly but maintained her composure best she could.

There was a high pitch shrill of a scream in the next room, and the very large gunman brought Sophie back into the living room kicking and writhing. Red, although bound, jumped up and threw herself at the gunman but was stuck in the face again by the same gunman. She was then brutally dragged over to the other side of the room by her hair. The gunman holding Sophie, threw her across the room, landing her onto the couch, and she bounce off, twisting and landed onto her feet with acrobatic ease next to her mother. And with her hands presently bound, Red lassoed her into a tight overhand embrace.

"Brat was trying to make a phone call," said the gunman.

"Oh you are a clever little girl aren't you?" said Uri. "And impressively acrobatic. Too bad you won't live long enough to join the circus."

"My daddy is coming," Sophie said calmly, looking up into the face of Uri. "And he's going to kick your ——"

"Sophie," snapped Red through the gag, fearing for her. "Shhh!" was all she could muster intelligibly.

She pulled Sophie's admonitory finger, which was pointing at Uri, down to her side and held Sophie tightly, shushing her softly in a hopeful bid for no further outburst.

"Ooo," Uri said in a mocked ghostly voice. "I'm shaking in my shoes. This child has more guts than the rest of you. Come to think of it Mr. Spooner, she looks a lot like you. Why is that?"

CHAPTER THIRTY-THREE

"Not the first time I heard that," said James with his arms still held in capitulation, the barrel of the gunman's pistol still at his head.

"Mr. Spooner, it's not enough that you are sleeping with my wife —— and by the way Veronica, your hair looks lovely down like that —— but you have another woman and a child as well. What kind of sick, twisted and perverted situation is this?" he said with more curiosity than disdain. "I must say, I'm intrigued by your lack of moral conviction. But I must inform you, if you had plan on marrying her, she will not take your name. You're better off with the other one," he indicated with a nod in Red's direction. "Is this what you have been holding out on me for Veronica Thealcey?" he redirected. "All those months of sleeping alone. So this is the reason, a ménage à trois. I should have finished him off when Blacky didn't. Did you think I wouldn't know. I've known long before the night you called Frank Nefer."

At the mention of this, James had an idea that Frank Nefer, who supposedly dinged his car that day in the Barnes and Nobel parking lot, had been keeping tabs on Veronica. Perhaps even viewed the pair of them through the large windows of the building.

"Yes my dear Veronica," Uri continued uninterrupted by James' thread of thought. "He works for me and so does Detective Matlock, who has been very helpful in keeping track of Blacky, and what a treat it was to find out that your beau here is related to Blacky. It's a small world after all, my dear sweet Jezebel."

Then his voice turned venomous.

"And when I'm finished with you, you'd wish the world was much larger and that I had killed you with the others. Oh, don't look so surprise. Yes you'll all die here as soon as I get my property. Speaking of meeting one's end, Mr. Frederick was —"

James lurched forward at the sound of his father's name and was struck with a smarting blow in the back of the head.

"Move again," said Uri. "and you'll be the first."

James stood motionless to keep from being struck again or worst. He could not take another blow to the head. It was getting in the way of his thought process, and he was desperately searching his brain for a solution to how he was going to get them out of this unfortunate situation. Perhaps it was the recent traumatic events he had endured that desensitized him, bestowing upon him a surprising acuteness of clarity and steadied his nerves. He was astonished to see that his heart beat was not in the very least elevated. This must be how it feels to exist in Black's world for too long, calm in the face of danger and embracing it.

"Like I was saying," continued Uri. "Mr. Frederick — by the way, I thoroughly enjoyed that internet scandal — was a surprisingly brave man. Would you like to know how he died? He did not scream as most men I have killed. He fought pretty hard until he met the tip of my knife. I like to get close up and watch the light in the eyes extinguish," he added with a deep relishing groan. "The last breath he uttered was *Jamie*."

James thought sickly of Uri's delight in his father's death. Uri's head was tilted upward in exquisite recollection, then he turned his face to James.

CHAPTER THIRTY-THREE

"You piece of sh——"

James received another incredibly excruciating blow to the back of the head, and his knees buckled. His hot-headedness was again hindering his ability to figure a way out of their present circumstance. And with a tremendous effort to remain standing, he reach deep inside himself and summoned the strength. He thought of Veronica, Red and Sophie, how helpless they were and how dear they were to him. He must not fail them.

"You know why I killed your father," he said, his breath drawing closer into James' ear. "Because he was the farthest away from your family, proving to Blacky that no matter who or where, I can get to them. Now," he added, his demeanor changing, his face now contorted with contained rage, "where is the list?"

"The what?" said James at a lost, still shaking off the affects of the last blow.

"The list, the list," he snapped. "I've been waiting for that list for too long now. It contains the addresses of people who possess some of the most luxurious cars on the market. I have the keys. But as a business man who keeps his word always with his clients, I'll be needing the cars yesterday. And something tells me that Blacky has given it to you for safe keeping. That little stunt he pulled that night at the pier didn't fool me in the least. No matter, when he's brought here, one of you will surrender it to me."

"I have no idea what you are talking ——"

James' voice tailed away, his eyes became transfixed forward. He had been struck surprisingly with the overwhelming possibility, that this mysterious list was in his possession. He remembered searching frantically for his mobile in the glove compartment the night of his arrest and came across an envelop that boldly read on the outside, *the list*. How oddly fortunate was this. James thought Blacky must have placed it there the day the pair went to restaurant Siam for a bite to eat. The more comprehension dawned, the more James' eyes began to widen,.

"That's it, Mr. Spooner. Coming back to you now, is it?"

"No," said James with perfect indifference. "Still don't know what you are talking about."

"Don't be coy with me pretty-boy. Perhaps this will loosen your tongue."

And Uri began to reach into his blazer, only to be forestalled by the slow draw of a deep and familiar voice.

"I have it," came Blacky's voice from the back room; his gun in hand preceded him as he slowly stepped out, pointing it at Uri. "But do you think killing my uncle would somehow impress me or make me more incline to acquiesce? No. You thought I'd be so stricken with fear that I would give you what you want. Wrong on all accounts. So," he added with a deadpan stare. "I am going to tell you only once, and I pray for your sake you comply. Let Spooner and the ladies go, and I'll consider not putting a couple of hot ones in you."

James saw that Blacky's finger was ready at the trigger.

"Now," James said with a grin of immense pride creasing his face, "that's the Blacky I know."

CHAPTER THIRTY-THREE

"Shut it," said the man holding the gun to James' head and arm-roping him now around the neck in an effort to keep most himself out of Blacky's deadly cross-hairs.

"It's going to be alright Rose," said Blacky addressing Red.

James looked perplexed. "*Rose*?"

"You plan on saving him and the girls?" said Uri, laughing sinisterly with an expression that made him look quite mad. "You're only one man against, oh let's see," he cast around mockingly, "four of mine. How about this," he added, his face now drained of all emotion and voice icy. "You put your gun down and surrender the list, and I will consider not killing this lot," he gestured with an airy wave of the hand to Veronica, Red and Sophie.

"I have a better idea," began Blacky. "Seeing as how the ladies are unable to vote at the moment, it now rests on how Spooner feels. It's not up to me. So Spooner," he redirected, "I never..."

"Never ever, Blacky?" said James.

"Never."

"Light his ass up," he said as the room darkened.

A shot rang out no sooner than James' eyes were closed, and he thought he heard a fleeting sound or felt something passing very near his ear. He then felt the tightened grip of Uri's man releasing him. He opened his eyes just in time to see Blacky train his weapon on another gunman, firing while simultaneously reaching with lightening speed behind his back and pulling out a second weapon, tossing it to James. He caught it and heard a third man fall to the floor from Blacky's prodigious skill. James spun right to fire upon the forth, who had however promptly snatched up Sophie from Red's arms and was using her as a reluctant shield. She squirmed, struggled, kicked, and flailed in his arms.

"Let me go! Let me go!"

"Spooner no!" shouted Blacky.

And James swung around automatically, turning his attention to Uri and pointing the gun with deadly intent. His fingers tightened around the trigger.

"I want to kill you so bad, my d——"

"Easy, playah. I know he killed uncle Alex, and I'm sorry. But as you can see he's unarmed," said Blacky slightly surprised by what would had been a colorful choice of words, yet all the same proud of James.

"Oh, believe me, he's armed," said James.

Blacky's eyes were still glued to the man holding a struggling Sophie.

"Then if he even blinks... feel free. Now," he addressed the man holding Sophie. "Get your hands off my child, or..." and Blacky cocked his gun with deliberate intent.

James' eyes lit with understanding, and it all began to make since: *My daddy is coming* Sophie had said; the seven years Blacky and Red both were gone; his referring to her fondly as Rose; the reason why she would not tell him about Sophie's father; the shadows he saw cast upon the curtains the night he visited his mother and Red, and the look of expecting someone other than

James that night — they had had a lover's quarrel; Red's eagerness to defend Blacky's behavior, the daredevilries of Sophie and her incredibly strong family resemblance, all of which presently made perfect sense. He thought, why hadn't he put the pieces together by now. Red... Sophie... His train of thought was interrupted.

"Bravo Mr. Blacky," said Uri unconcernedly, his men at his feet and his arms low in front of himself with his fingers interlocked. "You *are* every bit of the man your reputation claims. However, I didn't know you were a family man. Didn't see that one coming."

"Umm," moaned Veronica into her gagged mouth.

"It's going to be alright, Veronica," said James softly.

"It's too late for that Veronica," said Uri reading her anguished look. "What? Did you think I would stop all this and let you come home to me? Do you think I would want you after you have been with this —"

"Careful Uri," interjected Blacky sharply, "If Spooner doesn't kill you for what you're about to say, I promise I will have no problem blowing your damn head off."

"He's not a killer," said Uri. "I know when I see a killer. His father, now there was a man who had blood on his hands. I can see in your eyes that you are nothing like him."

"Oh do try me," said James.

Then Blacky shook his head almost imperceptibly at Sophie, and she stop writhing.

"I told you," (Bang!) came Blacky discharging his weapon. "Get your hands of my child."

It had happened in the blink of an eye, and the man fell suddenly to the floor releasing Sophie. She popped up from the floor like a jack-in-the-box and ran into her father's open arms. Outside, Willoughby was barking again, and Veronica and Red were still seated in their places, screaming frantically behind their gags.

"It's okay. It's okay," said Blacky releasing Sophie and cutting Veronica's and Red's bonds with a small knife he pulled out of his boot.

But they were still hysterical, Veronica more than Red. James was distracted long enough for Uri to remove his pistol from his blazer. James saw the look in Veronica's eyes and turned his attention once again to an armed Uri and pulled the trigger. Nothing happened. The gun did not fire. Blacky caught sight of Uri from the corner of his eye and realized he could not get a shot off fast enough. He, therefore, pulled Sophie out of the line of fire to protect her with one great embrace, turning his back to Uri. Uri with murder in his eyes, now squeezed the trigger. He shot Blacky in the back once, twice, and then a third time. Blacky toppled and slumped lifelessly over Sophie. Veronica and Red were screaming much louder. And outside, Willoughby barks became even more ferocious.

"Mr. Spooner," began Uri with his gun presently pointed at James. "Next time you threaten to kill someone, make sure you take the safety off."

CHAPTER THIRTY-THREE

Bang! A shot rang out and Veronica and Red shrilled even louder in terror. James jerked his entire body in reflex, but there was no pain. He was still standing.

Then Uri coughed up a massive amount of blood, dropped his weapon, and sputtered, "Ver—— Ver——"

He fell to his knees, revealing a massive Rock standing in the foyer with gun in hand.

"Rock?" said James shaken and surprised yet a thousand times thankful to see him.

Mr. Berchmier entered the room suddenly and unexpectedly from the back. He had a snub nose pistol in hand pointing it at Rock. In that fleeting moment, James thought he must have apparently heard the gun fire and came to aid. He was wearing pink fluffy slippers and a matching chiffon nightgown with feathers along the edges. It was James' guest that it must have been the first thing he grabbed and undoubtedly was wearing Mrs. Hawthorne's tight gown. It was barely draped over his white t-shirt, white socks with ankle gun holster, and white boxers emblazoned with BIG PAPA on the front. And at present, this odd gender bending attire caught them all off guard. James was thankful for this; it appeared to have kept Rock from shooting him on sight.

"No, no more shooting!" said James with his arms held up. "It's okay, we're all on the same side."

They lowered their weapons, and James cast Mr. Berchmier a raised eyebrow before turning in Rock's direction.

"Tell Blacky," began Rock, "*Smoke says, debt paid in full.*"

And he promptly vacated the house, leaving a puzzled yet gratified James turning on his heels again and heading towards Veronica. Red rushed over to Blacky screaming his name, pulling him off a struggling Sophie and cradling him in her arms.

"Daddy," said Sophie gasping breathlessly. "Daddy please... please get...," she began to sob. "Get up daddy."

Veronica was in shock of what had just transpired. She painfully remember how it felt to hold James bleeding in her arms. She thankfully turned towards him, and threw herself at him in a great embrace, kissing him hard. His strong arms gathered her tightly. Her ordeal was over, and she once again felt safe.

Mr. Berchmier knelt, pulled Blacky's cell phone out of his jacket and dialed a long number. It was not your typical 911 call. It was much more of an official call for help.

"What are you doing," said Red sobbing, her tear streaked cheek pressed against Blacky's bald head.

"They need to know," he said softly. Then with his voice more urgent he said into the phone, "I am a retired federal agent service number 2744722. I have with me a federal agent down. I repeat, federal agent down, code name Blacky."

34

One of the Good Guys

Several hours later and what seemed like a million inquiries posed by FBI agents, James found himself yet again answering the same tedious questions. He was just as confused about what was going on as Veronica, Elizabeth, Red, and Sophie were and had some questions of his own.

"And then Rock shot Uri," repeated Capt. Mahony, staring into James' eyes. "That's how it happened?"

"Yes Capt. Mahony, just like I said it did," breathed James after what seemed the umpteenth time explaining it to another person. "Now please, will you tell me what's going on with Blacky? And what has he to do with the police department and the FBI?"

Hours ago, Blacky had been rushed away by ambulance, leaving many unanswered questions as to his health and to his association with local and federal law enforcement. Veronica, Red, and Sophie were presently being cared for in the bedroom by Elizabeth, who had promptly arrived after receiving a call regarding the shooting. She appointed herself the buffer for those who would seize the opportunity of unnecessarily questioning the shaken women and child.

Mr. Berchmier, who after calling the authorities and immediately dashing back to Mrs. Hawthorne's home to change into his own gender specific clothes, was now in the living room conversing with three very official looking men in suits.

Mahony steered James towards the front door for a more private chat on the patio. On their way out, they past Mr. Berchmier, who was engaged in a lengthy account of what had happened from his perspective. James felt Berchmier seemed to enjoy the excitement by how exuberantly he was expressing himself. He obviously missed his days in the bureau.

"Then I said to Marry —— Mrs. Hawthorne, the kind woman who lives next door," he indicates with his finger, "that her scones were the best I had tasted in years. That's when I heard the gun shots and immediately engaged the situation."

Out on the patio, James imperceptibly chuckled to himself, thinking how Mr. Berchmier had obviously omitted a few kinks in the details.

"What I'm going to tell you" began Mahony, "is highly confidential. I'm sharing this with you, because I believe after all you have gone through, you are owe an explanation. Blacky is an FBI agent. He was working in conjunction with our department to put a stop to the rash of car thefts committed by a notorious criminal. And believe me, this spree has been going on in this area for quite some time. He was therefore sent here because of his familiarity with the streets. But I was unaware of Mr.

Berchmier's association with the FBI. I have just been told that he trained Blacky seven years ago at Quantico. I must admit, that one caught me off guard. Interesting."

He paused, then continued.

"Nonetheless, Blacky was assigned the task of helping bust up the car theft ring. So he spent time in prison undercover, getting close to dangerous criminals and gaining an unsavory reputation. The FBI would, from time to time, pull him out of prison for debriefing, under cover of placing him in solitary for assaulting a guard or any act which would warrant his isolation. To the FBI's. great fortune, they followed the ring to Rock and Smoke's stomping ground. As you know, Blacky has been associated with Rock and Smoke's gang. It was the perfect setup for us, you see. But your presence did little to help our investigation. Blacky was hiding in the trunk of your car the night you got arrested and insisted on me letting you out. He assured me he would make sure that you stayed out of trouble. Yes, that's right," he added to James' quizzical look that was beginning to dawn with astonished understanding. "Blacky was the one who sprung you and relayed to me as well, that one of my detectives was present when you were pulled over and also on the pier that night. Since I've been promoted, I've been cleaning up the corruption in my department, and I owe you a bit of thanks for inadvertently helping to flush out a dirty officer. I'm sure you know that I'm talking about Detective Matlock. He is now in custody. According to his our phone taps, Detective Matlock had been tailing Blacky and passing information onto Uri Sergei. This is how Uri Sergei found out all about you, but this you already know."

James nodded.

"Matlock was there the night at the docks, and that's when I became highly suspicious of him. I had given him strict orders to stay away from you and Blacky. It was when he did not engage after the shooting that I was absolutely certain he was on the take. Although Blacky was wired and was in constant communication with us and the FBI, Matlock should have showed up, particularly after you, a civilian, was in direr need of help. Nonetheless, it was not fatal and Uri Sergei got away."

"And at the funeral," said James, "he was there to see you. Blacky I mean."

"Correct. He could have chosen a better place. Somewhere no one would put two and two together, but he was insistent on meeting there. He wanted to pay his respects to your father. Again, my condolences."

"Thank you."

"But you guys got in a fight and drew too much attention to yourselves. Blacky did not want to continue with the investigation. The death of your father disturbed him immensely, and he feared for the lives of your entire family. He told me that he was going to talk with his superiors and call the entire investigation off because he believed his cover was blown. Remember, he was still being tailed by Matlock, that is, whenever Matlock could keep up. And Blacky was the first to suspect him. But his superiors told him to stay the course."

"I remember," said James. That's when I walked in on his phone conversation. I thought I heard him say he didn't want to do it anymore. His family was in danger. But I was too angry with him to even notice."

"I'm sure he understood," said Mahony.

"What about those people Blacky killed?"

"They were Max's old gang and the FBI's official report states it was done in self defense. They were at the scene first, implementing damage control. The press reported whatever they were told. Bottom line, Blacky is one of the good guys, and that's all I can tell you."

"That's more than enough, Capt. Mahony. Thank you for clearing it all up for me. Oh, and you will find the evidence of how my father was killed on the answering machine in the foyer."

"Thank you. I was going to ask you for it. I'll see to it that it's brought to light, and Uri Sergei is named as the real killer. Now, I know it seems like a lot of hoopla was made about this precious list, but the names and addresses on it are real, and I prefer that it doesn't fall in the wrong hands. So James, if you please, give me the list, and you can go inside to be with your family."

Epilogue

Seven Years Later

The afternoon's cloud strewn sky was a brilliant forget-me-not that stretched far and wide as the eyes could see. Trees reached their leaf baring limbs towards the wide and inviting sky, casting their shadows upon May bloomed flowers below, which were all abuzz with hummingbirds, bees, and butterflies hovering about their vivid and illustrious colors, hopefully to sample their alluring nectar.

A nearby stream that reflected the firmament, flowed along the banks of gigantic smooth rocks, where stood a massive and ancient tree. Its wooden make-shift swing that hung low with braided ropes, wobbled animatedly above a foot worn spot in the grass. Its occupant had abandoned it moments ago and presently sprinted up a path towards a yellow and white ranch style home, which porch stretched around its entire girth.

His companion, who stood at the bank of the stream skipping rocks across the surface of the water with skillful and incredible accuracy, turned and dashed off in his direction.

EPILOGUE

"They're here! They're here!" yelled the boy nearest the house.

"Frederick James O'Neil, slow down sweetie," issued a concern woman's voice from one of the kitchen windows of the house.

But he had reached an alarming speed and leapt high into the air, sailing more than three meters across the remaining path then landed frog-like onto the porch at the foot of his cousin.

"Nice one," said a very pretty teenager who stood over him smiling.

She bore a pair of white headphone cords that dangled loosely from her ears, converging into one single wire and connecting itself at the end to a white phone with red glitter which was held securely in her hand. Her well manicured fingernails were besprinkled with tiny red and gold decals of glittering stars that matched her impeccably white besprinkled sneakers. She wore red shorts and a matching t-shirt that had splattered across the front in large bold white letters blaring: **PETA, People Eating Tasty Animals.**

"I'm a ninja," said Frederick snapping to his feet and posing heroically.

"Yes you are," she said parroting his excitement. "I bet you can do a flip out of the swing too."

"Don't encourage him Sophie," said Red approaching from inside the doorway of the house and laughing, yet managing an undertone of sternness.

"I can do it!" said Sophie's younger brother Max, bounding up the stairs as well and adopting his own heroic pose.

"You'll do no such thing," said his mother, finally exiting the house onto the porch with a platter holding a pitcher of lemonade and clear plastic cups. "Now the two of you go wash your hands," she added to the pair of miniature heroes. "I don't know how you two get yourselves in such a grubby state."

"They're boys, Rose," said a laughing Blacky, following closely on the heels of Red then kissing the back of her neck. "Mmm, you smell good."

"Alright now, that's how you got those two," said James, who was sitting over in a large comfortable chair with his two year old son Benjamin, writing in his journal and presently pointing his pen at Sophie and Max. "One... two... Need I say more?"

"Did someone say that they're here?" said Veronica, exiting the house unexpectedly onto the porch as well with one hand supporting her lower lumbar and staring for the approaching car in the distance. "Elizabeth and Olivia said dinner is nearly ready," she addressed the group at large, her stomach sticking out so far that she looked as though she was pregnant with twins.

"Yeah, look who's talking," said Blacky in response to James' comment. "One... two... Need I say more?" he added, cutting his eye at a pregnant Veronica then giving James a pointed look.

"I know, right?" agreed James with a wide and happy grin.

And they all broke out in chuckles, Veronica at a lost, missing the joke yet joining in their contagious laughter. James stood to kiss her and offered a helpful hand, caressing her back with one, and with the other, aiding her into the nearby seat.

"What? What are we laughing at?" she said brightly with a slightly bemused expression.

"Blacky called us baby makers," he said still chortling.

"This is the last one, *Mr. Baby Maker.*"

"Sure it is," piped up Blacky. "You two keep working on that mantra."

Finally the window tinted cherry sports car pulled up to the drive. Its license plates read WIL-2-LIV. William stepped out of the small car, tussling with bags and seemingly talking to himself, and everyone greeted him first with shout-outs and waves. Frederick and Max, whose attention spans were known to wander, dashed over to William and tackled him with all the grace that rough boys possessed.

"Umph," said William, bracing himself against the force of the pair's launch and gathering them into a great hug.

"What you bring us, cousin William," said Frederick and Max looking up at him.

"Oh, and how have the pair of you been," said William sternly, reminding them of their often abandoned etiquette and simultaneously releasing them from his embrace.

"Oh, pardon me," Frederick said with a perfect imitation of William's British accent. "Where are our manners? 'Tis ever so delightful to see you again. Did you have a wonderful flight in, cousin William?"

"Would you like us to carry your bags for you or perhaps park your car for you, sir?" said Max in a Yorkshire accent, curtsying then bowing low as though he was saluting an audience.

"The pair of you are quite a team!" said William, roaring with laughter. "You sure know how to take a mickey out."

And he reached into one of his bags and removed two extendable plastic light sabers and handed them one each in turn.

"There you go, young master Jedi knights."

"Wow, no way!" the both exclaimed, extending their light sabers and running off somewhere private, undoubtedly to dual in secret, away from the intervening concerns of overly protective adults.

"You're welcome!" called William to the pair."

And the boys' faint thank you's came from around the other side of the house accompanied with battle cries and grunts.

Anita Forman stepped out of the passenger side of the car. She appeared impatient with William.

"No, I can manage just fine," she said, righting herself and tossing her compact and lipstick in her purse then beaming and waving to everyone.

"Good," said William.

The pair proceeded up the walk with baggage and all. Sophie was the next to receive them, followed closely by Blacky and Red. Everyone greeted them properly with hugs and kisses, and lessening their loads. James, who was carrying Benjamin, welcomed Anita and William both with an embrace. Benjamin pushed them apart in protest of his personal space being violated by their hugs. Veronica was once again on her feet, awaiting at the bottom of the porch with one arm out expectantly, the other against her back.

"Welcome to our humble abode William, Anita," she said, bestowing a kiss on both their cheeks in turn. "You are absolutely beaming. How was your trip?"

"My first time, and I thoroughly enjoyed it," said Anita.

"Easy for you to say," said William non too crossly. "You know how the airport security is, nearly had me naked. I kept shedding clothes every time that damn thing went off. And then the security idiot kept pointing that wand dangerously close to my crotch. Why don't they just require full body searches and have done with it. Next time I'll go naked. Seems to have worked for you in the past," he finished with a smirk in James' direction.

James laughed.

"You're all a glow and look as though you are ready," said Anita, touching Veronica's stomach.

"She's ready to come any time now —— any time," said Veronica referring to her unborn child.

"And my dear Aunt Catalina, how is she?" James asked, passing a struggling Benjamin into the arms of his favorite cousin Sophie.

"Mom's doing fine," began William, "and she says hello. She has also signed the publishing company over to me, and now you and I will be working together, just like old times, mate. And how goes catching the bad guys, Blacky?"

"While you were gone, I put in my resignation after the Smoke case was closed and now live the life of leisure."

"Excellent." said William, thumping him on the back rather exuberantly.

Blacky coughed.

"And you William, you should get rid of that death trap of a match box. You can't put a family in that little thing," said Veronica with a slight wink.

"She's got a point," said Red.

"Your right, and that may be sooner than you think," said William grinning widely.

And Anita stuck out her hand in her contained excitement, wiggling her fingers vigorously, and drawing attention to an enormous diamond ring on her finger to general astonishment.

"Surprise!" she said.

"We're getting married and you're all are invited," said William.

"Kept that to yourselves long enough," said James.

They all congratulated the pair and proceeded up the steps of the house to the calls of Olivia and the aroma of a savory feast awaiting. And under cover of a protracted and clamorous welcome, William whispered to James.

"I scattered the ashes over your mother's grave, mate."

"Thanks, man. I know he would have wanted it that way."

Inside, the family all filed into the great dining room beneath a large ornate fan light, which hung from the ceiling, illuminating the whole of the room. It particularly reflected in an enormous rectangular marble veneer table, centered in the room. The table cast the ceiling's reflection, as well as the room's and that of everyone as they took their seats. Elizabeth and Olivia placed the last of the platters on the table and joined the rest.

"Smells wonderful mom," said James.

"Yes," said Blacky, "Mom, you and Aunt Elizabeth have outdone yourselves again."

Their bright thank you's were chorused between fussing over Benjamin and preparing the children's plates.

Everyone was talking at the same time and carrying on several different conversations with one another, everyone but James, who sat smiling at Veronica across the table.

"Jamie?"

"Yes, Veronica my love."

They stared a each other for a moment, and to them the voices around the table seemed to diminish in their intense gaze.

"I know what you're thinking, Jamie."

"Why Mrs. O'Neil, I think you're blushing."

"Have you given any thought as to what you will name the baby?" cut in Anita, unaware of their flirtation.

"Yes, but it's a secret," said Veronica, still locked in a gaze with James.

And the protest broke out at the table, everyone now plying James and Veronica with questions regarding the name of their soon to arrive family addition.

But James was pleasantly off contemplating something it had taken him years to finally fully appreciate, something his father had said: *Moments in the sun belong(s)* —with and without the *s— to you.* He smiled, realizing each of them: his mother Elizabeth; aunt Olivia; Blacky, Red, Sophie, and Max; his absent aunt Catalina; William and Anita; his beautiful wife Veronica, and children Frederick, Benjamin and the soon to arrive new addition, had given him precious moments in his life, shining moments of love, of happiness. He could not believe that it took him this long to truly appreciate an assertion that was so simple. The world is not as he thought it was, in chaos, but rather held together by precious moments. He now felt the joys of life were always before him, adding meaning and continuity. Surely difficult times come, but also good times as well. And he was certain that it is both sorrow and joy that makes the moments precious. One cannot be without the other. Sorrow carves out in our hearts a chasm, only to be filled, if we so desire, with happiness. The deeper our sorrows, the deeper the joy we feel.

And his smiled grew larger with immense contentment, wondering how his parents, whose love for one another brought him into being, would think to see their beautiful family together at last.

"Jamie sweetie," a soft and distant voice called, pulling him out of his reverie.

"Yes, my love," answered James again across a table of laughter and loud chattering voices, yet still his and Veronica's voices stood out for one another crystal clear.

“My word, after all these years, I still don’t know where you go when you zone out like that.

“Moments, my love,” he said smiling contently. “Moments in the sun.”

THE RISE OF

A SPECIAL PREVIEW

BOOK TWO OF MOMENTS IN THE SUN

Prologue

The Missing Years

Within the seven years of James and Veronica's pleasant and quieted ease of life, the pair raised a family of two boys, Frederick and Benjamin, and later —— as previously revealed —— a soon to arrive new addition. Their lives had settled into a peaceful state, while James' cousin Blacky, despite his promise to Red, sought a life of excitement before settling down to marry. Although they finally married, and a big to-do was made of it before Blacky caved into the ancient and sacred institution, Red's disapprobation for Blacky's hunger for excitement grew. And sensing this, he felt that it would satisfy her if he chose a job that seemed less dangerous. So Blacky took up with what he called a boring desk job with the local law enforcement to be closer to their new home in Hampton Roads. This was obviously a cover to appease his thrill seeking needs by remaining in the thick of all things dangerous. The drama which unfolded those seven years before his resignation from the police force, was no less hazardous than those of his FBI days. And the more he came home late from his supposed desk job bruised and battered, with nightmares to add, the more Red began to suspect.

Chasing Nightmares

The crisp afternoon air wafted the smell of bagels, sweet pastries, and a number of delicious entrees from several restaurants, about Stephen O'Neil's senses. He was standing on the corner of the very busy Virginia Beach Boulevard and Constitution Drive. He checked the safety on his weapon and thought of the shooting which occurred at his cousin's home a few weeks ago. Stephen spent his time in bed with nothing but a book of sudoku puzzles, which he promptly within a few days managed to devour and a television to aid him in his recovery. It was within those drawn out and tedious days of his convalescence that he had promised Red he would hang his hat and settle down. But Stephen was not satisfied with a life of hanging around the house nor was he able to find a job that suited him. He therefore found himself once again as Blacky the street thug, presently in the thick of some dangerous mix.

"What you got for me?"

"If they find out that I'm talking to you, Blacky, they would kill me."

"Well Two-Pound... I'll kill you if you don't. So pick your poison."

"You're still an ass, Blacky."

"So I'm —— "

Blacky's attention was diverted by a gentleman standing in the door of a restaurant across the street, The Macaroni Grill. The man's eyes widen in astonishment, and he pointed at Blacky in dire accusation.

"Five-O!" he bellowed, then set off running at top speed.

"What?" spluttered Two-Pound sneering.

But Blacky had dashed of in the direction of the runner. He crossed the busy highway, weaving in and out of moving cars, some slamming on breaks just in time. He proceeded toward the intersection after the runner. Blacky was nearly struck by a car, but his powerful legs catapulted him into the air, and he landed on the hood of the car, now even more determined. He could not let this guy get away. His cover was shot to hell and it would be beyond retrieve if he did not stop the runner. He jumped from the hood of the car, whipping his gun out with lightening speed, and the sound of the traffic fell away. His concentration was focused on his assailant.

"Just a nick in the leg to slow him down," he said with a steady aim.

And just as the perfect time to pull the trigger presented itself, the sound of an enormous horn blared in Blacky's ears, and he turned to face a speeding bus five inches away from him.

Blacky suddenly awoke drenched in sweat and panting for air.

"Bad dream again? I swear that desk job of yours has got you twitchy."

"I'm okay, Rose. Go back to sleep."

But she had not stirred much after his sudden awakening. She lay there still, her breath steady. Blacky, however, was shaken from his dream and worried that Red would find out about his dangerous assignments if the nightmares continued.

www.ingramcontent.com/pod-product-compliance
Lightning Source LLC
Chambersburg PA
CBHW020737020826
48980CB00018B/589/J
9780978842055